Praise for Ally Blue's *Closer*

"CLOSER is an exciting addition to the BCPI series, from the first chapter I was sucked in by Ally Blue's usual strong characterisation and descriptive turn of phrase. The storyline itself is thrilling and at times very dark, keeping me glued to my screen until the end."

~ *Barbara Small, Paranormal Romance Reviews*

"In this episode, the Bo and Sam relationship and lovemaking continues to be intense, with a nail biting, well written storyline that causes your neck hair to stand on end."

~ *Chocolate Minx, Literary Nymphs Reviews*

"As usual, Sam and Bo are hot enough to singe your fingers while reading and the mystery scary enough to make you keep all the lights on while you read."

~ *Sabella, Joyfully Reviewed*

Look for these titles by *Ally Blue*

Now Available:

Bay City Paranormal Investigations Series:
Oleander House (Book 1)
What Hides Inside (Book 2)
Twilight (Book 3)
Closer (Book 4)
An Inner Darkness (Book 5)

Print Anthologies:
Hearts from The Ashes
Temperature's Rising

Willow Bend
Love's Evolution
Eros Rising
Catching a Buzz
Fireflies
The Happy Onion
Untamed Heart
Where the Heart Is

Closer

Ally Blue

A SAMHAIN PUBLISHING, LTD. publication.

Samhain Publishing, Ltd.
577 Mulberry Street, Suite 1520
Macon, GA 31201
www.samhainpublishing.com

Closer
Copyright © 2009 by Ally Blue
Print ISBN: 978-1-60504-144-5
Digital ISBN: 1-59998-948-4

Editing by Sasha Knight
Cover by Anne Cain

First Samhain Publishing, Ltd. electronic publication: May 2008
First Samhain Publishing, Ltd. print publication: April 2009

Dedication

To the J_A_W_breakers, as always, for keeping me sane, and especially to Kimber, for giving me the idea!

Chapter One

Panting, Sam Raintree wiped the sweat from his brow before it could drip into his eyes. "Bo?"

"Almost there," Bo answered, his voice breathless.

Sam nodded and kept moving. The pace was almost more than he could handle, but he wasn't about to say so. Dr. Bo Broussard might be Sam's boss as well as his lover, but Sam would rather collapse from exertion than admit he couldn't keep up with Bo. Not when it came to *this*.

The problem was, Sam felt like collapse was imminent. His heart hammered so hard and fast he was afraid it might explode, and his breath came in ragged gasps.

Normally, he didn't get this tired and winded so quickly. He blamed the heat. Or the sand. Or both.

Maybe doing it on the beach had been a bad idea.

Bo shot him a devilish grin. "We can stop. If you want."

Encouraged by Bo's flushed face and heaving chest, Sam shook his head. He was grateful for the burning in his lungs, because it kept him from begging Bo to finish it already.

The seconds passed in silence, broken only by harsh gasps and the sigh of sea oats in the hot breeze. Just when Sam thought he had to stop or die, Bo called out the words Sam had been longing to hear. "That's half an hour."

Instantly, Sam stopped running and leaned over, hands on his knees, gulping air as fast as he could.

"Keep moving," Bo ordered, though he sounded nearly as out of breath as Sam felt. "Not good to stop like that."

Groaning, Sam straightened up and forced himself into a brisk walk. "Bastard."

"Hey, you made me do hill repeats last week. I owed you the most torturous run I could come up with."

Sam had to laugh. For one of their runs together the previous week, he'd managed to find the longest, steepest hill in Mobile and led Bo in a grueling set of runs up the slope and down again. "Yeah, well, I think running an hour in the sand beats hill repeats hands down. Especially when it's this hot."

"I think you may be right, actually." Bo lifted the waist-length black braid from his back, lacing his fingers together on top of his head to hold it up. "Ready to head back?"

Sam grimaced, but nodded. "The sooner we get back to the house, the sooner we can get a shower and a cold drink."

"Those aren't the only things I want." Letting his braid drop, Bo reached over and smacked Sam's ass. "Come on."

One look at the hungry gleam in Bo's dark eyes told Sam exactly what he wanted. Anticipation gave Sam the energy to face the long run back. Following Bo, he turned and forced his feet to move faster.

By the time they reached the house where they were staying, Sam's feet ached and a painful stitch was running up his side. He dragged himself up the steps to the covered porch and fell into the nearest chair.

"Damn, Bo. You about killed me." Sam snatched a damp beach towel from the porch railing and mopped the sweat from his face. "How's your leg? Okay?"

"It's fine, just like it's been ever since we left Sunset Lodge." Bo shook his head. "You worry too much."

It was true, Sam knew. The near-fatal bite Bo had sustained from the otherworldly creature at South Bay High over six months ago had been healed for ages, and had only bothered him when they'd been near the closed portal at Sunset Lodge. He hadn't experienced so much as a twinge since they'd left the Lodge. But then again, they hadn't run across any more portals since then. The fear of what might happen to Bo next time they did was a constant, nagging presence in Sam's mind.

"I know." Sam took Bo's hand, pulling him closer. "I try not to worry about you, but it isn't easy."

Bo didn't say anything, but the look in his eyes spoke volumes. He'd been quite vocal about his own concerns for Sam's well-being. Since Sunset Lodge they'd had more than their share of fights where Bo had wheedled, begged and finally ordered Sam to seek out the treatment that just might break his psychic connection to the interdimensional portals. Sam had consistently refused, on the grounds that destroying his ability to open and close the portals would leave them all vulnerable to the nightmare things living on the other side.

Sam had come to regret sharing his theory about his psychic abilities with Bo—that they might, just possibly, be a rare form of epilepsy, and thus treatable with anticonvulsant drugs. It was only a theory, and a far-fetched one at that, but Bo had clung to it with dogged determination. Though he no longer brought up the subject, it hung dark and heavy between them, and Sam wished it wouldn't.

"Next time we go for a run here, let's go out on the road, where it's halfway shady," Sam suggested in an attempt to dispel the cloud of tension. "The beach is too damn hot."

Laughing, Bo plopped onto Sam's lap, making him feel a thousand times better. "Agreed. I haven't run on the beach in years. It's harder than I remembered it being." He tucked a finger under Sam's chin, lifted his face and pressed a swift, salty kiss to his lips. "We'll take tomorrow off, then do a road run the next day."

That suited Sam just fine. They still had ten days of a two-week vacation left. Both of them had agreed not to slack off on their running just because they were on vacation, but Sam figured he'd rather get fat than put himself through another hellish hour like the one he'd just endured. Jogging along in the shade on a surface that didn't shift with each step sounded like pure luxury in comparison.

"You're on." Smiling, Sam licked a drop of sweat from Bo's throat. "It was really nice of Andre's sister to let us use her house for free."

"It certainly was." Bo wound an arm around Sam's shoulders and rested his cheek against Sam's head. "Especially since between everyone at BCPI, we're taking up a whole month when they could've potentially rented it out."

"I just hope we don't go back to work as sunburned as David and Cecile did. And they were only here for a week." Sam nuzzled under Bo's arm, breathing in the luscious scent of healthy, sweaty man. Bo let out a yip. Chuckling, Sam wrapped both arms around Bo and snuggled him close. "God, it's beautiful here. Perfect for getting away from everything."

Bo nodded his silent agreement against Sam's hair. The house was situated on a long stretch of beach between the town of Gulf Shores and the end of the narrow peninsula jutting into the mouth of Mobile Bay. Fifteen miles from town, the houses were set among the pines behind the dune line and spaced far apart. Though he and Bo could see the cedar shingle roofs of their closest neighbors through the trees, the place was private enough that even Bo felt comfortable kissing on the porch, or holding Sam's hand as they strolled the beach at sunset.

Bay City Paranormal Investigations had been swamped with high profile cases for months. They had all been on the ragged edge of burnout when the sister of BCPI co-owner Andre Meloy had offered to let the entire group take turns vacationing at her family's beach house. Bo had agreed right away, without argument, which went to show how exhausted he was. The cases at Oleander House, South Bay High and Sunset Lodge had made BCPI the most sought-after paranormal investigations company in the southeast, and they were all feeling the strain.

Sam and Bo sat there for several minutes, not speaking, just watching the afternoon sun sparkling on the calm blue green water. Sam rested his head against Bo's chest and let Bo's heartbeat lull him into a half-trance. After all he and Bo had been through in the past eight months, two weeks alone to do as they pleased was nothing short of nirvana.

Eventually, Bo levered himself off Sam's lap. "Come on," he said, taking Sam's hands. "Let's go take a shower."

Grinning, Sam let Bo pull him to his feet. "Together?"

"Is there any other way?" Bo pressed close, tongue flicking over Sam's lips. "I have to say, showering with you is my second favorite thing about living together."

Sam cupped Bo's cheek and rubbed at the corner of his mouth with his thumb. "What's your first favorite thing?"

The teasing light died from Bo's eyes, replaced by a solemn tenderness which made Sam's stomach flutter. "My favorite thing of all is going to sleep with you every night, and waking up with you every morning." His fingers traced the line of Sam's jaw, the touch soft and reverent. "I love knowing you're mine, and I'm yours. It sounds maudlin, I know, but it's true."

Sam swallowed the sudden lump in his throat. "It's not maudlin. I feel the same way." Three and a half months after the fact, the day Bo had moved in with Sam still counted as the happiest day of his life.

With a sweet smile, Bo tilted his head to capture Sam's mouth in a deep kiss. When they drew apart, Sam was so hard it hurt, and he could feel Bo's erection digging into his hip.

He grabbed Bo's ass in both hands and squeezed. "Shower now?"

"Shower now, yes." Bo squirmed out of Sam's grip, took his hand and dragged him toward the French doors. He arched a dark brow over his shoulder at Sam. "I want you to fuck me. Think you're *up* to it?"

Laughing, Sam squeezed Bo's fingers. "Smartass. You know I am."

The heat in Bo's eyes could've burned down the building. "I'm counting on it."

ॐ

Two hours later, clean, dressed and sated—temporarily, at least—Sam and Bo sat side by side on the rattan love seat on the upstairs porch, watching a thunderstorm roll in across the water. Over the Gulf of Mexico, the sky loomed black and ominous. The sun still shining on the inland side lent a weird green glow to the rippling water and turned the sand blinding white.

As the first scattered raindrops clinked on the blue metal roof of the house, a bolt of lightning cut a brilliant zigzag between the clouds and the water. A moment later, thunder rumbled across the sky. The sun was blotted out as the storm rushed in and the rain began in earnest.

"I love this porch," Sam declared, not for the first time. The house had deep covered porches running all the way around both levels. The second story had proven to be the perfect spot from which to watch the brief but violent storms that buffeted the beach most afternoons. Sam had been captivated from the first by the fiercely beautiful spectacle. "I love the sound of the rain on the roof."

"Mm-hm." Bo laid his head on Sam's shoulder and squeezed Sam's thigh. "Wonder how everyone's doing at work?"

"You're not supposed to be thinking of work. You're supposed to be relaxing."

"I *am* relaxing. But you know how busy we've been lately. I'm just worried about my team, that's all."

Winding Bo's braid around his hand, Sam gave a gentle tug, forcing Bo's head back so Sam could look him in the eye. "Stop worrying. I'm sure they're fine."

Bo bit his lip in that unconsciously sexy way which always made Sam's insides twist. "I'm sure you're right. But maybe I should check on them, just to make sure."

Sam was already shaking his head before Bo finished speaking. "No, you shouldn't. Andre's in charge, and you know as well as I do that he's perfectly capable of handling whatever comes up. Plus Danny's full time now, which means everybody else is free to concentrate on the active investigations."

Bo nodded, the furrows smoothing from his brow. He'd hired Danica "call me Danny" McClellan as a receptionist-slash-secretary after the Sunset Lodge case touched off a barrage of new cases. A fifty-one-year-old widow with a grown daughter, Danny had over twenty years of secretarial experience under her belt. Since she'd joined the group, the office had become

15

more organized and well run than it had ever been. Between her and Andre, Sam had no doubt the rest of the crew would be fine in his and Bo's absence.

Smiling, Bo slid a hand around the back of Sam's head and brought their mouths together. They shared a languid kiss as the thunder boomed and the rain pelted the roof. When they broke apart, Bo rose to his feet.

"I'm just going to call real quick," he said, leaning down to peck Sam on the nose. "I'll be right back."

"Bo, come on..."

"It won't take but a minute."

Before Sam could argue, Bo had the sliding glass door open and was already inside. Sighing, Sam stood and followed him into the enormous master bedroom.

Bo was sitting on the side of the king-sized bed, dialing the phone. Sam wandered over and sat beside him as he pressed the handset to his ear.

"Workaholic," Sam murmured, bending to mouth the curve of Bo's bare shoulder.

Bo ignored him, but Sam saw the gooseflesh pebbling Bo's arms. He grinned.

"Hi, Danny," Bo said into the phone. "It's Bo... Yes, we're having a wonderful time, thank you for asking. Is Andre there?... Okay, thanks." He elbowed Sam, who was tracing a single finger up and down his spine. "Stop that."

"Oh, am I distracting you from the work you're not supposed to be doing?" Dipping his finger below the waistband of Bo's indecently tiny cut-offs, Sam caressed the top of Bo's crease with a feather-light touch. "Oops."

Bo glared and opened his mouth, no doubt to reprimand Sam, then snapped it shut again. Sam heard Andre's deep voice faintly through the mouthpiece of the phone.

"Hi, Andre." Bo sounded just breathless enough to make Sam feel mischievous. "No, we're fine. Having a...oh...a wonderful time."

Stop that! he mouthed, pushing on Sam's chest. His pupils were dilated and a pink flush colored his cheeks. Grinning, Sam shook his head, ducked under Bo's arm and caught one brown nipple between his teeth. Bo squeaked.

"No, I'm okay," Bo said in answer to whatever Andre had asked. "Sam doesn't think I ought to be calling y'all, so he's being a pain in the ass."

Letting go of Bo's nipple, Sam sat up. "I was a pain in the ass earlier, in the shower," he called loudly enough for Andre to hear. "Right now I'm being a pain in the nipple, to punish him for working on vacation."

Masculine laughter drifted from the mouthpiece. Groaning, Bo covered his eyes with his free hand. "Ignore him, Andre. I'm not working, just checking in." He dropped his hand from his face and aimed a halfhearted kick at Sam's ankle. "So how's everything going? Y'all doing okay?"

Bo fell silent, listening. He leaned back on one hand, legs falling open. Judging by the intent expression on Bo's face, Sam figured whatever Andre was saying must be pretty interesting. Sam, however, couldn't care less. All he cared about right then was the denim-clad V between Bo's thighs.

Sliding to the floor, Sam knelt between Bo's legs, bent forward and rubbed his cheek against Bo's crotch. Bo's scent, clean and musky and deliciously male, made his head spin.

"Fuck," Bo hissed as Sam's tongue traced the swell of his cock through the shorts. "No, Andre, not that... The case sounds interesting. What are the details?... Oh no, I swear I won't interrupt our vacation with work. Sam would kill me."

Damn right. Staring up into Bo's glazed eyes, Sam undid the battered shorts and pulled out Bo's hardening prick. He licked at the head, tearing a harsh gasp from Bo's throat.

Bo's hips lifted in silent invitation. Not one to waste an opportunity, Sam worked the shorts down Bo's legs and pulled them off. Bo flopped onto his back, legs bending up and spreading, the phone still pressed to his ear.

"Uh. Yeah. S-so you're starting—*Jesus,* Sam—you're starting the day after tomorrow?... Uh-huh... Well, then why don't you—" Bo broke off, letting out a sharp cry when Sam stopped sucking his balls and bit one firm butt cheek hard.

Sam indulged in a moment of smug satisfaction before taking Bo's now-full-blown erection into his mouth. He shut his eyes and let Bo's taste and smell and the feel of his skin fill his senses.

Through the rush of his lust-quickened pulse in his ears, Sam thought he heard *come on out* and *plenty of room* and a not-quite-coherent promise not to do something or other before the phone bounced off the carpet and Bo's fingers tangled in his hair.

A thread of suspicion wormed through the haze of desire fogging Sam's brain. He ignored it. Whatever Bo had just agreed to, he'd find out—and they'd probably argue about it—later. Right now, he wanted to wring as much pleasure as possible from this one perfect moment.

Something told him it might be his last chance for a while.

Chapter Two

"Excuse me. What'd you just say?"

"I said, I told Andre they could all stay here."

"That's what I thought you said." Sam watched, stunned, while Bo stirred spaghetti sauce as calmly as if he hadn't just ruined their vacation. "Would you mind explaining why the hell you did that?"

"It made sense. They're going to be investigating Fort Medina, and it's just a few miles down the road from us." Bo spooned up some sauce, took a tiny sip, and added a sprinkling of oregano from the arsenal of spices lined up beside the stove.

"They could've stayed in a hotel."

"If they found a vacancy within twenty miles at this time of year, it would be a minor miracle. Besides, even the cheapest places would run us at least one hundred and fifty dollars a night for two rooms, and they're going to be investigating several nights. BCPI can't afford it right now."

"This is supposed to be our vacation." Leaning his back against the counter, Sam crossed his arms and fixed Bo with a look he refused to call a pout. "It was supposed to be just us. Two weeks, alone, with no work or anything. We've only been here four days, and you're already inviting the whole fucking office over."

Bo shot a barbed glance at Sam. "Come on, Sam, be reasonable. Why should they drive back and forth from Mobile every night when we're so close to the site? There's plenty of room here for everyone to stay without us being crowded."

He was right. Dammit. Sam wrinkled his nose. "I was looking forward to having you to myself for a while, that's all. Half your mind's always on either work or—"

Sam bit off the rest of the sentence, but it was too late. Bo threw the spoon on the counter, splattering the green and white tiles with sauce, and whirled to face Sam. "Or what? What were you going to say?"

Sam shook his head. "Nothing."

"Like hell." Bo stalked up to Sam, dark eyes full of a dangerous glitter. "You were about to say, 'the kids', weren't you?"

Hanging his head, Sam studied a scuff mark on the white linoleum under his bare feet. He didn't say anything, but his silence was answer enough, and he knew it.

Sighing, Bo turned to lean against the counter beside Sam. "Christ, Sam. I can't believe you're still jealous of my kids. That is so fucking immature."

Sam didn't answer. As much as he hated to admit it, Bo was right. When Bo's divorce from Janine was finalized and she received full custody of their sons, leaving Bo with only twice-a-month weekend visits, a dark part of Sam had been relieved that he and Bo would be able to spend most of their time together without the kids around. He knew how important Bo's children were to him, and he tried his best to be supportive, but the selfish little boy in him burned with jealousy every time he had to share Bo's attention with Sean and Adrian. Being forced to share Bo with *work* during a time which was supposed to be theirs alone was just too much for him to stand.

When Bo pushed away from the counter and went to put the spaghetti noodles on to boil, Sam finally dared to speak. "I'm sorry, Bo. I don't like feeling that way, and I'm trying to get past it. It's just, we never have any time to ourselves. Not really. And Sean and Adrian aren't even the biggest part of that. The business is, and I know that once the rest of the crew gets here and starts working on the case, you won't be able to resist getting involved."

Bo laughed, but the sound held no humor. "Andre said the same thing. I promised him I'd stay out of it."

"You won't, though."

"You don't think I can keep a promise?"

"Not this one, no." Walking over to Bo, Sam stroked a hand down his naked back, where the muscles stood out hard and tense. "You mean well. You'll intend to keep your promise. But you won't be able to. Work's too important to you."

More important than me, said the black, bitter corner of Sam's heart. He kept that thought to himself.

Bo was silent for a long time, swirling the softening noodles through the boiling water. Just when Sam was starting to get seriously nervous, Bo spoke in a soft, sad voice that made Sam's heart ache.

"I love you, Sam. I want to be with you for the rest of my life. Why isn't that good enough? Will you not be happy until I give up everything else I care about?"

God, he's reading my mind. Torn between irritation and contrition, Sam rubbed both hands over his face. "I'm not asking you to give up anything. I wouldn't do that."

"I know." Putting down the spoon, more gently this time, Bo turned to meet Sam's gaze. "But you want me to anyway."

It was partly true, but not entirely. Sam wished he could

make Bo see that.

Cupping Bo's face in his hands, Sam leaned their foreheads together. "Sometimes I wish things were different, that's true. Sometimes I wish we could spend every minute together, and not even think of anything but each other. But I know that's not realistic for either of us, and I sure as hell don't want you to give up the things that are important to you. I really don't. I wish you could believe that."

Bo didn't say anything, just tipped his face up to capture Sam's mouth with his. Sam let himself sink into the kiss, ignoring for the moment the fact that nothing had been resolved. He and Bo both wanted to do better, and each wanted to believe in the other's sincerity. It would have to be enough, for now.

ଞ

The rest of the BCPI team arrived the next evening around sunset. By then, Sam had resigned himself to spending the remainder of their vacation with a houseful of people. At least these particular people were his and Bo's friends and would respect their privacy.

"Remember, no working," Sam reminded Bo as they walked out the front door to meet the SUV rolling up the long, shaded drive. "You can ask about the case, but you are *not* allowed to get involved."

Bo quirked an eyebrow at him. "Yes, sir."

They hadn't spoken of the upcoming investigation since the night before. Sam was half afraid the tension which had dissipated since then would come back when he reminded Bo of his promise to stay out of the current case. He was relieved to see no sign of anger in Bo's eyes, only a familiar simmering heat.

Growling, he grabbed Bo around the waist and bit his neck. Bo hitched his shoulder up, laughing, and Sam grinned. That was one of Bo's ticklish spots.

"I think I like you calling me 'sir'," Sam murmured, nuzzling behind Bo's ear.

"Yeah, well, don't get used to it." He shoved Sam away with a smile. "I get to be the boss again when we go back home."

"Oh, so I'm the boss now?"

"I wouldn't mind if you were, sometimes." Bo shot Sam a smoldering look. "When we're alone, if you know what I mean."

Sam thought he did, and the idea went straight to his crotch. He watched with something like panic as the SUV rolled to a stop in front of the house and all four doors flew open at once. If David or Dean noticed the sudden "problem" in his shorts, he'd never hear the end of it.

Orgy at the nursing home, he thought, holding his clasped hands in front of his crotch in what he hoped was a casual manner. *Rush Limbaugh in drag. Dick Cheney fucking Barbara Bush.*

The last mental image did it. Breathing a silent sigh of relief, he strode forward with Bo beside him.

"Hi, guys," he called. "Y'all are awfully late, aren't you? We expected you nearly two hours ago."

"We didn't get away as early as we wanted to. If it weren't for Danny I guess we'd still be there tying up loose ends." Andre wrapped his muscular arms around Sam and Bo and pulled them into a tight hug. "Thanks for letting us stay here. I know we're getting in the way of your vacation, but damn, it'll be good not to have to drive back and forth between here and Mobile every night."

"It's no problem." Bo shot a warning glance—entirely unnecessary, Sam thought—in Sam's direction before letting go of Andre to hug Cecile Langlois. "There's absolutely no reason not to share this place with y'all, it's huge."

"I can't believe I gave y'all my week here, and ended up staying here anyway. Must be karma or something." Grinning, Dean Delapore bounded up, flung himself at Sam and Bo and kissed them each on the cheek. "So. Y'all been having fun? You disturbing the neighbors every night?"

"Come on, the nearest neighbors have to be a quarter mile away," Bo protested, squirming out of Dean's grip with a laugh.

"So, what you're saying is, you're really loud, huh?" David Broom slapped Sam's back as he strolled toward the back of the SUV to help Andre get the equipment. "Nice hickey, Sam."

"He's lying," Bo muttered, grabbing Sam's hand before it could fly up to his neck. "You don't have any marks *there*."

Sam blushed, thinking of the giant purple bruise Bo had left on his inner thigh that morning.

Cecile hooked a hand through Sam's elbow and smiled up at him. "I know you probably weren't happy about this. Thank you for letting us stay."

Like I had a choice.

Sam shoved the uncharitable thought aside. He knew having the team stay here was the best option, and he knew his friends felt bad already about interrupting his and Bo's vacation. He didn't want to make them feel worse, when they were just doing their job. Just doing what the boss said.

"No problem." Sam patted her hand. "I can't wait to hear about the new case."

She gave him a stern look as they went to help unload the

SUV. "You *do* know that you and Bo aren't supposed to be working on this one, right?"

"I know. Believe me, I know. But that doesn't mean we don't want to hear about it." Glancing at Bo, who was deep in conversation with Andre, Sam leaned closer to Cecile. "Besides, you know as well as I do that Bo won't be able to resist. If he's in, I'm in."

Cecile didn't say anything. She didn't have to. They both knew Sam was right.

Between the six of them, they got all the luggage and equipment unloaded and stowed in the house within a few minutes. Once everyone got settled into their rooms—all on the first floor, Sam was pleased to note—the whole group converged on the back porch in the gathering dusk. Sam lit a couple of citronella candles to provide some light and keep away the mosquitoes.

"Okay," Bo said, claiming the chair between Sam and Andre. "Tell us all about this case."

"It's pretty simple, really." Leaning forward, Andre grabbed a handful of chips from the big bowl Bo had put in the middle of the round patio table. "Joanne Biggers is the current manager of Fort Medina. She called us the other day asking if we could investigate the fort's ghosts."

"The place has been haunted forever," Dean chimed in, taking a swig from his bottle of Corona. "It was built in the late sixteen hundreds, and it's been collecting ghost stories ever since. I remember going on a field trip there in eighth grade. It's a cool place. Really creepy."

"So it's just regular ghosts?" Sam asked. "Not...anything else?"

Not portals. Please. He figured it wasn't a portal case, or Bo would've already said something, but he had to ask. Just to put his mind at ease.

"No portals," David answered, blunt as always. "Just your garden-variety spooks."

"Mostly residuals, from the sound of it." Andre popped the last of his chips into his mouth, chewed and swallowed. "Although a couple of the reported sightings sound more like apparitions. Hopefully we'll find out soon enough."

Beneath the table, Bo's hand crept onto Sam's thigh and gave a gentle squeeze. Sam laid his hand over Bo's, grateful for that reassuring touch. Bo knew how much Sam dreaded the time when another interdimensional portal case would come along. Sam's dreams were still haunted by visions of Bo's near death after the creature from the other side bit him at South Bay High.

Cecile shifted in her seat, tucking one slender leg beneath her long gauze skirt. "We're meeting Joanne at the ticket office tomorrow night at nine o'clock. The fort's open to the public during the day. It closes at eight p.m. She'll give us the tour and show us where the major sightings have been. From that, we can hopefully get a good idea of how many nights the investigation might take."

Bo nodded, twirling the tail of his braid between his fingers. "Okay. Well, as y'all know, Sam and I are planning to sit this one out. But I'm always available if you need me."

"Boss-man, this one's a cakewalk. We can handle it, no problem." David scooped up a palmful of chips and crammed them into his mouth. "'Ou guys s'ay ou' o' th' case an' in bed."

Cecile smacked David on the shoulder while Dean and Sam snickered and Bo glared. "My God, David," she chastised. "Could you possibly be *less* refined?"

David shot her a cheerful leer. "You don't love me for my refinement, baby."

Chuckling, Andre shook his head. "The point David is so crudely attempting to make is, this is a pretty straightforward case, nothing complicated or dangerous. The folks at the fort are hoping that having us investigate will raise their profile as a tourist attraction and bring in more people, which is the main reason they asked us to come out. There won't be any reason for you and Sam to be involved."

Glancing sideways, Sam wondered if he imagined the disappointment on Bo's face. *Probably not.*

"They realize we can't do this if they'll only accept one answer, right?" Bo turned his palm up, lacing his fingers through Sam's. "If you find evidence, fine. If not, they need to know we won't fake it for them."

Andre made an impatient sound. "Give me some credit, Bo. I told them that, just like we tell everyone. They're fine with it. They figure this'll be good publicity whether we find anything or not."

Bo had the good grace to look sheepish. "Of course. Sorry, Andre."

"No problem," Andre answered with a dismissive wave of his hand. "I know how it is. It's hard to let go of control when you're used to having it."

The sentiment resonated in Sam's brain. As if reading his thoughts, Bo swiveled his head toward Sam. Their gazes locked, and the hunger in Bo's eyes sent a jolt up Sam's spine. Heat pooled between his legs. Suddenly he wanted nothing more than to drag Bo upstairs, rip his clothes off and make him lose control in the best possible way.

Later, he mouthed, and bumped Bo's leg with his. A tiny nod and an anticipatory twist of Bo's lips told Sam he understood.

"Bo? What do you think?"

Startled, Sam turned toward Dean's voice. Bo leaned forward to look at Dean, who sat on Sam's other side. "Sorry, what was that?"

Dean grinned. "I was asking what you thought of making the fort a site for the Scooby Tours, but it can wait. I can see y'all have other things to think about right now."

Thankfully, the increasing dimness hid the blush staining Sam's cheeks. At least he assumed it did. He knew Bo well enough to know his face was scarlet, but Sam couldn't see it in the flickering candlelight.

"No, that's fine." Bo's voice was firm, in spite of the faint tremor of his fingers where they gripped Sam's. "I think that's a fantastic idea, actually. If the fort checks out, we'll talk with Joanne about scheduling a tour."

Excitement fluttered in Sam's belly. In spite of his resentment of the case for intruding on his private time with Bo, a part of him wanted to be involved in this one. The fort sounded intriguing, not to mention rich in history. Holding one of their biannual investigations for paying amateur ghost hunters at the old fort sounded like fun. They only led the Scooby Tours—as Dean had dubbed them—at sites proven to be both paranormally active and safe, and the fort promised to be both.

"Cool." Rising to his feet, Dean stretched and let out what Sam was positive was a fake yawn. "Man, I'm wiped. Think I'll go get some shut-eye."

David gaped at him. "But if you go to sleep now you'll be up at the crack of dawn, and we're gonna have to stay up most of the night tomorrow. Why don't you stay up now and then you can sleep in in the morning?"

"Naw. I'm gonna just sleep for a few hours, then take a nap tomorrow afternoon. That way I'll be as well rested as I ever am, and by the time we head to the fort I'll be wide awake and ready to hunt some ghosts." Picking up his empty beer bottle, Dean gave Sam's arm a quick squeeze and headed toward the door. "'Night. See y'all in the morning."

A chorus of "good nights" followed him inside. Sam smiled at the wink Dean shot him. Dean's constant determination to create chances for Sam and Bo to be alone was sweet, but he was about as subtle as a wrecking ball.

Cecile watched Dean go with a knowing smile on her face. "He had a good idea there. I think I'll do the same."

David let out a long-suffering sigh as Cecile stood and tugged on his arm to make him follow. "All right, all right, we'll go away and leave the lovebirds alone to get their man-thing on. But I'd better get some s—"

"David," Cecile murmured, taking his hand.

"S...sugar," David amended. "Daddy better get some sugar for this, little girl."

The look he got in return was far from sweet, but it made David hum happily and follow Cecile like a well-trained puppy.

"Those two are like a couple of kids," Andre said, shaking his head as he watched them disappear inside. He sighed. "I miss Amy."

The confession shocked Sam with its sheer unexpectedness. Andre rarely mentioned Amy Landry, the lover he'd lost to the otherdimensional monster at Oleander House. He'd grieved for her in his quiet, stoic way, but he hadn't so much as mentioned her name in months. Seeing the sadness in his face right now made Sam's heart ache for him.

Bo laid a hand on Andre's shoulder. "You know you can talk to me—to any of us—any time you need to, right? We're your friends. We're here for you."

The corners of Andre's mouth lifted in a melancholy smile. "I could say the same for you. You and Amy were friends long before I even met her, but you don't talk about her any more than I do."

Bo's fingers tightened in Sam's grip. "You're right. I don't ever mention her anymore. But I miss her too."

"I guess we both just deal with it better in private, huh?"

"I guess so."

Silence fell. Sam kept quiet. He still felt some measure of responsibility for Amy's death, since his psychokinetic abilities had opened the portal which allowed the thing that killed Amy access to the human world. It had been an accident, and Sam knew that. But knowing the truth in his mind didn't stop the tiny shard of guilt from burrowing deep into his soul.

They sat there until the last of the sunset glow died and the candles had burned low. Beyond the faint circle of candlelight, the sea oats whispered in the breeze and insects sang beneath the pines. Sam drew a deep breath, letting the scent of the ocean dissolve the tension in his shoulders and the back of his neck. He wondered, not for the first time, if he'd ever be free of the guilt of Amy's death.

Sam had begun to slip into a doze when Bo stirred and pushed his chair away from the table. He stood, pulling Sam up with him. "Andre, I think Sam and I are going to bed now. Will you be okay?"

Andre nodded, the movement barely visible in the gloom. "I'm just going to sit out here for a while, if that's all right."

"Of course it is." Bo glanced at Sam with concern in his eyes. "Okay. Well. Good night, Andre."

Andre grunted in answer, his face turned toward the sea and his attention already a million miles away. Sam threw a worried glance over his shoulder at Andre as Bo opened the door.

"I hope he'll be all right," Sam said once he and Bo were inside. "I mean it always seems like he's doing okay, but it hasn't been that long, really. Not quite nine months."

"He's still healing. I suppose we all are." Bo stopped at the foot of the stairs, let go of Sam's hand and wound both arms around his waist. "I'm glad I have you, Sam. I know I never really shared my grief with you, but you helped me deal with it all the same, just by being there. Just by being in my life."

Bo's solemn confession made Sam feel warm all over. He pulled Bo close and kissed his brow. "I'm happy I could help you, even if I didn't know I was doing it at the time."

One of Bo's hands slid into Sam's hair. His lips brushed Sam's. "Let's go to bed now."

Humming, Sam cupped Bo's ass in both hands. "Are you tired?"

"Not really." Bo rocked his hips, pressing his groin against Sam's. "It was selfish of me to invite the group out here." He nipped Sam's bottom lip. "Aren't you angry?"

"I was, at first, but now..." Sam trailed off when he saw the wicked glitter in Bo's eyes. *Oh fuck. Is he asking for what I think he is?* "But, now," he continued, speaking slowly and watching Bo's face, "I'm even *more* angry."

"I don't blame you." Bo dipped his head and bit Sam's neck hard enough to hurt. "It was terrible of me to use my position as your boss that way." The tip of his tongue traced a wet path up Sam's throat. "To tell everyone they could come out here without even asking what you thought."

"Mmmmm. Yeah." Sam raised his chin for Bo's nips and kisses. "Terrible."

Bo lifted Sam's shirt, fingers skating along the skin over his ribs. "So what are you going to do about it?"

Grabbing Bo's braid, Sam yanked his head back to stare into his wide eyes. "I think I need to teach you a lesson. I think you need to be punished."

A hot flush crept up Bo's neck and into his cheeks. His eyes blazed. "Do it."

Sam's knees nearly buckled. He closed his eyes for a moment, trying to get control of himself. When he felt like he could move without his legs giving out, he extracted himself from Bo's embrace, took his hand and led him upstairs to the bedroom.

Inside the room, with the door shut and locked and the curtains drawn across the sliding glass door, Sam swept Bo into his arms and claimed his mouth in a deep, possessive kiss. Bo opened to him, eager as ever, needy little sounds bleeding from his lips.

"Take your clothes off." Sam let Bo go and stepped back, leaning against the wall and crossing his arms. "Right now."

Bo raised his eyebrows at Sam's commanding tone, but did as he was told. He undressed and stood naked with his hands at his side, his gaze fixed on Sam's face. The mix of bravado and uncertainty in his eyes made Sam's insides twist.

"God, you're beautiful." Sam closed the distance between them, took hold of Bo's braid and let it slide across his palm. "Take your hair down."

A sly smile curved Bo's mouth. "I think my hair is becoming a fetish for you." Pulling the rubber band off the end of the braid, Bo began unwinding it.

"*Becoming* a fetish? Hell, it's been my perverted obsession since day one."

With a soft laugh, Bo undid the last twists in the braid. His hair fell in a silky dark mass around his shoulders and down his back. Moving to stand behind Bo, Sam buried both hands in all that shining hair, lifted it to his face and drew a deep breath. The scents of salt air and shampoo conjured vivid memories of all the times they'd made love. All the times Bo's silky tresses had brushed Sam's chest, his stomach, his back, the insides of his thighs. Thinking of it brought a rush of heat through Sam's body.

Letting go of his double handful of hair, Sam clamped his hands onto Bo's hipbones and thrust his clothed crotch against Bo's bare butt. "God, I want to fuck you right now."

Bo turned his head and gave Sam a mischievous smile over his shoulder. "And that would be punishing me how, exactly?"

"You mean you *want* my cock up your ass?" Sam blinked, faking surprise.

"I do, yes. Very much." Bo ground his rear into Sam's privates, making them both moan. "But you were going to punish me for my transgressions, I believe. And fucking me is hardly a punishment."

Sam bit the insides of his cheeks, trying to hold back his amusement, then gave up and laughed out loud. "No offense, Bo, but you're terrible at roleplaying."

Chuckling, Bo settled against Sam's chest, his head falling back to rest on Sam's shoulder. "You're right. I'd much rather just say what I want. It's easier, and I don't feel like quite so much of an idiot."

"So what is it you want?" Sam brushed the hair from the back of Bo's neck, dipped his head and sucked up a mark on the dusky skin. "As if I didn't know already."

"If you already know, why don't you just do it?" Bo moaned low and rough when Sam's tongue pressed to his pulse point. "God, Sam. I shouldn't like it this much when you mark me."

Sam stomped down the automatic surge of irritation. So Bo felt uncomfortable sporting a bunch of love bites, so what? They could be seen as less than professional, and Bo was nothing if not a professional.

But we're not working right now. And he just said he liked being marked by you.

"Tell me what you want," Sam murmured against Bo's skin. He slid a hand down to cup Bo's balls. They felt hot and tight against his palm. "I won't do it until I hear you say it." He traced his fingertips up the length of Bo's shaft to stroke the satin skin at the tip.

Bo's breath hitched, his hips arching into Sam's touch. "I...I want you... *Fuck,* Sam, yes... Want you to...to spank me."

If it hadn't been for the pure need in Bo's voice, Sam would've been tempted to laugh again. He'd known what Bo was going to say—at least he'd been pretty sure, and he'd been right—but it was strange hearing his meticulous, methodical, bordering-on-control-freak lover admit he wanted to be spanked. Surreal didn't even begin to describe it. Before today, Sam hadn't seen the slightest indication of this sudden kink of Bo's.

Not that he minded. He couldn't pretend he'd never wanted to turn Bo over his knee. The man could be infuriating at times.

"Oh. I see." Sam splayed his free hand over Bo's left buttock, kneading the firm muscle. "So you want me to paddle your ass?"

"Yes." Bo's voice was a raspy whisper.

"Like this?" Sam gave the side of Bo's hip a sharp smack. Bo gasped, a tremor running up his body, and Sam grinned. "Oh yeah. You like that."

"I do." Bo's hand clamped onto the back of Sam's head, forcing his face down for a swift kiss. "I want to explore

34

everything with you, Sam. Just you. No one else, ever."

Sam's chest constricted. Only Bo could make kinky sex play seem almost sacred.

Lifting his hand to cup Bo's jaw, Sam kissed him again, taking it deeper this time. Bo's mouth opened wide to suck Sam's tongue in. His cock twitched in Sam's hand, a drop of moisture leaking out to trickle over Sam's fingers, and Sam nearly came in his shorts.

Sam broke the kiss, panting. Bo whimpered his protest, and Sam let out a breathless laugh. "Go put your hands on the wall and lean forward with your legs spread."

Bo obediently walked over and planted his palms on the pale green wall beside the door. His hair cascaded around him as he leaned forward and scooted his feet apart. He stared over his shoulder at Sam, his face red and his eyes heavy-lidded with desire. His ribs heaved with his quick, shallow breaths.

"Damn. You're a wet dream come to life, you know that?" Sam sauntered forward, doing his best to play it cool. Though he'd never played dominance and submission games before, instinct told him Bo needed him to be calm and in control. He caressed Bo's exposed ass, loving the way the smooth skin jumped at his touch. "Such a pretty ass. And it's all mine."

"Yours." Bo moaned, his head falling forward as Sam stroked his hole with one fingertip. "God, Sam, please."

Giving no warning, Sam lifted his hand and dealt a light slap to Bo's butt. Bo yipped, more in surprise than pain, Sam thought. Sam smoothed his fingers over the spot he'd hit. "Good?"

Bo nodded. "Harder."

Sam bit his lip. "Damn, I love it when you say 'harder' to me."

He smacked Bo's ass again, hard enough to make his palm sting. Bo gasped, fingers curling against the wall. "God."

Sam frowned. "You okay? I'll stop, just say the word." He stared at the red handprint on Bo's butt cheek and hoped he wouldn't want to stop.

The frantic look Bo aimed at him eased his mind considerably. "No! No, don't stop. Do it again."

Sam obliged, marking the other buttock this time. Bo's pleas for more continued, devolving from words into eloquent gasps and moans. Sam watched, fascinated, as the skin of Bo's ass turned a raw, fiery red under one open-handed blow after another.

The intensity of his own excitement shocked Sam. He never would've thought he'd be this turned on by spanking his lover, but there it was.

Bo's obvious enjoyment was probably what did it. Nothing excited Sam as much as seeing Bo lose himself in pleasure.

Sam finally had to stop, his palm burning and nearly as red as Bo's rear. Laying his other hand on Bo's ass, he raked his gaze up and down Bo's body. Bo was shaking all over, his breath coming short and fast. Precome dripped from the tip of his prick onto the floor. His butt felt hot to the touch.

"Sam," Bo moaned, arching his back to press his ass into Sam's hand. "Fuck me."

The suggestion went straight to Sam's cock, which lurched against the confining briefs. He kissed Bo's shoulder blade. "Gotta get the lube. Don't move."

Bo nodded. "Hurry."

Sam didn't want to take his hand off Bo's backside, but he had to if he wanted the lube. His psychokinetic abilities didn't allow him to fetch objects with his mind. He'd tried. It never worked.

Moving reluctantly away from Bo, Sam hurried to the bedside table, yanked the drawer open and fished out the half-empty tube of lubricant. He bounded back to his former position behind Bo and plastered himself to Bo's back, his arms winding around Bo's waist. "Miss me?"

"Uh-huh." Bo wriggled in Sam's embrace. "In me. Now."

Sam smirked into Bo's hair. "Bossy."

"Can't help it." Bo bumped his ass hard into Sam's crotch, making his vision blur. "God, *please!*"

Closing his eyes, Sam grabbed Bo's cock and squeezed hard, tearing a growl from his throat. "Fuck, I love it when you beg."

He opened his eyes again, let go of Bo's cock and stepped back enough to unbutton his shorts and slide the zipper down. He pulled his cock and balls free, mindful of the zipper. Flipping open the lube, he coated his fingers, shut the cap and stuck the tube in his back pocket. He didn't bother to warn Bo, just slid one slick digit through the ring of tight muscle into his rectum.

"Oooooh, God," Bo breathed, his hole clutching hard at Sam's finger. "Yes. Yes. More."

Sam inserted another finger and started pumping them in and out. "Bend over some more."

Groaning, Bo did as he was told, bending forward until his forehead rested on the wall. His anus clenched and relaxed as Sam stretched him. His body trembled. Sam could see the gooseflesh raising the fine dark hairs on his arms.

Sam reached between Bo's legs to stroke his prick with his free hand. He kept his gaze glued to his fingers in Bo's ass. *So fucking hot.*

He pressed deep to nail Bo's gland. Bo keened and clawed

the wall. "Fuck, Sam. Please."

"Yeah."

Tugging his fingers free of Bo's hole, Sam retrieved the lube from his pocket, opened it and squirted a generous amount into his hand. He closed the cap and tossed the tube on the floor with one hand while slicking his cock with the other. Spreading Bo's cheeks, he positioned the head of his prick at the stretched hole and pushed.

They groaned at the same time as Sam's cock slid deep into Bo's ass. Sam hung onto his control by sheer force of will. As always, the hot grip of Bo's body felt so good it was almost painful.

Bo turned his head to pin Sam with a dazed stare. He licked his lips, getting a strand of ebony hair caught in his mouth in the process. "Move," he whispered. "Fuck me."

The desperate need in Bo's voice sent a wave of heat through Sam's blood. Clamping his hands onto Bo's hipbones, Sam started thrusting in a strong, steady rhythm.

Sex with Bo was always incredible, but for some reason Sam found this particular scenario unbearably exciting. Maybe it was the contrast of his own fully clothed state with Bo's nudity, or the way Bo muttered half-coherent curses and praises and pleas for Sam to fuck him harder, to never stop. Sam didn't know. One thing he knew for sure, though—the sight of Bo's flaming red buttocks, the way they framed his hole with Sam's cock pistoning in and out, was by far the most erotic thing Sam had ever seen.

A shudder rippled through Bo's back muscles when Sam reached around and started jerking his prick. "Sam. Yes, God, 's good."

Leaning forward, Sam planted a hand on the wall beside Bo's and molded himself to Bo's back. "Come now."

To his surprise, Bo did, a breathless litany of "oh God, oh God" falling from his lips. Warm semen flowed over Sam's hand. Bo's insides convulsed around Sam's shaft, ripping his orgasm from him. He let it take him, closing his eyes and burying his face in Bo's hair as he shot deep inside Bo's body.

"Oh, my God." Bo laid both forearms on the wall with a contented sigh. "That was fantastic, Sam."

"Mmm. Was, wasn't it?" Sam laid his clean hand on Bo's butt. "You okay?"

"Fine." He wriggled his bottom against Sam's hand. "My ass feels hot."

"It *is* hot."

"So you keep telling me."

Sam snickered. "Not that. Although it really is the hottest ass I've ever seen." He stroked the overheated skin. "Your butt is actually much warmer than usual."

Humming, Bo tilted his head back to rub his cheek against Sam's. "From the spanking?"

"I assume so." A sudden idea struck Sam. He peeled himself off Bo's back and pulled out of him, hissing when Bo's hole clutched at the sensitive head of his prick. "Don't move."

Sam sank to his knees, wiping his sticky hand on his shorts. Bo ducked his head to peer at Sam from beneath one arm, a lecherous grin on his face. "Are you going to do what I think you are?"

Sam laughed. "Shut up."

Whatever Bo had been about to say next was lost in an undulating groan when Sam licked a wide, wet path up one crimson buttock. "Oooooooooh. Damn, that feels good."

Sam agreed, though his mouth was too busy to say so. He licked at the other cheek, then planted open-mouthed kisses along the edge of Bo's crease. The hot skin cooled beneath his lips and tongue. Above him, Bo practically purred.

Leaning sideways, Sam peeked around the bend of Bo's hip to catch a glimpse of his face. Bo's eyes were half-closed, his mouth curved into a lazy smile. "Mmm. Don't stop."

"Wasn't planning to."

Spreading Bo's ass cheeks, Sam lapped up the stream of semen dribbling from Bo's hole. He traced the loosened opening with the tip of his tongue, savoring the mingled tastes of Bo and himself. The ring of muscle fluttered and clenched at the soft touch.

Bo gasped when Sam's tongue wormed itself inside him. "Jesus, Sam. You're killing me here."

Retrieving his tongue, Sam leaned over to give Bo a blankly innocent look. "I thought you didn't want me to stop."

Bo groaned. "I don't. But you're going to have to. My legs aren't going to hold me up much longer if you keep that up."

"Ah. Okay." With one last flick of his tongue across Bo's hole, Sam pushed to his feet, wrapped his arms around Bo's chest and pulled him upright. "It's late, and we'll need to get up early if we want to get a run in before it gets too hot. You ready to hit the sack?"

"More than ready." Bo turned in Sam's embrace and kissed his chin. "I really am sorry I asked everyone out here without consulting you, Sam. It was selfish of me."

Smiling, Sam lifted a hand to caress Bo's cheek. "To be honest, it kind of was. And I wasn't happy at first. But you were right. It didn't make any sense for them to drive back and forth to Mobile when we're staying not five miles from the fort."

Bo nodded. "Thank you for being so understanding. I promise I won't let their investigation interfere with our time together."

Sam wasn't sure he believed Bo's promise, but what choice did he have? Bo believed it, Sam was certain of that. He would just have to trust his lover and hope for the best.

Slipping his hand up to cup the back of Bo's head, Sam tilted Bo's head for a kiss. "Come on. I'll wash you off."

They headed for the bathroom with their arms around each other. Sam nuzzled Bo's hair and tried not to think of what the next day might bring.

Chapter Three

Sam wasn't sure whose idea it had been to take the road to Fort Medina for their morning run. He thought maybe Bo had first brought it up, pointing out that the road was more heavily shaded in that direction. At seven a.m. the day had already promised to be fine and hot, so running in the shade sounded like a good plan.

However, Sam himself was the one who'd suggested taking a look at the fort as long as they were headed in that direction. Bo had eagerly agreed, and now here they stood, the locked gate in front of them and a stretch of deserted road and pine forest behind them, staring across the empty parking lot at the entrance to the old brick structure.

"Dean was right," Sam said, hooking his fingers in the chainlink fence. "It looks spooky, even in daylight."

"Yeah. I wonder what it must be like at night, with no one here and everything pitch dark?" Bo grinned, eyes sparkling. "It would be fun to come out with the group tonight, just for a little while."

Sam shot Bo a stern look. "No. You promised."

"I promised not to get involved in the investigation." Bo shrugged, his gaze fixed on the fort's arched entryway. "I was just thinking it would be interesting to see the place at night, that's all. We certainly don't have to."

"Damn right we don't." Turning away from Bo's wistful expression, Sam studied the high walls of weathered brick.

It really is a cool place, the insatiably curious investigator in his brain prodded. *So much history here. So much to see, and to learn. What sorts of ghosts must haunt this place? Don't you want to find out?*

Sam scowled, irritated with himself. The rest of the team would gladly fill Bo and himself in on what they found during the investigation. Why, Sam wondered, couldn't his adventurous streak just calm the fuck down and leave him alone?

Bo's hand cupped his ass and squeezed, bringing him out of his thoughts. "Come on, Sam. Let's head back. I'll fix omelets for breakfast."

"Okay." Snaking an arm around Bo's waist, Sam pulled him close for a quick, sweat-tinged kiss. "I love you."

Laughing, Bo kissed Sam again and nuzzled his cheek. "I love you too. Now come on. We have a lot of swimming and lying in the sun to do, and we're falling behind schedule."

Sam shook his head as they drew apart. "You and your schedules."

"What can I say, I'm anal like that."

"You're anal lots of ways."

Bo arched an eyebrow at him and started jogging back down the road without another word. With one last glance over his shoulder at the fort, Sam followed. Soon enough the fence and the parking lot were out of sight behind them.

ॐ

"Did you bring the thermal imaging camera?"

"Yes, Dean's got it."

"What about the new power cable for the laptop? You know the old one won't stay plugged in anymore."

"It's with the laptop."

"Well what about—"

"Okay, stop it." Setting the bag full of flashlights and extra batteries in the back of the SUV, Andre turned and aimed a glare at Bo, who stood behind him. "We have everything we need, Bo. We didn't forget anything, and believe it or not we know what to do without you instructing us every step of the way."

It was eight forty-five, and the team was preparing to leave for the fort. For the past couple of hours, Bo had been following Andre around peppering him with questions about their plans for the evening. Sam had watched Andre's irritation at Bo grow, wondering when he'd finally explode.

Andre's level of control was impressive. Hopefully Bo would stop while he was ahead.

"I know that." Bo sidestepped Andre, leaned into the SUV and opened one of the bags. "This doesn't look like enough cord to me. The fort's a big place."

Andre shook his head and turned a pleading look to Sam. "Can't you do anything with him?"

Sam snorted. "What makes you think he'll listen to me?"

"'Cause you're fucking him, my man," David supplied, coming around the back of the SUV at that moment with a bulky duffle bag slung over one shoulder. "Sex is a powerful motivator."

Bo paled, then flushed crimson. "Okay. Well. Good luck tonight, Andre. Tell us all about it tomorrow, okay?"

Andre nodded. "Sure thing." He reached out and laid a

hand on Bo's arm. "Hey, Bo—"

"I'm, uh, just going to finish cleaning up the kitchen. See y'all tomorrow." Turning on his heel, Bo strode back toward the house, braid swinging. His tension showed clear as day in his hunched shoulders and stiff back.

Sam shook his head. It could've gone worse. At least Bo would probably be back to normal once everyone else left.

With a deep sigh, Andre turned to David. "You and your big mouth. Why'd you have to say that?"

"Oh come on, how long's he known me? If he hasn't figured out I'm a smartass by now he's not nearly as bright as I'd always thought." David hefted the bag into the rear of the vehicle and mopped the sweat from his forehead with the bottom of his T-shirt. "That's the last of the equipment."

"Okay." Andre glanced at his watch. "I'll round up the rest of the crew and we'll go." He poked David in the chest with one thick finger. "And for God's sake, think before you talk next time, huh?"

Andre stalked off, grumbling under his breath. David scowled at his back. "Yessir, your highness. Geez."

Sam shut the SUV's tailgate and leaned against it. "Don't let him bug you. Bo's been a real pain in the ass tonight, asking questions and poking his nose in where he promised he wouldn't. It's getting on Andre's nerves."

"Yeah, I couldn't help noticing that. The old 'kick the dog' syndrome. And what fun it is to be the fucking dog." With a quick look around, David leaned closer and lowered his voice. "You don't think I really upset Bo, do you? I didn't mean to."

Chuckling, Sam patted David on the back. "Don't worry about it, he's fine. He just hates being reminded that everyone knows we're having sex."

David pretended to gag. "I'd rather not be reminded either, if it's all the same to you."

"Maybe you shouldn't bring it up, then." Sam looked up at the sound of the front door opening. Andre walked out into the yellow glow of the front porch light, followed by Cecile and Dean. Sam pushed away from the SUV. "Here comes the rest of the crew. Y'all have fun tonight."

"We will. And you do what you have to to improve the boss's mood, yeah?"

"Will do." Sam saluted, and David laughed.

After a flurry of goodbyes and promises to discuss their findings the next day, the group piled into the SUV and started down the drive. Sam stood at the edge of the driveway and watched the taillights disappear into the darkness. Part of him wished he was going with them, and not just because it sounded like an interesting case. Bo had been moody all day, and Sam didn't feel like facing it.

As if in answer to his thought, the front door opened and closed behind him. He heard the sound of bare feet through thin grass, then arms slipped around his waist and warm lips brushed the back of his neck.

"Hi, Bo," Sam said, laying his hands over Bo's where they rested on his stomach.

"Hi." Bo pressed his cheek to Sam's shoulder. "I'm sorry."

"For what?" Turning one of Bo's hands over, Sam stroked a thumb across his palm.

"For my attitude tonight. For driving Andre and everyone else to distraction over the case when I'd promised I wouldn't get involved."

"You *were* kind of irritating. But it's okay." Sam patted Bo's hand. "We all know you can't help yourself."

Bo's arms tightened around Sam's waist, but he didn't argue. "Want to go for a walk on the beach? It's a beautiful night." He bit Sam's shoulder, then soothed the sting with his tongue. "It's almost a full moon. Very romantic."

Turning in Bo's arms, Sam framed Bo's face in his hands and kissed him. "I'd love a romantic walk on the beach with you."

Bo smiled, brown eyes shining in the lamplight. "I love being here with you, Sam. It's nice to be able to kiss you or hold you whenever I want, and not have to worry about people seeing."

Sam squashed the swift flare of resentment. In the last few months, Bo had learned to relax and express his affection for Sam around the people they loved and trusted. It shouldn't matter that Bo still didn't feel comfortable holding hands when they walked down the street together, or greeting Sam with a kiss in public.

It *shouldn't* matter. But it did. Sam wished with all his heart that it didn't. More than that, he wished he could rid himself of the nagging fear of what it might mean—that he wasn't as important to Bo as Bo was to him.

Shaking off the unwelcome bitterness, Sam stepped out of Bo's arms and took his hand. "Do you have the house key?"

"Right here." Bo patted the back pocket of his shorts with his free hand. "The doors are already locked."

Sam laughed as they started down the path running through the pines down to the beach. "Pretty sure of me, weren't you?"

"You're a romantic at heart." Bo squeezed Sam's fingers. "I like that."

Sam didn't answer, just pulled Bo to him and wound an arm around his shoulders. They followed the path in silence, for which Sam was grateful. A deserted moonlit beach awaited them, and he hated to ruin the mood with the things he was afraid he might say.

∞

Sam woke from a dream of blackness and lung-crushing terror to find the other side of the bed empty.

He lay in the dense darkness, his heart hammering against his ribs and his right arm flung across the spot where Bo should be, and tried to get his bearings. To his left, the night sky showed as a star-pricked square in the glass doors between the partially open curtains. To his right, the clock radio on the bedside table told him it was three fifty-seven a.m. Light bled around the closed door leading to the upstairs hallway. Across the room, the bathroom door stood half open. It was dark inside.

"Bo?" he called softly. Maybe Bo had gotten up to go to the bathroom and had left the light off to keep from waking him. "You in there?"

No answer. Sam frowned at the dark blur of the ceiling fan. Where could Bo possibly have gone at almost four in the morning? He'd never had trouble sleeping before.

Wide awake and a little worried, Sam kicked free of the tangled covers and slipped out of bed. Groping on the chair next to the bed, he found his boxers and pulled them on, then started feeling his way to the door. He tripped over the sandals he'd left in the middle of the floor and nearly fell. Cursing under his breath, he stumbled to the door, opened it and shuffled into the hall. He squinted against the sudden brightness.

A faint murmur of voices drifted from downstairs. Bo

must've heard the rest of the group returning from the investigation and gone to talk to them.

For a moment Sam stood there, leaning against the doorframe and thinking. Wondering if he should join Bo and the others downstairs, or just go back to bed. He was angry. Angrier than he had any right to be, really. After all, was it so bad that Bo had woken up and wanted to know how the first night of the investigation went? Sam couldn't say for sure that he wouldn't have done the same himself if he'd been the one to wake up first.

Bo's voice rose above the others in a soft, excited laugh that melted some of Sam's anger. He loved that sound. The sound of Bo discovering something.

Before he'd consciously decided to, he found himself walking down the stairs. He stepped into the foyer, turned the corner into the living room and nearly walked right into Bo's back. Bo stood at Dean's right shoulder, peering at the thermal imaging camera.

Andre nodded from his spot perched on one of the tall chairs at the bar between the living room and kitchen. "Hey, Sam."

Turning, Bo took Sam's arm and pulled him close. "Sam. I'm sorry, I didn't mean to wake you." He tilted his head up to kiss Sam's lips. The gentle touch went a long way toward dispelling the resentment Sam still felt toward Bo for letting work get in the way of their private time.

Sam summoned a smile. "You didn't wake me. I just..." He stopped, his stomach curdling at the memory of the nightmare that had woken him. He couldn't recall details, but he remembered the horrible, paralyzing fear, and blackness that seemed almost alive. Describing it didn't even seem possible, and he didn't feel like trying. "I had to pee."

David, sprawled on the sofa beside Cecile, wrinkled his nose. "TMI, man."

Sam flipped him off and turned back to Bo, ignoring David's laughter. "So, what're y'all watching?"

"I got something interesting on the thermal." Dean insinuated himself between Sam and Bo and rewound the thermal video a few seconds. "Check it out."

Sam peered over Dean's shoulder at the video screen. Dean hit play. The blur of blue gray on the display resolved itself into what looked like a smooth wall and a rather rough floor.

"This is one of the old weapons bunkers," Dean explained as the image panned slowly to the right to reveal a corner of the room. "There's only one door into the room, and it's behind me at this point. Cecile's standing just outside the door, taking video of the hallway. Now watch."

Something small and bright red darted across the bottom of the picture. "That's just a rat or something," Sam said, gesturing at the display. "You must've heard it."

"Yeah, we did. That's not it. Just wait—" Dean pointed at the far left side of the screen. "There. Look."

Sam looked. On the wall to the left of the corner was the light blue figure of a man in a uniform. An old-fashioned musket was slung over his shoulder. He turned his head, seeming to stare right at the camera, though the cap he wore hid his face. As Sam watched, the figure faded and vanished.

"Wow." Reaching around Dean's arm, Sam rewound the video and started it again. "That's amazing."

"Isn't it?" Bo rested his chin on Sam's shoulder, watching with him. "It's clearly a human figure, in what looks like a Confederate soldier's uniform, but the heat signature indicates that it's not much warmer than the wall."

"Dean and I tested to see if it might be his own body heat reflecting off the wall," Cecile chimed in from the sofa. "But it didn't work. Even his reflection was hotter than whatever this was."

"And I had to get really close to the wall to make it reflect me at all," Dean added. "Way closer than I was standing when I was filming. The walls at the fort are all stone or brick, so they don't reflect well. This one was actually one of the smoother ones, because it had been painted at one point."

"Pretty impressive." Halting the video again, Sam glanced over at Andre. "Did y'all get anything else?"

Andre shrugged. "Hopefully. We had a few personal experiences, but we won't know if we caught anything else concrete until we review the rest of the video and audio."

"Which we're going to have to start doing in a few hours." Rising to his feet, David held a hand down for Cecile and hauled her up. "We're off to bed. See y'all this afternoon."

David and Cecile exited amid a chorus of good nights. Cecile squeezed Sam's arm as she passed, and Sam gave her a smile in return.

Yawning, Sam laid an arm around Bo's shoulders. "I'm going back to bed, Bo, you coming?"

Bo hesitated. The desire to start watching videos right away was clear as day on his face, and Sam's heart plummeted to his feet.

Sam let his arm slip from around Bo and stepped back. "Okay. Guess I'll see you later today."

Sam turned and walked away without looking back. He was torn between fury and sorrow, and didn't understand why either emotion was so strong. Evidence as good as Dean's thermal video was rare, and Sam knew how excited Bo got about those things. Hell, they all did, Sam himself no less than any of the others. So why was he so upset about Bo wanting to go ahead and delve into the data from the night's work?

Because he'd rather do that than come back to bed with you, that's why.

Grimacing, Sam started up the stairs. He wished he could stop feeling so resentful of work. He loved his job. He'd loved it ever since he'd first arrived at Oleander House all those months ago for his first case with Bay City Paranormal. Bo felt the same, and Sam knew that. Their mutual love for their work was one of the things which had drawn them together in the first place. He hated that the business had begun to come between him and Bo.

No. That wasn't right. The business hadn't come between them. He'd *let* it come between them, for no reason at all other than his childish need to be first in Bo's heart.

"Fuck, Sam," he sighed, walking into the bedroom and kicking the door shut. He flopped on top of the wadded-up covers. "Why can't you just grow up? Why are you pouting like some stupid kid?"

Having no answer for that, he fell into bed and willed his body to relax.

He'd begun to doze off when the bedroom door opened. A shirtless silhouette in battered denim shorts slipped inside. Sam heard the sound of a zipper, then a muffled thump of fabric hitting the floor. Seconds later, the mattress dipped and a warm naked body molded itself to his. Bo laid his head on Sam's chest, and Sam wrapped an arm around him.

"Find anything else?" Sam asked, resting his cheek against Bo's hair.

"I don't know. I didn't stay to see."

"You didn't?"

"No."

"Why not?" Sam wasn't sure the question was a good idea, but he wanted to know. He wondered if he was just being a masochist.

For a moment Bo was silent, one finger idly circling Sam's nipple. "Do you want the truth?"

Sam frowned. "Of course I do."

"You were angry with me. And I didn't want you to be. When I know you're upset with me about something, it makes me feel literally sick." He cuddled closer, his hair tickling Sam's skin. "What have I done, Sam?"

The undercurrent of sadness in Bo's voice made Sam ache inside. He wound both arms around Bo and kissed the top of his head. "You haven't done anything. It's me. I'm tired, and it's making me act like a prick. I'm sorry."

Lifting a hand, Bo curled his fingers around Sam's forearm. "You don't need to be jealous of Bay City Paranormal, you know."

"I'm not jealous."

"Yes, you are. And I'm telling you right now, you shouldn't be." Bo raised his head and tucked a hand under his chin. His face was a blur in the darkness of the room. "I've put a great deal of my time and energy into this business. I'm proud of it, and I love it. But I love you more."

Sam's throat went tight. He knew what Bo was saying, and the knowledge of what Bo was offering to sacrifice for him was humbling.

Tangling his fingers in Bo's hair, Sam pulled him in for a soft, slow kiss. "I meant what I said before," he whispered against Bo's mouth. "I'd never ask you to give up the things that are important to you. I don't *want* you to. Whatever makes you happy, that's what I want."

Sam felt Bo's lips curve into a smile. They kissed again, then Bo settled back into Sam's embrace. Sam lay awake for a long time, trying to convince himself that he'd told Bo the truth.

Chapter Four

When Sam woke again, it was almost nine a.m. and Bo's side of the bed was cold. Rubbing sleep from his eyes, Sam hauled himself out of bed, went to the sliding glass door and pushed the curtains the rest of the way open.

It looked like another beautiful day in the making, sunny and perfect. A single wispy cloud floated across the deep azure sky. Beyond the dunes, the Gulf glittered like a jewel against the blinding white sand. A pelican plummeted into a turquoise swell, emerging moments later with a fish clutched in its beak. The sleek silver body flashed in the sun as it struggled in the bird's grip. The pelican swallowed its meal with a toss of its head, then rose into the air.

Sam watched the bird cut a graceful arc across the sky to the west. For some reason, the casual display of predator versus prey reminded him of the creatures from the portals. The things which could cross the boundaries between dimensions and snuff out a human life with as little effort as a man crushing a bug beneath his shoe. The thought chilled Sam to the marrow.

"No portals here," he reminded himself. "You don't need to worry about that right now."

Shaking off the uneasy feeling in the pit of his stomach, Sam went over to the dresser. He took off his boxers and kicked them into the corner where his and Bo's dirty clothes had been collecting. A moment's digging in the middle drawer turned up a pair of black and purple board shorts he'd forgotten he'd brought. He pulled them on, then left the bedroom and followed the mouthwatering aromas of sausage and fresh-brewed coffee down the stairs.

Andre and Bo sat huddled together at the table in the breakfast nook. They seemed to be holding a whispered argument. Bo sat hunched over, his back to Sam. The muscles in his bare shoulders stood out hard and tense. Andre wore an expression of helpless frustration with which Sam was all too familiar. He'd had enough disagreements with Bo to know just how Andre felt right now.

Sam shuffled into the room, and the whispers stopped as if a switch had been flipped. He shook his head. "Don't stop fighting on my account."

Bo stood and snagged Sam by the waist as he passed. "Good morning, Sam," he said, pressing close for a kiss. "I made biscuits, sausage and gravy, and I can fix you some eggs if you want."

Sam studied Bo's face. He was smiling, but he looked tired, and a stubborn crease marred the skin between his brows. Slipping an arm around him, Sam smoothed his thumb over Bo's forehead. "What's wrong, Bo?"

"He wants to come with us tonight," Andre burst out, cutting off anything Bo might have said. Pushing his chair back, Andre rose and pointed a stern finger at Bo. "You promised you wouldn't do this."

"I'm not surprised. Disappointed, yeah, but not surprised. I knew he couldn't hold out long." Sam raised his eyebrows at Bo, who blushed and scowled at the floor. "Actually, Bo, I'm kind of surprised you lasted *this* long."

Bo darted a sheepish look at him. "Okay, fine, you're right. I can't stop thinking about the case, and I'm dying to be a part of it." He touched Sam's cheek. "Come on, Sam. Can you honestly say you have no desire whatsoever to get involved?"

Sam wanted to claim he had no such wish, but he knew that would be a lie. As much as it galled him, he was itching to explore Fort Medina along with the rest of the team.

He sighed. "Dammit."

"I knew it." Bo's grin threatened to split his face in half. He slung his free arm around Sam's neck and bit his chin. "Let's go to the fort tonight and help with the investigation. Maybe if we get it out of our systems now, we'll be able to stay away the rest of the time. What do you think?"

"I think when you say 'we' what you really mean is *you.* I think you're projecting your own inability to control your workaholism onto me." Sam laid a finger across Bo's lips to stop the protest he knew was coming. "But I also think you have a point. I *am* curious about the place, and I'd like to be part of the investigation, if only for one night. I could live without it, but I'm not sure I could live with *you* living without it."

Bo snatched Sam's hand away from his mouth and laced their fingers together. "Does that string of insults mean you agree with me?"

"It's not insulting if it's the truth," Sam pointed out. "But yeah, I guess I sort of agree with you."

Behind Bo, Andre picked up his coffee mug and strolled into the kitchen. "Sam, you're as bad as he is."

Bo let go of Sam and followed Andre into the kitchen. Sam trailed behind them.

"Is it all right if we come, Andre?" Bo opened the cabinet beside the refrigerator and handed Sam a blue mug with cartoon dolphins capering across it. "You're the group leader on this case, so it's your call."

Andre laughed. "You know as well as I do that you wouldn't stay away if I asked you to. You'd play the 'boss' card."

Sam snickered as he poured coffee into his mug. "He's got you figured out, Bo."

Bo glared at him. "I would not do any such thing. If Andre would rather not have us on the team, we'll stay here."

"And put up with the tension and fighting from you being forced to stay here and be good? No thanks." Andre held out his mug for Sam to refill. "Seriously, I don't mind at all if y'all come with us, and I'm sure the rest of the team feels the same. The more the merrier."

Bo's eyes narrowed, but he nodded. "Thank you, Andre."

Sam stirred caramel-flavored creamer into his coffee, set the mug on the counter and took the clean plate Bo had left beside the stove. "What time do we start tonight?" he asked, piling his plate with biscuits and sausage and spooning gravy over it all.

"Eight-thirty. That's the earliest we can set up and get started after they close for the day." Andre held a hand out. "Will you hand me a piece of sausage?"

Grabbing a crisp brown patty off the platter, Sam laid it in Andre's palm. "How many nights is the investigation going to run? Or is that worked out yet?" He picked up his laden plate and started wolfing down his breakfast.

"We've arranged five nights at the fort, six hours each night including set-up and take-down." Andre bit into his sausage, chewed and swallowed. "I doubt we would've done any more than that even if Joanne had been able to be there any longer, which she couldn't. This is a relatively simple case. Five nights ought to give us plenty to work with."

Bo nodded, winding the tail of his braid around one hand. "So, y'all didn't sense anything out of the ordinary there?"

"Since when are residual hauntings and apparitions ordinary?" Sam asked with his mouth full.

Chuckling, Andre hooked his fingers through the handle of his coffee mug. "I guess they're only ordinary to professional paranormal investigators. But I believe I know what Bo means. Come on, let's go sit down." He strolled out of the kitchen and into the breakfast nook without waiting for an answer.

Bo went first. Sam followed, watching the hypnotic glide of Bo's walk, the flex of firm buttocks and long legs barely hidden by the clinging red swim trunks he wore. Sliding into the chair beside Bo's, Sam set his plate and mug on the table, reached over and squeezed Bo's thigh. Bo shot him a wicked grin in return, the sight causing a familiar clutching heat in Sam's gut.

"To answer your question," Andre said, sitting across the table and leaning his elbows on it, "no, Cecile and I didn't sense anything other than the general feeling of age and death that we get in any place with a history as long and bloody as the fort's. There was no sense of anything intelligent or in any way malicious." He turned a solemn look to Sam. "We didn't sense the sort of energy we've come to associate with portals."

A vague tension Sam hadn't realized he'd been carrying eased from his body. "Good. I really don't feel like dealing with any more of those right now." He traced the thin line of the scar on Bo's thigh with his thumb.

Bo's hand covered Sam's. "What about the EMF levels?"

Andre shifted in his chair, looking uncomfortable. "It was high. Four point three to four point seven, on average, though it varied from spot to spot."

Sam's stomach knotted. Every portal they'd dealt with so far had been associated with high natural electromagnetic field levels. In fact, most had opened in the presence of EMF significantly weaker than this one.

Turning Sam's hand over, Bo wove his fingers through Sam's. "But you didn't sense anything that would indicate portal activity."

Andre shook his head. "Definitely not."

Glancing at Sam, Bo squeezed his hand. "It'll be okay, Sam."

God, I hope so. "Promise me you'll tell us right away if your leg bothers you even a little."

"I promise." Bo bumped Sam's shoulder with his. "Don't worry, okay? Lots of places have a strong electromagnetic field. That alone doesn't mean there's any potential for a portal to form."

It was true. Although every portal they'd encountered had been in an area of high EMF levels, they didn't have nearly enough evidence to conclude that elevated EMF alone could create the potential for a portal. They'd only dealt with three of the interdimensional gateways, and one had already been permanently closed when they found it. That wasn't enough data upon which to base any conclusions, or even any solid theories. All they had so far was speculation, and Sam refused to let mere speculation worry him.

He forced a smile. "You're right. Plus, if there was a portal there, or ever *had* been, I'm sure Andre and Cecile would've picked up on it."

"Yeah, we would have." Lifting his mug, Andre took a long swallow of coffee. "Well. I don't know about you two, but I could use a little time on the beach before we start slogging through all the tapes and stuff from last night. Anyone up for a swim?"

"Me!" Dean bounded out of the hallway leading to the bedrooms and made a beeline for the kitchen. "Food first, though. I smell Bo's cooking."

Spearing a chunk of sausage on his fork, Sam quirked an eyebrow at Dean across the counter. "Where the hell did you get that?"

"Get what?" Dean grabbed a plate out of the cabinet and started piling it with food. "Oh wait, you mean this?" He pointed the spoon at a fading purplish mark on his collarbone, splattering himself with gravy in the process. He snatched the hand towel off the oven door handle and swabbed his chest clean. "I got it from Suzanne, last weekend. She's a good lay, but a little too rough. You should see the bite mark she left on my ass."

"Actually, I was talking about that tiny piece of fabric you're almost wearing," Sam clarified, raising his voice over Andre and Bo's laughter. "And I *did* see the bite mark. We all did, since your butt's hanging out of that thing."

"This *thing* is called a thong." Plate in one hand and a steaming coffee mug in the other, Dean sauntered into the breakfast nook. He set the dishes on the table and shimmied his hips. "Sexy, huh?"

Sam eyed the emerald green triangle barely covering Dean's privates. "Yeah. Although, I'm not sure who you're being sexy for."

With a shrug, Dean plopped into the chair beside Sam and tucked into his breakfast. "Hey, you never know who you might meet on the beach."

"One of those college boys staying next door, maybe?" Bo asked, looking amused.

An evil grin curved Dean's mouth. "Maybe."

"What if they're straight?" Sam picked up the last biscuit on his plate and bit off half of it.

Dean smirked over the rim of his coffee mug. "Nobody's *that* straight."

"You really need to work on your self-esteem problem, Dean." Draining his cup, Andre pushed his chair back and stood. "Okay, I'm going to go get changed. Into something more substantial than what *some* people are wearing, you'll all be glad to know."

"You just wish you had the balls to show off that fine bod in something like this," Dean declared, pointing his fork at Andre. "You'd look *way* too hot."

Andre patted Dean's tousled hair as he passed. "You know what, the thought of you staring at my ass all day and thinking it's hot is enough to keep me out of thongs forever."

Dean stuck his tongue out at Andre's retreating back, then turned his attention back to his plateful of food. "So. Y'all talked yourselves into coming to the fort with us yet?" He forked up a huge mouthful of gravy-covered biscuit and shoved it into his mouth.

"We did, actually," Bo answered, darting a surprised look at Sam. "Just now."

"You mean *you* did." Sam gestured at Bo with his half-empty mug. "I'm just going along with it to keep you happy."

Dean swallowed his mouthful and licked a stray drop of gravy from the corner of his mouth. "Oh please, Sam. You know damn well you wanted to come." He grinned, gray green eyes sparkling. "To the fort, I mean."

Groaning, Bo rubbed a hand over his eyes. "And on that note, I'm going to head on down to the beach."

"We'll be out in a few minutes." Sam gulped the rest of his coffee while Bo shoved his chair back and stood. "Where's the sunblock? Do I need to run upstairs and get it?"

"No, it's still out on the porch." Bo leaned over to kiss Sam. His braid fell forward, tickling Sam's chest. "Our towels are out there too." He straightened up. "Dean, there're several clean beach towels in the laundry room, if y'all need them."

"Cool, thanks." Lifting his mug, Dean blew on the coffee and took a sip. His gaze followed Bo out the French doors and onto the porch. "How big a fight was it?"

"Not that big, really. You were right about me wanting to go to the fort. That makes it kind of hard for me to yell at him about it." Sam stared out the window, hands folded on the table. "I won't lie to you, I was upset at first about y'all coming to stay here. This was supposed to be our time, you know? Just Bo and me. No work, no kids, nothing to do but just be together."

Putting his fork down, Dean laid a hand on Sam's arm. "I'm sorry."

Sam gave him a fond smile. "It's okay. Like I told Bo, I realized he was right to invite you. It didn't make sense for y'all to drive back and forth every night or spend money on a hotel when you could stay here. And Bo and I can still have our time together. We're hoping going on the case tonight'll get the urge to explore out of our systems."

Dean shook his head. "I don't know, Sam. Knowing the two of you, I think it'll just make it worse."

Sam didn't answer, and was glad Dean didn't push the issue. He had a sneaking suspicion his friend was right.

୧ଓ

At nine-thirty that night, the group stood in a huddle beneath the arch of the short tunnel forming the entrance to

Fort Medina. They'd set up cameras in strategic locations throughout the fort—with the help of what seemed like miles of extension cords—and were preparing to begin the night's investigation.

Sam gazed around at the fort's moonlit center pentangle and the high brick walls surrounding it. His stomach churned with a mixture of sadness and excitement. The fact that he and Bo had ended up here after all hurt, because it meant being with Sam hadn't been enough to keep Bo away. On the other hand, this place pulsed with the palpable energy of the centuries. The need to dive headfirst into it, to see and hear and *learn*, itched along Sam's palms.

Bo's hand closed around his arm, breaking his thoughts. He turned to meet Bo's smiling face. The childlike gleam in those brown eyes made Sam's heart lurch.

We both want to be here. Stop worrying. Sam returned Bo's smile. For a moment, the familiar thrill of a new case reverberated between them. It felt good.

"Okay, people. Equipment check." Andre pointed his pencil at Dean. "Thermal?"

"Got it." Dean patted the canvas bag hanging from his right shoulder. "I have extra batteries for all the gadgets in here too."

"Excellent." Tapping the pencil on his clipboard, Andre turned his attention to David. "Video?"

David saluted. "Video cameras ready for action, substitute boss-man."

"EMF and audio recorders are ready too." Cecile looked up from the powerful laptop they'd set up on a long table Joanne Biggers had provided for them. "All the stationary cameras are showing nice, clear pictures."

"Good thing for us they wired this place for electricity when they opened it to the public," David said, leaning against the wall and crossing his arms.

"Speaking of which, are all the floodlights off inside the fort?" Andre glanced at Cecile, eyebrows raised. "Cecile?"

"They should be," she answered. "Joanne turned them all off from the office right after we finished setting up."

Andre nodded. "Good. They're so bright they'd drown out anything we managed to catch on tape."

"What would you like Sam and me to do?" Bo asked. He gave his braid a tug.

"I'd like to check out the psychic energy here, if that's okay," Sam spoke up before Andre could say anything. "Bo can bring a notebook and record whatever I pick up."

"I have a better idea. How about if *you* take the notebook, and I take a video camera and audio recorder?" Bo nodded toward the equipment lined up on the table. "That way if you sense something, we can try to get some concrete evidence of it."

Sam gave Bo a sharp look. Bo stared back. His expression was relaxed, but the glint in his eyes warned of dire consequences if Sam protested. Clearly, Bo knew Sam had been trying to keep their workload to a minimum. Bo wasn't having it, and Sam knew from experience that he would argue his position all night if need be. The last thing Sam wanted right now was to fight with Bo over what they would and would not do in this investigation, and Bo knew it.

Sam sighed. "Okay."

"Great. Let's grab our stuff and get going." Setting his clipboard and pencil on the table, Andre picked up one of the video cameras. "Teams are David and Cecile, Sam and Bo, Dean and me. We have stationary cameras set up in all the main hotspots, but I want everyone to take a handheld video camera anyway, along with EMF detectors and an audio recorder.

Dean, you take the thermal first. We'll meet back here in an hour to touch base and you can give it to Cecile then."

"Gotcha." Dean took the small two-way radio from his belt and switched it on. "We still using channel two?"

"Yes." Andre turned on his own radio. "Come on, Dean. You and I will start from this first room on the left. David and Cecile, y'all start on the right. Sam and Bo, you can start up on top of the wall, if you want. The steps are across the courtyard from here."

With that, the group claimed the necessary equipment from the table and broke up to begin the night's work. Sam fished a notebook and pen out of a canvas bag lying beside the table. He trailed behind Bo as they crossed the five-cornered courtyard. The place looked eerie and mysterious in the moonlight.

On the other side, they stopped at the bottom of a flight of steep, narrow stone steps. Sam gazed up at the shape of the brick rampart against the night sky. "I think I'll leave off tuning into the psychic channel until we get up there."

"I think that's a good idea." Bo looked the steps up and down, lips pursed. "Look at this, Sam, there's a trough worn right down the middle."

Sam looked. Bo was right. Each step dipped in the center, the stone glinting where centuries of passing feet had worn it smooth. "We'd better be careful climbing these."

"Absolutely." Tucking the audio recorder into the front pocket of his jeans, Bo took Sam's hand and squeezed, then let go. "I'll go first."

Sam ascended the steps behind Bo, one hand clutching his notebook and pen and the other pressed to the wall for balance. The brick was cool and rough under Sam's palm. He let his psychic senses stretch just a little. The residual energy from hundreds—maybe thousands—of deaths swirled through him, making his head swim. He closed his mind to it. Falling down the stairs was not an idea which appealed to him.

Bo turned a stern look to him as he stepped out onto the wide rampart running the full length of the high wall. "I thought you were going to wait until we got up here."

Sam widened his eyes. "I just wanted to see if I could sense anything. How'd you know what I was doing, anyway?"

"I looked back and you didn't notice. You had that spaced-out look in your eyes."

"Oh."

"Did you feel anything?"

Sam smiled at the excited sparkle in Bo's eyes. "Nothing unexpected. Just the normal energy from all the people who've lived and died here."

Bo's relief was clear, even in the dark. "Good. Let me know if that changes." Switching on the video camera, Bo panned slowly from the steps out over the courtyard. "This is Sam and Bo, Fort Medina, Alabama, walkway on top of the wall," he recited for the record. "Date is May sixteenth, two thousand and five. Time is nine-forty-two p.m."

While Bo filmed, Sam wandered over to a deep, narrow notch in the wall. Pressing his free hand against the cool brick, he shut his eyes and let his awareness expand. Years upon years of death left behind a crackling energy which crawled over Sam's skin like a swarm of ants. As odd and uncomfortable as the sensation could be at times, it was by now a familiar one to Sam. There was nothing sinister in it.

"There's a lot of energy here," Sam murmured, opening his eyes and pacing down the walkway away from the steps. "But nothing specific. Have there been sightings here?"

"According to Andre, a headless male figure is often seen

here, just standing at the top of the steps for a moment before fading away."

"Creepy."

"Yes. According to the stories, a soldier was beheaded here during the Civil War. His head rolled down the steps and left bloodstains you can still see in the daylight."

Sam turned to face Bo. "Do bloodstains last that long?"

"I have no idea." Bo glanced away from the camera and grinned. "David thinks they paint over the stains from time to time so they can show people and tell the story of the soldier and his ghost."

"You know what, for once I think David's cynicism might be right on target."

"Maybe so. I—" Bo staggered, his shoulder hitting the wall. "Oh. Damn."

Alarmed, Sam hurried to his side. "What's wrong? Is it your leg?"

"No. It aches a little, but no more than it usually does. I just..." Bo leaned against the wall, brow furrowed. "I don't know."

Sam took the camera from Bo's shaking hand and switched it off. "Tell me what happened."

Bo closed his eyes, his head resting against the bricks behind him. "I saw something. Or rather, I suppose you could say I saw *nothing*. For a split second, I felt like I wasn't here, but someplace else. Someplace cold and dark, where the air was too heavy to breathe." He opened his eyes, staring at Sam with a blend of wonder and dread. "It was so strange, Sam. I felt like I was there forever, but it was all over in less time than it takes to blink, and I knew that."

The hairs stood up on the back of Sam's neck. "I had a

dream like that earlier. It woke me up when you were downstairs talking to everyone else after they came back from last night's investigation."

Bo's expression hardened. "We're both getting too much sun and not enough rest, and it's causing us to hallucinate."

Sam frowned. "Maybe so, but we don't *know* that. After everything we've experienced in the past few months, we shouldn't be so quick to dismiss this as imagination."

"Not imagination. Hallucination. There's a difference." Pushing away from the wall, Bo held out his hand. "Give me the camera, and we'll continue our sweep up here."

Sam handed over the camera, then grabbed Bo's arm to stop him from moving away. "Bo, come on. Don't you think we ought to at least consider the possibilities here? You just had a...I don't know, a vision or something, that was exactly the same as my dream. Don't you think that's enough to act on?"

"Act on how, exactly? What do you suggest we do?"

"Leave," Sam said with a sudden rush of conviction. "Right now. And stay away."

The look in Bo's eyes told Sam what he was going to say before he ever spoke. "No. That's ridiculous. We're not leaving. Whether we come back or not is another question, but at this point I think we should, if only to prove to you that there's no danger here."

Anger and frustration heated Sam's cheeks. "I don't know why you bother to ask my opinion, when it obviously doesn't matter to you what I think."

Bo snatched his arm away from Sam's hand. "Did you sense anything when I had that hallucination? Anything at all?"

"No. Not that that proves anything." Sam crossed his arms and glared at Bo. "And I notice you didn't even bother to try and convince me you *do* care what I think."

Bo's eyes narrowed. For a second, Sam thought the argument was about to degenerate into blows. Then the hard, angry expression melted from Bo's face. He closed the distance between them, wound his free arm around Sam's neck and kissed him.

"I do care what you think," Bo declared, his voice soft but firm. "I know I'm opinionated and overbearing at times, but your opinion is always important to me. *You* are important to me. Never doubt that."

Sam nodded and forced a smile, but his heart wasn't in it. He knew Bo loved him, and that he was important in Bo's life. But when it came to this particular incident, it was clear that his opinion didn't even register with Bo.

It wasn't the first time, and it wouldn't be the last. When Bo made up his mind about something, there was no getting through to him. Either he talked himself into changing his own outlook, or it didn't happen. Sam knew that and accepted it as one of the less endearing aspects of Bo's personality, but accepting it didn't make it any easier to deal with.

If Bo noticed Sam's strained smile, he didn't let on. He kissed Sam again, fingers caressing his neck, then stepped back. "Okay. Enough of that for now. Let's finish this up."

Sam pretended to fall into the half-trance from which he normally connected to the realm of psychic energy, but he couldn't concentrate enough to actually do it. Instead, he watched Bo through slitted eyelids.

Something wasn't right. He couldn't pinpoint what, exactly, but the certainty that everything had just changed in a fundamental way hooked its talons into his gut and wouldn't let go.

The worst part was, he knew he would figure it out

eventually, and part of him very much didn't want to know.

Chapter Five

The remainder of the night passed without further incident. They wandered the fort separately from the rest of the team, Bo filming while Sam watched him. After the first few minutes, Sam kept his psychic senses partially open, hoping to catch any changes if Bo should have another episode.

A couple of times, Sam saw Bo freeze and stiffen for a moment. Sam let his mind fully open to whatever might be there at those moments, even though Bo never mentioned any more visions. The fort's energy pulsed and shifted to the extent that Sam couldn't be entirely sure what he did and didn't feel, but he never sensed anything alarming, and after a while he began to relax a bit.

Not that he was letting it go. He didn't feel safe brushing the issue aside, considering BCPI's experience with the portals and how little they truly knew about the phenomenon. Later, when they were alone, he planned to pin Bo down and have a serious talk. Now, however, wasn't the time. He'd learned the hard way that pushing Bo about such a subject in the middle of an investigation caused more problems than it solved.

The group assembled at the entry arch at two a.m. and went to work taking down the cameras and putting away the equipment. They worked silently, all anxious to finish and get back to the house.

Sam yawned as he slung the bag full of extension cords into the back of the SUV. "Damn, I'm beat. I hate investigating at night."

"You said it, brother." David hefted two bulky camera cases into the vehicle. "That's the last of it. Where's Andre and Bo? I need to get in bed in the next ten minutes or I'm gonna collapse and sleep wherever I fall down."

"I think they're talking to Joanne." Sam stepped back and slammed the tailgate shut. He turned around just in time to see Bo and Andre exit the ticket office, followed by a middle-aged woman in a calico dress. "Never mind, here they come."

Bo, Andre and Joanne walked up as Cecile and Dean joined Sam and David at the back of the SUV. "Hey, Joanne," Dean said. "Thanks for letting us use that table."

"Sure thing." She smiled, crinkling the corners of her eyes. "It's in the office, so y'all can use it any time you want."

"That's very good of you, thank you." Andre stuck his hand out. "Same time tomorrow night?"

She took his hand and shook it. "That'll be fine. See you then."

The group called goodbyes as she hurried to her battered old blue Subaru, got in and cranked the engine. She drove away, waving out the open window.

"Are we ready to go?" Cecile yawned and leaned against David's shoulder. "I'm worn out."

Andre nodded. "We're ready."

Sam pulled up the middle seat so Cecile and David could crawl into the rear, then locked it back into place and climbed into the middle seat beside Bo. "So, did y'all experience anything interesting?"

"I'll say." David leaned forward, folding his arms on the

back of Sam's seat as Andre pulled out of the parking lot. "We saw a mist form in one of the bunkers. I got it on video, and Cecile asked some questions to see if we could catch some EVPs. It was the same bunker where you got that thermal, Dean. May have been the same dude."

"Cool." Twisting around, Dean peered over the back of his seat at David. "Get this, y'all, I caught footage of the headless soldier."

"Oh man, awesome!" David held his hand up over Sam's shoulder, and Dean reached over to high-five him. "We didn't see anything there."

"Yeah, well, I hope the video comes out okay. I saw it pretty well, but it's probably a residual, and you know how those are. They don't always show up well on video."

"We'll see, I guess." Andre glanced over his shoulder, a crease between his brows. "Sam and Cecile, did either of you feel a..." He paused, clearly searching for the right word. "A change in the energy of the fort? Nothing spectacular, just a very brief blip before it went back to normal?"

"I did, yes," Cecile answered, her tone thoughtful. "Twice. Well, maybe three, I'm not sure. The psychic energy here is very strong, and it seemed to fluctuate a lot tonight, so it's difficult to tell, really."

The hairs stood up along Sam's arms. "When did y'all feel this?"

"I don't remember." A car pulled out of a nearby drive behind them, its headlights illuminating Andre's frown in the rearview mirror. "I wrote it down, though. I can look it up later when we're going through the data from tonight."

"Same here." Cecile shifted in her seat, her skirt rustling. "Sam? Did you feel it?"

"No, I didn't," he admitted. "Like you said, the energy of

this place is kind of hard to read."

Bo gave him a sharp look, and Sam felt his cheeks flush under that penetrating gaze. Bo knew him well enough to figure out *why* he'd missed something the other psychics had felt. The hard, tight set to Bo's features told Sam he'd be hearing exactly what Bo thought of that later.

Sam stifled a groan. He wasn't in the mood for a lecture from Bo.

The rest of the short ride home passed in silence. Andre pulled into the circular drive of his sister's beach house and parked right in front of the door. "Okay. Let's get unloaded as fast as we can. I'm about to fall asleep here."

"You and everybody else." Dean opened the passenger side door and stumbled out, yawning. "Damn."

The group piled out of the SUV and re-converged at the back. David opened the tailgate while Bo dug the house key out of his pocket and went to unlock the front door. Taking two large equipment bags out of the SUV, Sam followed Bo into the house. By the time he set his burden down in the living room, Bo had already gone back outside to help carry things in.

They passed each other on the front porch as Sam was going out and Bo was coming in with a camera case in each hand. Sam caught Bo's arm. "Bo, we need to talk."

"You're damn right, we do." Bo shook loose of Sam's grip, dark eyes snapping. "Upstairs, after we unload."

Swallowing his growing anger, Sam nodded. "Fine. But you're not the only one with something to say."

He strode out the door before Bo could retort. Cecile gave him a concerned look as he walked past her toward the SUV. He pretended not to see. Cecile had been a good friend and confidante to him ever since Oleander House, but he didn't feel like telling her about his latest conflict with Bo. He didn't even

75

know what to tell himself, never mind anyone else. When he thought about it, he could find no good reason why he and Bo should be so angry with each other, but for his own part he couldn't seem to help it. Something about Bo destroyed his ability to think logically, reducing him to gut reaction. It was frustrating as hell.

Within ten minutes, all the equipment was unloaded and stashed in the corner of the living room where the group had set up shop. Sam said good night to his friends, then stalked up the stairs with Bo at his heels. He could feel the others watching them, most likely wondering what he and Bo were fighting about this time. He didn't think he could explain it even if he wanted to.

Inside the bedroom, Bo shut the door and leaned against it, arms crossed. "Explain to me why you felt you had to watch me instead of reading the fort's psychic energy like you were supposed to be doing."

"Because you were deliberately ignoring something that might be important." Sam dropped into the rattan chair next to the sliding glass doors and leveled a pointed stare at Bo. "I kept my senses partially extended. But after that vision you had—"

"Hallucination."

"Vision. After you brushed it off and pretended it was nothing, even though it was *exactly* like the dream I had, I wanted to keep an eye on you, and I couldn't do that if I was in full psychic mode."

"It *was* nothing. I was fine then, and I'm fine now." Bo pointed an accusing finger at Sam. "You had a job to do, Sam, and you didn't do it. There's no excuse for that."

At that, Sam's control snapped. He jumped to his feet, crossed the room in a few strides and grabbed Bo by the shoulders. "We weren't even supposed to *be* there, Bo! *You* fucking dragged us out there, then you have the fucking nerve to tell me I'm not doing my job?" He shoved Bo hard against the wall, then let go and backed away. "Fuck you."

Bo stood stock-still, hands hanging by his sides, eyeing Sam warily. "You wanted to go as much as I did."

"Yeah, I wanted to go, sure. The difference is, it wouldn't have bothered me if we didn't go. You just wouldn't fucking leave it alone."

Silence. They stared at each other, neither speaking. Neither giving any ground. Suddenly Sam felt horribly tired. Turning away, he went to the sliding glass doors, opened them and walked out onto the porch.

He leaned against the rail and gazed into the darkness. The night air felt wonderfully cool on his face. He could smell the ocean, could hear the whisper of the waves on the sand, but he couldn't see a thing past the glow of light spilling across the sand from the house. A thick cloud cover had rolled in over the last couple of hours, obscuring the moon and stars. The blackness mirrored Sam's mood.

Footsteps sounded behind him. He didn't turn around, but when Bo's arms enclosed him, he laid his hands over Bo's and leaned back into his lover's embrace.

"I shouldn't have said that," Bo murmured against Sam's ear. "You're right, we were only there because I insisted. I had no right to accuse you of not doing your job. Especially when you're one of the most conscientious workers I've ever known."

"No, you really didn't have any right to say that to me." Sam lifted one of Bo's hands and kissed his knuckles. "I have to tell you the truth here. It really worried me that you wouldn't even consider the possibility of what you experienced having any kind of significance. After Oleander House, and especially after that thing bit you at South Bay High, I'd think you'd at least want to keep an open mind. You could be in danger here."

"What kind of danger are you afraid of, Sam?" Bo tilted his head sideways and rested his cheek against Sam's shoulder. "I don't feel as if my safety is threatened, if that makes you feel any better."

"It doesn't."

"Then tell me what you're afraid is going to happen to me. Help me understand."

Sam stared into the night, trying to find the words to articulate his fears. Everything he could think of to say sounded paranoid, even to him.

"I don't know," he admitted at last. "It's just that you've never had any experiences like that before, and this one just happened to be exactly like my dream. When that happened at Oleander House, when we all had the same dreams, Amy died."

Bo's arms tightened around Sam's waist. "This isn't the same. Whatever it was that happened to me at the fort, it was only for a second. I didn't actually *see* anything, I just felt as if I were somewhere else. Something like that can be attributed to a thousand different causes."

"What about what Cecile and Andre felt?"

"You didn't feel it, and you're the one who's usually the most sensitive to the..." Bo trailed off, his body shifting. "To changes in a place's energy. Even without your senses in full use, I'm positive you would've noticed if it were anything strong enough to be dangerous. Besides, Cecile and Andre both agreed that it's difficult to get an accurate psychic reading at the fort."

Sam laughed in spite of himself. "There's no such thing as an 'accurate' psychic reading."

Bo's soft chuckle vibrated against Sam's back. "You know what I mean."

"Yeah." Turning in Bo's arms, Sam framed Bo's face in his hands. "Maybe you're right. Maybe I'm letting past experiences cloud my judgment in this case."

"That's all it is." Bo's hands covered Sam's, holding Sam's palms to his cheeks. "After all we've been through in the past few months with the portals, I can't really blame you." He leaned forward and pressed a swift kiss to Sam's lips. "I'm not in any danger at the fort, Sam. None of us are."

Sam wasn't sure he believed that, but he had to admit Bo had a point. It was possible that Sam's mind, fueled by memories of Bo's near death, was making connections that weren't there.

Dropping his hands to Bo's hips, Sam pulled him close. "Just promise me you'll tell me if you have any more of those visions, okay?"

"Hallucinations," Bo corrected with a grin. He molded his body to Sam's. "Let's go to bed."

One of Bo's legs slipped between Sam's. A firm thigh pressed against his balls. Sam gulped. "Promise me first."

For a second, Bo's eyes hardened. Then his mouth curved into the smile that always made Sam's knees weak. Bo stepped back, letting his hands slide down to grasp Sam's. "Whatever you want, Sam. Now come to bed."

Sam's feet were moving before he gave them permission, led by the promise of a different sort in Bo's smile. He followed Bo inside, shut the door and drew the curtains.

Later, lying wide awake with Bo sleeping beside him, Sam realized Bo hadn't promised him anything at all.

&

Sam jolted awake, his heart slamming against his ribs. The first dawn light leaked around the curtains to lend a dim illumination to the room. Sam sat up and looked around, trying to figure out what had woken him. The dream he'd been yanked out of was just as horrible as the one from the previous morning, but it wasn't what had disturbed Sam's sleep. It was something else, some sort of noise or movement in the bedroom.

A low, ragged moan drifted from the pile of covers bunched on the other side of the bed. Bo's body jerked, throwing off the corner of the bedspread which had obscured his face. His brows were drawn together in fear or pain, or both. Little whimpers bled from his open mouth. When Sam laid a hand on Bo's bare shoulder, he could feel Bo trembling.

Sam frowned. In the short time he'd shared Bo's bed, the man had never suffered nightmares. The fact that he seemed to be having one now of all times made Sam feel cold all over.

"Bo, wake up." He gave Bo's shoulder a shake.

With a sharp cry, Bo shot to a sitting position, panting like he'd just sprinted a mile. His wide-eyed gaze darted around the room. The fear melted from his eyes when they met Sam's.

"Fuck." He flopped onto his back. "God, I'm glad you woke me up."

"You've never had nightmares before," Sam pointed out, keeping his tone carefully neutral. He lay down beside Bo and propped himself up on one elbow. "What was it about?"

"Damned if I know." Bo tugged at a lock of tangled black hair lying across his chest. "I don't remember anything specific. Just...weird images. They were terrifying when I was dreaming them, but I couldn't even tell you what they were now."

"Strangely enough, I just woke up from another dream like I had yesterday morning. And now you're having them too."

Sam licked his lips, hoping his next words didn't touch off an angry tirade. "Was this nightmare anything like what you saw at the fort?"

"Not really, except for the general sense of fear, and not being able to breathe properly." Bo darted a pointed look at him. "I know what you're thinking, Sam, but I really don't believe the two are related. I don't usually have nightmares, that's true, but I have had a few in my life. The hallucinations I had last night probably triggered one, that's all."

A hard chill raced up Sam's spine. "I thought you said it only happened once."

"It did."

"Then why did you just say 'hallucinations', plural, like it happened more than once?"

A muscle twitched in Bo's jaw. "I didn't mean to say that. I meant to say 'hallucination', singular."

"But—"

"For God's sake, Sam, drop it!"

Anger and frustration boiled up inside Sam and bubbled over. He kept his voice calm with an effort. "I will not drop it. This is important. I'm sure of it."

Sighing, Bo pressed both palms to his eyes. "Look. I know you're worried, and I understand why. But *one* strange feeling during the investigation and one nightmare do not add up to anything dangerous, or even concerning."

"Even though I had a very similar dream yesterday morning, and again just now?" Sam persisted. "Even after the dreams at Oleander House?"

"This is nothing like Oleander House." Turning onto his side, Bo folded an arm beneath his head and gazed into Sam's eyes with a pleading expression. "Don't you think I'd tell you if I felt this was anything to worry about? Do you really think I'd put everyone in danger by keeping it to myself?"

"No, of course not." Sam tucked Bo's hair behind his ear, fingers brushing his neck. "But I don't think you're seeing this situation clearly."

Bo's fingers curled, bunching the sheet between them. He looked away. "What makes you think I'm not being clearheaded about this?"

"I don't know, exactly." It was hard for Sam to say, but it was true. He couldn't lie to Bo, no matter how difficult it might be to tell the truth. "All I know is, you're not acting like yourself. And that worries me."

With an impatient noise, Bo kicked the covers aside and started to get up. Sam wrapped both arms around his waist and rolled on top of him, pinning him to the bed.

"Let me up," Bo growled, dark eyes flashing.

"No."

"Sam..."

Fisting a hand in Bo's hair, Sam leaned down and kissed him until the angry tension melted from his body and his mouth opened beneath Sam's.

The kiss went on for endless, blissful minutes. Sam didn't break it until Bo's legs opened to cradle Sam in the space between his thighs. Drawing back, Sam stared down into Bo's heavy-lidded eyes. Bo's pupils were dilated, his breath coming short and quick. The sight made Sam's chest ache.

"I love you," Sam said, putting his whole heart into the simple sentiment. "Maybe these dreams and visions of yours mean something, and maybe they don't. I think they do, but I don't know for sure. All I know is, I'll do anything to keep you safe. Even risk you hating me."

The lingering anger in Bo's eyes faded into a familiar affection. He reached up and laid both palms on Sam's cheeks. "I could never hate you. I'm grateful every single day to have you in my life."

Sam's throat closed up. He couldn't say what he felt right then, but he thought Bo understood.

Bo's gaze dipped to Sam's mouth. When he looked up again, lust had replaced the tenderness in his eyes. Sam's body responded with a predictable rush of desire. He tilted his hips, rubbing his naked prick against Bo's equally bare crotch. Bo moaned, low and rough. His thighs slid against Sam's ribs, one heel lodging in the small of Sam's back. Sam could feel Bo's cock filling, the hardness pressing against Sam's own growing erection.

A tiny corner of Sam's brain wanted to disentangle himself from Bo's arms and legs and continue the conversation Sam was beginning to realize Bo had successfully distracted him from. But the clutch of Bo's limbs around him, the increasingly frantic movement of Bo's hips and the needy little sounds he made, silenced that part of Sam's mind. One arm beneath Bo's neck and the other braced on the bed, Sam took Bo's mouth in a bruising kiss as they thrust against one another.

It was over far too fast. Bo shook and whimpered when he came, his teeth digging into Sam's shoulder as his semen spread between them and mingled with Sam's. Sam collapsed onto his side with Bo still plastered against him. He pressed a kiss to Bo's forehead and let his eyes close.

When Sam woke again, late morning light flooded the room. Bo was gone. Once again, nothing had been resolved between them. With a deep sigh, Sam hauled himself out of bed and went to get dressed.

Chapter Six

Jogging along in the humid shade of the live oaks lining the footpath, Sam stared at Bo's bare back with a mixture of irritation and longing. Dragging Bo away from evidence review for a run had been hard. Convincing him to try the recreational pathways through the nearby public park instead of running to the fort again had been even worse. Bo had eventually agreed, but only after Sam accused him of having an unhealthy obsession with the fort.

He hadn't spoken a word to Sam since. They'd run in silence, with Bo staying several strides ahead. Sam couldn't help but wonder if keeping Bo away from everything to do with the case had been worth it. He missed their usual camaraderie, the way they'd tease and prod each other to keep up the pace and pass the time.

Stop blaming yourself. He's the one being unreasonable. He is obsessed with the Fort Medina case, he just won't admit it. It's not your fault he's acting like a child.

Bo turned a sharp corner of the path and disappeared from Sam's view. Wiping the sweat from his eyes, Sam forced his feet to move faster. His limbs felt slow and heavy in the sticky afternoon heat. He and Bo were usually pretty evenly matched in their running pace, but today Sam struggled constantly to keep up with Bo. He didn't know whether he was slower than usual or Bo was faster, but it was frustrating either way. For reasons he couldn't define, he was anxious to keep Bo in sight.

Putting on a brief burst of speed, Sam rounded the bend. He nearly plowed into Bo, who was standing stiff and still in the middle of the path, head bowed and hands clenched at his sides. He didn't even look up when Sam skidded to a halt beside him.

Sam touched Bo's arm. "Bo? Are you okay?"

No answer. Heart galloping and mouth dry, Sam walked around until he could see Bo's face. Bo's eyes were wide and blank, staring at the ground.

Sam's stomach knotted. He grabbed Bo's shoulders. "Bo!"

Bo gave a violent start. His head snapped up. "What? What's wrong?"

"You tell me." Sam let go of Bo and stepped back, watching Bo's face. "You were just standing there, staring at the ground. You didn't even answer me when I asked if you were okay."

Fear flashed through Bo's eyes before his expression closed down. "Oh, that. I felt dizzy and sick all of a sudden, so I stopped. I heard you, I just couldn't answer. I felt like I was going to pass out." He rubbed the back of his neck and looked away. "I didn't mean to worry you. Sorry."

He's lying. To Sam's knowledge, Bo hadn't lied to him about anything in months. Not since the first days they'd known each other, when Bo had tried to deny his sexuality and his attraction to Sam. It was disheartening to think he would do so now, but Sam was certain that was exactly what he was doing.

"It must be the heat," Sam said, and wondered why he wasn't confronting Bo with his deception. Maybe he was just tired of fighting. "Let's sit down and let you cool off for a minute. You can have the rest of my water."

They walked over to a nearby bench half-hidden in the trees and sat. Sam handed Bo his mostly full water bottle. Bo's fingers brushed Sam's as he took it, sending sparks up Sam's arm. Bo put the bottle to his lips, tilted his head back and drank. Sam watched his throat work and had to fight off the urge to gather Bo into his arms and plaster kisses to his sweat-slick skin.

Bo lowered the bottle with a sigh and leaned back against the bench. "Thanks. That helped. I guess I was setting too hard a pace for this heat."

"It's supposed to be a record high for today's date." Sam stared into the shadows beneath the oaks. A squirrel darted through the undergrowth and raced up a tree with a scrabble of claws on bark. "Want to go for a swim when we get back?"

Bo was silent for a moment. Sam clasped his hands together so hard his knuckles turned white. *Please say yes. Don't go back to helping review the evidence from last night. Just spend some time with me, please, please…*

"Okay, sure. A swim'll be perfect today."

Turning, Sam caught Bo's gaze. Bo's smile thawed some of the apprehension lodged like a ball of ice in Sam's gut.

Sam took Bo's hand in his and squeezed. "Thank you."

"What for?" Bo asked, his expression puzzled.

For not brushing me off so you could work on the case. For putting us first for a change.

Sam swallowed. "For spending time with me today. It means a lot to me."

Without even checking to see if anyone was around, Bo leaned forward and captured Sam's mouth in a swift, hungry kiss. He nipped Sam's lip as they drew apart, and rested his forehead against Sam's.

"I want to spend time with you," Bo murmured, long fingers caressing Sam's cheek. "I love you. I'm sorry I've been such a prick lately. I don't know why I've been acting that way."

It was on the tip of Sam's tongue to bring up Bo's dreams and visions, but he kept it to himself. He didn't want to dredge up that argument again, just when Bo seemed to be coming back to him. He didn't have anything concrete to go on anyway, merely a vague sense of connection between Fort Medina and the strange things Bo had experienced. There was no reason to suspect that any of it had anything to do with the interdimensional gateways, or the things living on the other side. The fact that Sam believed it did probably said more about his own state of mind than anything else.

Staring into Bo's eyes, Sam made a silent vow not to bring it up again until he had solid evidence, something Bo's scientific mind couldn't ignore. With any luck, there wouldn't be any need for such evidence. Sam hoped not, because finding concrete proof would mean Bo was in danger, and Sam didn't want to face that again.

Forcing a smile, Sam pulled back. "You feeling better now? Ready to head back?"

"Yes, on both counts." Bo stood, one hand on Sam's shoulder to steady himself. "Let's keep the pace slow this time. I'm a little shaky still."

"Sure thing. You were almost too fast for me to keep up with you before." Sam rose, lifting Bo's hand from his shoulder and winding their fingers together. He kissed Bo's knuckles before letting go. "Would you rather walk?"

"No, I can handle a slow jog." Bo gave Sam a wry grin. "I promise I'll tell you if I need to walk."

Let's hope you can keep this *promise.* Sam bit back the bitter words before they could emerge. "All right. You set the pace."

With a nod, Bo started down the path in the direction from which they'd come. He smacked Sam's ass and arched an eyebrow at him. Sam followed, savoring the change in Bo's mood and hoping it would last. He had a feeling it wouldn't, but you never knew. Stranger things had happened.

ಬ

David, Cecile and Andre were still going over evidence from the previous two nights when Sam and Bo returned. Andre sat on the edge of a chair, headphones on, frowning at the laptop screen. He glanced at them and nodded before turning his attention back to his work. David, sprawled on his stomach on the carpet with the thermal camera in front of him, acknowledged Sam and Bo's return with a distracted wave.

Cecile stopped the audio recorder in her hand and took her earbuds out. "Hi, guys. Did you have a good run?"

"It was all right," Sam told her, mopping sweat from his brow. "Hot."

"*Very* hot, especially for mid-May." Bo brushed his fingers across the back of Sam's hand as he headed for the kitchen. "I'm getting some Gatorade, Sam, you want some?"

"What flavor do we have?"

"Hang on." Sam heard the refrigerator door open, then the sound of glass and plastic being shuffled around. "All that's left is lemon-lime."

Sam wrinkled his nose. "I hate lemon-lime. It tastes like sweat."

Bo's laugh floated from the kitchen. "That's because it's meant to replace the electrolytes you lose through sweating."

"Just bring me a bottle of water, if you don't mind."

"Okay."

The refrigerator door banged shut, and Bo came back into the living room with a plastic bottle in each hand. He handed the bottle of water to Sam, then twisted the top off his Gatorade and gulped half of it in a few long swallows. Sam drank the cold water gratefully.

"Where's Dean?" Bo flopped onto one of the chairs around the dining table, holding his sweating bottle to his forehead.

"Outside someplace." Chuckling, Cecile tucked her legs beneath her. "We all went out on the beach for a walk earlier, just for a little break, and we met up with those college kids staying next door. One of those boys was completely smitten with Dean. They're out there talking still."

"Talking, my ass." David glanced up and grinned, blue eyes glinting. "I'd bet my last dollar Dean's got that kid's cock down his throat by now."

"David!" Cecile uncurled one leg and aimed a barefoot kick at David's forehead. "Don't be crude."

"What? It's true!" He grabbed her foot and bit her big toe, making her squeal.

"You don't know that." Shaking her head, Cecile retrieved her foot before David could bite her again. "In any case, Bo, Dean is outside with his new friend."

Andre stopped the video he was watching and pulled his headphones off. "Just for the record, Bo, I told him he could stay out there for a while. He was up working today before any of the rest of us."

Bo gave Andre an affronted look. "I wasn't going to say anything."

Andre raised a skeptical eyebrow, but kept quiet. He put

his headphones back on then restarted the video.

Scowling at Andre, Bo turned back to Cecile. "Have y'all found anything since Sam and I left?"

"Nothing we didn't already know about. You already know about the EVPs."

Sam and Bo both nodded. Cecile had captured three distinct voices on her audio recorder the night before—two different male voices and one female. The woman seemed to be speaking French. Even though he hadn't been happy about Bo doing evidence review—and dragging him into it as well—Sam had been just as excited as the rest of the group about the find.

"What about the headless soldier?" Bo asked. "How did that footage come out?"

Cecile shrugged. "We could make out the shape, but it isn't as distinct as we would've liked."

"That's not surprising. At least Dean got footage of it, even if it isn't very clear." Bo pulled on the end of his braid. "So, there's nothing unexpected?"

Bo's tone was casual, but Sam heard the real question lurking behind the seemingly innocent inquiry. He shot Bo a stormy glare. Bo ignored it.

"No," Cecile answered. "Of course we haven't reviewed everything yet, but we've been over the thermal and audio and most of the video from the time when Andre and I felt that weird change in the fort's energy, and nothing's showed up so far."

The smile that curled Bo's lips seemed triumphant to the point of gloating. Sam bit his tongue. He wasn't about to let Bo goad him into another fight.

Downing the rest of his water, Sam crushed the bottle and tossed it across the room into the bucket they were using as a recycling bin. "Okay, I'm going for a swim. Bo?"

"Definitely." Bo toed off his running shoes, peeled off the sweaty socks and rose to his feet. "Cecile, we'll be back later."

"Take your time. Y'all are still on vacation." She put the earbuds back in and started the audio, shooing them away with one slender hand. "Go on."

Pulling off his own shoes and socks and setting them with Bo's beside the back door, Sam followed Bo outside. He grabbed a foam raft and tucked it under his arm before leaving the relative cool of the back porch. Fierce heat wrapped around him like a blanket as he and Bo stepped out into the sun.

"My God, I think it's gotten hotter." Bo grinned. "Ready?"

"Ready."

They ran across the burning sand and splashed into the ocean. The blue green water felt wonderfully cool on Sam's overheated skin. Hooking his arms over the raft, he dug his feet into the sandy seafloor and let his body go limp.

Bo ducked underwater and popped to the surface next to Sam. "That feels absolutely fantastic."

"Mm-hm." Sam folded his arms on top of the raft and laid his cheek against them. "Pour some water on my head."

"You could've just gone under like I did," Bo pointed out with a laugh. Cupping his hands, he scooped a double palmful of water and dumped it over Sam's head. "Better?"

Sam shut his eyes against the salty trickle. The sun glowed red through his closed lids. "Yeah. Do it again."

Chuckling, Bo dumped more water over Sam's head, kissed his shoulder and swam off. Sam stayed where he was, toes buried in the sand and head pillowed on his arms, and let the gentle swells rock him into a contented doze. He felt lazy and relaxed, the tension of the past couple of days fading in the sunshine and sea breeze. The ocean's cool liquid embrace around his lower body formed a delicious contrast to the heat pressing like a weight on his shoulders and upper back. The only sounds were the sigh of the waves on the shore and the splashing of Bo's arms and legs as he swam.

Sam couldn't remember the last time he'd felt so peaceful. He wished he could shrinkwrap this moment and keep it forever.

A sudden chorus of whoops and laughter broke through Sam's torpor. He cranked his eyelids to half-mast just in time to see a group of young men and women race down the beach and into the water. It was the people from the house next door. Sam grinned when he realized one of the boys was missing. *Wonder what sort of perversions Dean's talked him into?*

A cool, wet hand planted itself between his shoulder blades. He yelped. "Cold!"

Bo laughed, fingertips drawing chilly patterns on Sam's back. "I see one of our neighbors is missing."

"I noticed that, yeah." Yawning, Sam stretched his arms out across the raft. "What do you think they're doing?"

"You mean what do I think our resident charmer is doing with his barely legal new friend?"

Sam snickered. "Yeah."

"Hm. Well, I imagine they're..."

Bo trailed off into silence. Frowning, Sam twisted his head around. Bo was staring into the middle distance, his features slack.

Fear clutched at Sam's insides. "Bo?"

Bo blinked, and his eyes focused on Sam's face. He smiled. "Sorry. I was just thinking."

Suspicious, Sam narrowed his eyes. "About what?"

"Nothing, really. Just hoping Dean's summer fling really *is* legal. I'd hate for him to get in trouble."

Bo radiated sincerity, but Sam didn't buy it. He'd seen that blank look on Bo's face before, at the fort and again on the run that morning.

He's still seeing those things, and he's lying about it again to hide it from me.

The thought of another argument turned Sam's stomach, but he couldn't let Bo lie about something this potentially important without calling him on it.

Could he? Would it be so bad to let it go? He'd promised himself he wouldn't bring it up again. Wouldn't it be better to keep his worries to himself?

The memory of the nightmarish otherdimensional creature sinking its teeth into Bo's leg was answer enough to that question.

Sam straightened up and squared his shoulders, bracing himself for a fight. "Bo, listen—"

He broke off when Bo grinned and ducked beneath the water. Sighing, Sam draped his upper body across the raft again. He stared morosely down the beach, where the group from the house next door was having a noisy chicken fight in the calm water. He wished he and Bo could relax and have fun together like that, without work and lies and hard feelings getting in the way.

Fingers curled over the waistband of Sam's shorts. He didn't have time to react before the garment was yanked down. His cheeks were spread and a slick tongue pressed against his hole.

"Oh fuck," Sam breathed, fingers clenching on the raft. What in the hell did Bo think he was doing?

The tongue went away, and a second later Bo's head broke

the water to Sam's right. Eyes sparkling with a rare playfulness, he traced a single fingertip over Sam's hole.

Sam swallowed, one eye on Bo and the other on the group roughhousing not that far away. "What are you doing?"

Bo flashed an evil smile. "Don't move."

"What do you mean, don't move? What—?" Sam let out a squeak when Bo's finger breached him. "God. Oh, fuck."

"Not here, people are watching." Bo's finger slid deeper. His free hand wrapped around Sam's prick, which stiffened at his touch. "You like this, don't you? I know I do. I think I'll bring you off right here, right now. Just like this."

Caught between shock and arousal, Sam couldn't do anything but gape. Holding hands in public was usually a huge deal to Bo. Now, here he was fingering Sam's ass and jerking him off outside in broad daylight, not fifteen yards from a crowd of strangers, with only a flimsy raft and a few feet of crystal clear water as cover. It was so out of character for Bo that Sam had no idea how to react.

"Bo, come on. You...you can't distract me this way." Sam wished his voice wouldn't shake so much. It ruined the effect.

Smiling, Bo shook his head. "Sam?"

"Uh?"

"Shut up."

Sam gasped, hips jerking as Bo's finger curled to nail his gland. Regardless of what his mind thought, his body evidently knew what it wanted, and what it wanted was for Bo to keep doing what he was doing. He shut up.

Keeping his left hand clutched around the edge of the raft, Sam plunged his right hand beneath the surface of the water and into Bo's shorts. His fingers grasped the familiar steely length of Bo's shaft and went to work.

"Oh yeah, that's it." Bo's eyelids fluttered closed, then shot open again. "So hot, Sam."

"Tell me what's hot," Sam demanded, his voice breathless with rising excitement. "Say it."

Bo flushed deep red. Holding his gaze, Sam thrust back with a moan, driving Bo's finger in to the hilt. The catch in Bo's breath and the pulse of his cock in Sam's fist told Sam how excited he was. Sam held his breath and managed not to beg. Hearing Bo talk dirty turned him on beyond belief.

Bo leaned closer. His wet braid swung over his shoulder to slap Sam's arm. "I like how hard your cock is in my hand," he said, his voice soft and husky. He pinched the underside of Sam's glans, sending electricity shooting through him. "I like the way your hole grabs my finger, so fucking tight it almost cuts off the circulation." He pumped his finger in, out, in again, twisting with each stroke. "I love how hot and soft you are inside."

"God, yes." Sam's hips rocked between the finger inside him and the hand around his prick. "Close, Bo."

Bo's low groan said he was just as close to the edge as Sam. He pulled his finger out of Sam's hole and pushed two in. It burned a little, with only salt water to ease the movement, but the way Bo massaged Sam's gland felt amazing, and the excitement of doing this in public—kind of—was dizzying. Sam swallowed a cry.

"Almost there." Dipping his head, Bo bit Sam's shoulder. "Harder."

Sam obediently tightened his hand around Bo's cock, pulling as hard and fast as he could. It was all he could do to maintain any sort of rhythm. The feel of Bo's fingers caressing him inside and out threatened to wash him away in a tide of sensation.

Bo rested his forehead against Sam's. His breath stuttered warm and moist on Sam's face, his eyes wide and burning. "I love you," he whispered, and came in Sam's hand.

The depth of emotion in Bo's eyes, more than the practiced touch of his hands, was what pushed Sam over the edge and sent him tumbling. He bit his tongue and panted through an orgasm so intense his vision went white. His shaft jerked in Bo's palm, his hole convulsing around Bo's fingers. One of the girls from the group next door glanced over at them, but Sam couldn't bring himself to care. It took all his strength to stop himself from kissing Bo.

Sam had no idea how much time passed before Bo's fingers finally slipped out of him. "Oh, my God." Bo fell forward onto the raft beside Sam, causing Sam's hand to pull free of his shorts. "I've never done anything like that where people might see."

"I know." Sam reached down to pull up his shorts, then rested both elbows on the raft. "I'm not complaining, believe me, but what brought that on all of a sudden?"

Bo shrugged. "Not a clue. But damn, it was exciting." He shot Sam a sly smile. "You're just so incredibly sexy, I couldn't help myself."

Sam knew better. Yes, Bo loved him, and they shared a powerful physical attraction, but there was no way Bo would've initiated any sort of sexual contact in public under normal circumstances. He'd been trying to stop Sam from questioning him once again about the things he kept seeing. Sam knew it, knew he should call Bo on it, but he didn't have the strength to ruin this moment between them.

The movement hidden by the raft, Sam slipped his arm around Bo's hips. Bo slid closer until his shoulder and arm were flush against Sam's side. They didn't speak, just stood there in the afternoon sun as their mingled semen dissolved into the water around them.

℘

They stayed out for a while longer, taking turns lounging on the raft. When Sam's skin began to turn pink, Bo snatched the raft out from under him, took his hand and dragged him out of the water. The kids from next door were still swimming. The missing boy had emerged bruised and flushed from the dunes just a few minutes before, looking blissfully dazed. He grinned and waved from his spot sprawled on a beach towel next to the water as Sam and Bo left the ocean and started toward the house. Sam waved back, chuckling.

"Did you see that kid?" he asked, winding his fingers through Bo's as they reached the porch steps. "Did they have sex, or a fist fight?"

Bo laughed. "It was only a few love bites."

"A few thousand, you mean. Who knew Dean was so rough?"

Bo raised his eyebrows, and Sam blushed. Even though Bo knew Sam had gone to bed with Dean—once, when Bo had broken up with him—it made Sam uncomfortable to think about it. He didn't regret it, exactly, because it had indirectly brought Bo back to him. It just felt strange to talk about that part of his history with Dean when the man was such a close friend to him, and to Bo.

On the porch, Sam grabbed two towels and handed one to Bo. They dried off, then went into the house. David, Dean and Cecile were huddled behind Andre, who sat cross-legged on the floor with the laptop open on the coffee table in front of him.

Dean glanced up and flashed them a grin. "Hey, y'all."

"Hi." Sam rubbed his dripping hair with the towel. He returned Dean's smile. "You look like you've been making out in the sand with a college boy."

"You're a perceptive guy, Sam." Dean's tongue darted out, licking a smear of white from the corner of his mouth. "I'll tell you all about it later. Right now, y'all have to come see this."

Bo glanced at Sam with a mix of apprehension and excitement before turning his attention back to Dean. "What is it?"

Andre looked up. "This is the video you took last night, Bo. We found something."

Chapter Seven

Sam's mouth went dry. Letting the towel fall to the floor, he grabbed Bo's hand again and pulled him over to join the crowd around the coffee table. "What? What'd you find?"

"I'm not sure. It's nothing concrete, just a..." Andre shook his head. "I don't even know what to call it. You'll just have to watch. Here."

Sam shifted from foot to foot while Andre backed up the video to the right spot. He'd never wanted to be wrong so badly in his life. He would gladly put up with Bo's overdeveloped work ethic if it meant Bo was in no danger at the fort.

Well, maybe "gladly" was too strong a word. But there was no doubt he preferred to have Bo safe, even if it meant he couldn't have as much of Bo's time as he wanted.

"Okay, here we go," Andre announced. "Watch down in the right-hand corner."

He clicked "play". Sam stared at the screen. His own face drifted by on camera, looking distracted. He heard Bo's voice talking about David's theory of the bloodstains being painted over, heard his own voice answering. His fingers tightened around Bo's. The moment of Bo's vision was coming.

On screen, Bo's voice faltered. The picture jerked and dipped.

"There." Andre halted the video. "Did you see it?"

"No." Bo let go of Sam's hand and leaned forward over Andre's shoulder. "Replay it frame by frame."

Andre went back a few seconds, then restarted the video in slow motion. Sam kept his gaze glued to the screen. Just as the picture jerked and bobbed, Sam saw it—a strange, swirling blur in the lower right corner, as if the scene were a painting where the colors had run together. The hairs on his arms stood up.

"You saw it that time, right?" David asked, shooting Sam a questioning look.

Sam nodded. "Yeah."

Frowning, Bo shook his head. "All I saw was movement artifact."

Dean gaped at him. "Seriously? You didn't see that in the corner?"

"I saw that, yes."

"And?"

"And, it's a blur." Bo gestured toward the screen. "I stumbled, my shoulder hit the wall, and that jogged the camera. I really don't think there's any more to it than that."

Andre stopped the video and looked up at Bo. "I see your point, but this doesn't look to me like something you'd normally see from camera movement."

"Well, yeah, but it still *could* be the camera moving," David added, rubbing his chin. "I mean, it does look unusual to me, but you gotta admit we really can't rule out movement as the cause. Especially since it only lasts like half a second. Even frame by frame there's only a few shots of it."

"Thank you, David." Bo gave Sam an I-told-you-so look. He didn't say a word about the strange vision which had caused him to stumble in the first place, and Sam knew if he were to spill the beans Bo would make him suffer for it.

Feeling trapped and irritated, Sam stalked across the room to snatch his beach towel off the floor. "I'm going to take a shower."

He hung the towel over the back of a chair and strode out of the room. Bo didn't follow. Sam wasn't sure why he'd expected him to.

Once he got upstairs Sam opted for a bath instead of a shower, and lingered far longer than he should have. He tried to tell himself he wasn't waiting for Bo to join him, but he was, and there was no point in pretending otherwise.

When the water became uncomfortably tepid and Sam's fingers and toes were pruned and corpse-white, he gave up. He opened the drain, climbed out and dried off, then went into the bedroom to get dressed.

He put on his favorite black cargo shorts and the threadbare red Wintzell's Oyster House T-shirt he'd borrowed from Bo months ago and ended up keeping. Bo called it Sam's security blanket, claiming he wore it whenever he was feeling down or needed reassurance about something. Sam supposed that was true. At least, it was true at the moment. Right now, he felt angry and afraid, and utterly helpless in the face of Bo's stubborn refusal to acknowledge that anything out of the ordinary might be happening to him.

But what if he's right? Maybe it really is nothing. Maybe you're so afraid of losing him that you're seeing monsters where there aren't any.

Sam let out a deep sigh. His emotions were jumbled, his thoughts confused, and he just wanted the whole problem to go the fuck away.

Thunder rumbled in the distance. Drawn by the promise of the violent weather which always calmed his mind, Sam wandered onto the porch. The wind had picked up, whipping the crests of the choppy waves into foaming whitecaps. Lightning flashed against the blackness gathering on the horizon.

As he watched, gunmetal gray clouds swallowed the blue sky bit by bit. The lightning streaked closer and closer. Thunder shook the house. A few lone drops spattered the porch railing, bringing with them the sharp, earthy scent of the approaching rain. Finally, the clouds blotted out the sun and the rain pelted down, swathing the world in a silver-gray curtain. Sam fell into a chair and settled in to watch the storm.

The rain had tapered to a light drizzle and scattered sunlight had begun to break through the clouds by the time Bo joined Sam on the porch. He sat in the chair beside Sam's, reached over and took Sam's hand. Their fingers intertwined, and Sam felt better.

"You're still going to the fort tonight, aren't you?" Sam asked eventually. He didn't look at Bo, just stared out over the ocean. The water was rough and gray in the wake of the storm.

Bo was silent for a moment, his thumb rubbing absent circles on the back of Sam's hand. "I'd like to."

"I figured." Gripping Bo's hand tighter, Sam turned to meet his gaze. "I wish you wouldn't, Bo. I don't know why I feel so apprehensive about you being there, but I do."

"Is it just me you feel that way about?"

"Yeah. When I think about the rest of the group—including me—being there, it doesn't bother me. The rest of us feel safe to me. But you don't." Sam curled one leg into the chair beneath him. "I realize I have nothing really concrete to base that on. The blur on the video is inconclusive, I know, even though it seems completely wrong to be the result of camera movement.

Even those...visions, spells, whatever they are you keep having, don't prove anything."

"That's only happened to me once. But you're right, it proves nothing. I'm glad you're finally seeing that."

Sam stared at their clasped hands, choosing his words carefully. "It's happened at least twice since last night," he said, keeping the anger and frustration from his voice with a huge effort. "This morning while we were running, then again in the water."

"No, it hasn't."

"Yes, it has. Don't lie to me."

"I'm not—"

Sam silenced Bo's protest with a savage glare. He snatched his hand from Bo's grip. "Just stop it, Bo. I thought you trusted me more than this. If you don't, fine, whatever, I'll live. Just don't sit there and lie to my face."

Silence. Bo's eyes searched Sam's face. In the distance, a low rumble sounded as the storm moved north.

"Okay," Bo spoke up at last. His voice was soft and shaky. "You're right. I've had more of those...whatever they are. I have no idea what to call them."

Drawing his legs up, Sam wrapped his arms around his bent knees. "Why couldn't you tell me that before? Didn't you think I'd understand?"

"That's not it at all." Bo tugged hard on the end of his braid. "I dismissed what happened as a result of too little sleep. I haven't actually *seen* anything, even though I called it a hallucination before. It was nothing but a very strange, very brief feeling of being somewhere else. It wasn't that I didn't trust you to understand. I knew you would. It's just that I truly didn't think anything of it, and I didn't want to worry you unnecessarily."

"So what changed your mind about telling me?"

Bo grinned, and the unexpected change of expression was like the sun shining after the storm. "You mean other than your incessant nagging?"

Sam had to laugh. "Yes, other than that, since I know you well enough to know nagging never works."

"Because it's happened too often to dismiss it anymore. Once is a random event. Twice is a coincidence. More than that is a pattern." Rising to his feet, Bo started pacing a tight circle on the damp boards of the porch. "I still don't think it has anything to do with the fort, or with any potential portals."

"How'd you know that's what I was thinking?" Sam uncurled his legs and planted one bare foot on Bo's knee, stopping his pacing.

"Because I know you." Bo shot a fond look at Sam. "I suppose I can't blame you, really, after all we've seen and experienced in relation to the portals."

Snagging Bo's wrist with one hand, Sam pulled him onto his lap. "If what you've been experiencing isn't related to the portals, what do you think it is? I'm assuming you don't still think it's just exhaustion or whatever."

Bo's brow furrowed. He wound an arm around Sam's shoulder, fingers playing with the tendrils of hair curling against his nape. "Honestly? I don't know. Whatever's causing these episodes, they don't seem to be particularly dangerous. But if they continue, I'll go see my doctor after we get home. And I don't think I should be driving right now, just in case."

"I agree." Filled with a mingling of relief and renewed worry, Sam wrapped both arms around Bo and held him tight. He buried his face in the curve of Bo's neck. "Let's go back home, right now. Today. You can call your doctor, and I'll take you to see him. Let's find out what the fuck's going on."

Bo rested his cheek against Sam's hair. "It's Friday afternoon, Sam. Even if I were to get hold of my doctor this late, there's no way I could get in to see him until Monday. We might as well stay. If I'm still having the episodes then, we'll head back to Mobile and I'll go to the doctor. Okay?"

It wasn't okay, really, but Sam knew better than to argue. Bo had his mind made up, and nothing short of a catastrophic event would change it. Sam figured it was better to stay here and keep a close eye on Bo than to force the issue and end up spending the next few days with a tight-lipped and angry lover and no real change in the situation.

"All right," Sam agreed. "But I still don't think you should keep going to the fort."

"Whatever is causing me to feel these strange things, Sam, it's nothing to do with the fort." Bo's voice was surprisingly calm, his fingers gentle and soothing in Sam's hair.

"Maybe not. I don't know. I just don't feel good about you being there." Turning his head, Sam pressed a soft kiss to Bo's throat. "Please, Bo, don't go there."

Bo sighed. Straightening up in Sam's lap, he cradled Sam's face in his hands and stared into his eyes. "They need us. Andre won't say so, but they do. Fort Medina is too big for four people to cover."

"Andre wouldn't have accepted the job if he didn't think they could do it without us. You know that."

Something hard and desperate flitted through Bo's eyes and was gone before Sam could grasp it, replaced by a sincerity Sam suspected wasn't entirely genuine. "I tell you what, Sam. Let's go tonight, and see what happens. If I keep having those hallucinations, we'll stay out of the investigation from now on."

"Promise?"

"Yes. I promise."

Sam studied Bo's face. He seemed to mean what he said, but his eyes were shuttered, and Sam had the uneasy feeling Bo would break this promise like he'd broken the one he made to stay out of the case in the first place.

He's going to go whether you like it or not. Go with him, and watch him. Maybe he's right, anyway. You have no proof that any of this is caused by potential portals, or anything else out of the ordinary.

"I don't like it," Sam told him. "But I don't really have a choice, do I? You'll do what you please no matter what I think."

He hadn't meant for the words to sound as bitter as they did, but there it was. He *was* bitter, and a little hurt. Why shouldn't Bo know that?

To Sam's surprise, Bo didn't respond with clipped, angry rebuttals like he usually did. Instead, he leaned down and kissed Sam's lips, the touch lingering and tender. Sam closed his eyes and let the feeling carry him away.

"I'm so sorry," Bo murmured as they drew apart. He stroked Sam's face. "I seem to say that a lot lately, don't I? But it's true. I'm sorry for whatever I've done to make you think I don't care about your needs, or your opinion. I do care. I wish you could believe that."

Sam smiled, but there was no joy in it. "So do I."

For a second, Bo seemed torn between guilt and indignation. He opened his mouth, closed it again, then shook his head. "Okay. I'm going to start dinner. I'll call you when it's ready."

Pushing to his feet, Bo dropped a kiss on Sam's forehead and walked back into the house. Sam didn't try to stop him.

❦

At eight-thirty that night, the group piled into the SUV for the trip to the fort. Sam sat in the back with Dean, staring at Bo's profile. Bo was in the front beside Andre, who was driving as he usually did. They were talking. Discussing the case, Sam figured, though he made no attempt to listen. The only reason he'd come tonight was to keep two sharp eyes on Bo. If he'd thought anything short of physical restraint would've kept Bo away, neither of them would be here.

Not that he hadn't considered it. Watching Bo load equipment into the SUV, eyes gleaming with anticipation, Sam had been sorely tempted to throw Bo over his shoulder, carry him inside and tie him to a chair until the rest of the group returned from the night's work. The fear of Bo leaving him, for good this time, was the only thing that stopped him.

Fucking pathetic, Sam, he chided himself, watching Bo's fingers toy with the tail of his braid. *When did you get to be so whipped?*

An elbow nudged his arm. He turned to meet Dean's worried gaze. "What?" he snapped, and instantly regretted it. After all, Dean had done nothing to deserve being yelled at. "I'm sorry, Dean. What is it?"

Dean's eyebrows went up. "I'd ask what's making you so damn cranky, but I bet I know."

Sam sighed and leaned back to let his head rest against the back of the seat. "Bo and I had another fight."

"Thought so. About the fort?"

"Yeah. Well, mostly."

"You didn't think he should go, but he ignored you." It wasn't a question.

"Got it in one." Sam let out a sharp, humorless laugh. "The hell of it is, he wasn't even unpleasant. He was so sweet to me. He told me how much he loves me, and how important I am to him, and he apologized yet again for how he was acting. But here we are anyway. Nothing changes, ever."

Dean was quiet for a moment, watching Sam's face. "Don't take this the wrong way, but don't you think you're overreacting a little?"

Sam shot a glare at Dean. "No, I'm not."

"Then explain it to me." Dean twisted in his seat to face Sam. "I understand why you're upset about this. Y'all were supposed to be here on vacation, and now we're here and Bo's gotten all caught up in our new case. It sucks, but frankly I don't see why you're this upset about it. What's really going on, Sam? Tell me."

Sam sat up straight and glanced toward the front of the vehicle. David and Cecile were both leaning forward from the middle seats, involved in an intense discussion with Bo and Andre.

Moving closer to Dean, Sam lowered his voice to a near-whisper. "You remember that weird blur on the video Bo took last night?"

"Yeah. Bo said he stumbled and that's what made the camera move and the picture blur." Dean shrugged. "Made sense, actually."

"But he didn't just stumble. He had a... Well, he called it a hallucination. I don't know what to call it, but it sure as hell wasn't normal."

Dean stared at him, eyes wide. "What did he see?"

"He said he didn't see anything, but he felt like he was somewhere else. He said it was dark and hard to breathe."

Frowning, Dean brushed a lock of hair out of his eyes. "That's definitely not normal."

"Tell me about it."

"How long did it last?"

"Only for a split second. But Bo said he felt as if he was there in that other place for ages, even though he knew it was practically no time at all."

"Huh." Dean glanced at Bo. "Let me guess. That wasn't the only time it happened."

"Right again. It happened again this morning on our run, and again while we were swimming."

"And nothing like that has ever happened to him before?"

"No. And he had a nightmare last night that was very similar to the vision or whatever it was he had."

"Wow."

"Yeah." Sam picked at a loose thread in the hem of his shorts. "I had the same dream the night before, Dean. Exactly the same. The last time that sort of thing happened was at Oleander House."

"Christ." Dean ran a hand through his hair. "What do you think it means?"

Sam shook his head. "I don't know. Maybe nothing. But I don't like it. The whole thing feels wrong." Closing his eyes, he leaned his head against the window. "He's in danger at the fort. None of the rest of us are. Just him. I know it. I can feel it. And he won't listen."

A warm hand enfolded Sam's. He opened his eyes. Dean was gazing at him with determination on his face. "I know you're already planning to stick close to him tonight. If anything happens, if he has another one of those spells, note the exact time, and note anything at all that you pick up with your psychic senses at that time. We'll look for any fluctuations in the fort's energy field and see if they coincide. If we find any sort of correlation, we'll confront him. I'll help you."

Sam's vision blurred. He blinked away the sudden stinging behind his eyelids. "Thank you," he said, and squeezed Dean's hand.

৪০

At the fort, Bo suggested a switch in teams. Sam wasn't surprised, considering, but it hurt anyway. To his profound relief, Andre vetoed the idea with a decisive "no", and, when Bo tried to argue with him, a threatening glower.

The entire team—Bo included—had learned not to argue with Andre when he gave them what David called simply *That Look*. Bo shut up and followed Sam to the old living quarters lining the inside of the fort's northern wall.

Two hours later, Bo still hadn't stopped muttering under his breath about Andre's curt dismissal of his suggestions, and Sam's nerves were worn ragged. Listening to Bo's constant complaining was bad enough. Knowing that the reason for it was because he didn't want to be with Sam was downright painful.

As they entered a tiny, windowless room carved into one wall of a larger space, Bo grumbled about no one listening to him. It was just loud enough for Sam to know he was supposed to hear it, and something inside him snapped.

Stalking over to Bo, he snatched the thermal camera from his hand and switched it off. "All right, that's it. If you have something to say to me, just fucking say it already. I'm sick of listening to you whine like a little kid."

Bo's eyes narrowed. "Okay. Fine. I was *trying* not to hurt your feelings—"

"Bullshit," Sam spat. "Did you really think I wasn't going to notice your fucking passive-aggressive bitching? You *knew* I would hear, especially that last bit."

In the glow of Sam's flashlight, a muscle in Bo's jaw twitched. His eyes burned. "As. I. Was. Saying," he ground out between clenched teeth. "I didn't want to hurt your feelings, but I really thought it would be better for everyone if you and I were teamed with other people tonight."

"Yeah, because you didn't want me to see if you had another episode like you had before. What a big fucking surprise that was." Sam started pacing, and let out a bitter laugh when he realized he'd picked up one of Bo's nervous habits. "What the hell is happening to you, Bo? You're the most stubborn person I've ever known in my life, but you've never been one to completely dismiss something like this. At Sunset Lodge, you were smart enough to recognize that your leg wasn't behaving normally, and you acted accordingly. You kept Dean and me informed, and let us know what was going on. Why can't you do that now?"

Bo crossed his arms. His eyes glittered with a dangerous light. "This is a completely different situation."

"No, it isn't, dammit! It's the same! If anything, this is worse because you're seeing and feeling things that can't be explained away by a four-hour hike or anything else." Sam pushed a frustrated hand through his hair. "The worst part is, you're shutting me out. That scares me."

Bo pressed his lips together and dropped his gaze to the dirt floor. He didn't say a word. Everything about him shouted *don't touch* loud and clear. Sam wanted to scream at him, to shake him and hit him, anything at all to break through the wall he'd built between them in the last twenty-four hours and bring him back.

"Bo, please," Sam said, though he didn't know what he was pleading for.

Raising his head, Bo looked at Sam. For a moment, Sam thought he saw contrition in the dark depths of Bo's eyes.

Bo's lips parted. He took a step forward, faltered and stopped.

Something dark and strange fluttered on the edge of Sam's psychic perception. Something with a hint of the familiar, setting off alarm bells in his head.

"Bo," he whispered. "We need to get out of here."

Bo didn't answer. His eyes were empty, his expression blank.

Sam's mouth went dry. *Oh, Christ.*

Even as Sam dropped the flashlight and lunged forward, Bo's knees buckled.

Chapter Eight

Sam snaked his arm around Bo's waist and eased them both to the floor, still clutching the thermal camera in his other hand. His heart hammered so hard he could hear the rush of blood in his ears. "Bo? Can you hear me?"

No answer. Sam set the camera on the floor and peered into Bo's face by the light of the flashlight, which had come to rest in the corner. The beam pointed toward a spot on the wall to Sam's left, but it was still strong enough to see by.

Bo's eyes were half closed and rolled back so that only the whites showed. Sam pressed two shaking fingers to the pulse point in Bo's throat. At first he felt nothing. After a panicked second he found the pulse, weak and far too fast, but there. Bo's breathing was rapid and shallow, and sweat dotted his forehead.

Feeling as if he'd fallen into a bad dream, Sam pulled the radio off the waistband of his shorts and thumbed the button. "Dean, come in, this is Sam." Dean, with his background as an ER nurse's assistant, would know what to do.

There was a burst of static, followed by Dean's voice. "This is Dean, go ahead."

"Bo passed out, and he's not waking up." Sam hated the quaver in his voice, but he couldn't help it. He hadn't been this scared since November, sitting in the surgery waiting room at

Mobile General waiting to hear whether Bo was alive or dead. "C-Can... Can you come?"

"Where are you?"

Dean radiated calm competence even over the radio. Some of Sam's fear seeped away. "In the living quarters. The last room on the east end. There's a little closet-sized room off to the side."

"I know the place, Andre and I were there last night. I'm on my way." Dean was already shouting instructions to Andre before the radio cut off.

As Sam set the radio on the floor beside the camera, Bo stirred in his arms. Brown eyes blinked and snapped into focus. Bo glanced around, looking confused. "Sam? Why are we on the floor?"

Sam smiled, dizzy with relief. "You passed out. Scared the crap out of me."

Bo's brow furrowed. "But why would I—?" He stopped, understanding dawning on his face. "Oh. I remember now."

"You had one of those visions, didn't you?" Sam stroked a stray lock of ebony hair from Bo's face. "Are you okay? What did you see this time?"

"That's not what happened. I just suddenly felt really weak and dizzy. Maybe I'm coming down with a virus or something. I feel a little feverish, actually." Bo sat up, one arm winding around Sam's shoulders. "Help me up?"

Sam stared into Bo's eyes. Bo's gaze skittered away, telling Sam all he needed to know. Bo had always been a terrible liar.

Then again, Bo had always been a terrible patient as well. Maybe he just didn't want Sam to see how bad he actually felt.

Not that that scenario was any more comforting.

"Stay there," Sam ordered. "Dean's on his way, let him

check you over before you try to do anything."

Bo shook his head, but didn't argue. "That's probably a good idea. I'm not sure my legs'll hold me up at the moment."

Concerned, Sam laid a hand on Bo's forehead. The skin was damp with sweat and surprisingly hot. *Maybe it really is just a virus. A fever can make you feel pretty weird.*

It was almost enough to convince Sam he was wrong. Almost. The juxtaposition of the ominous psychic disturbance he'd just experienced with Bo's most recent lapse in consciousness practically screamed *danger*.

Footsteps pounded through the doorway of the larger room at Sam's back. Dean came flying into the little room and dropped to his knees beside Bo. "Hey," he panted. "Sam said you passed out. What happened?"

"Sam and I were..." Bo glanced at Sam, his expression unreadable. "We were talking. And I suddenly felt very weak, nauseated and dizzy. I knew I was about to pass out, but I couldn't seem to move. Luckily, Sam caught me before I could fall."

Pursing his lips, Dean shone his flashlight on Bo's face. "You look flushed. How do you feel now?"

"Still weak. Shaky. But not sick or dizzy anymore."

Dean pressed two fingers to Bo's wrist. "Your pulse is awfully rapid."

"He said he felt feverish," Sam supplied. "He does feel pretty warm to me."

"Hm." Dean held the backs of his fingers to Bo's forehead. "Yeah, you definitely feel like you have a fever."

"So you think that may have been what caused me to pass out?" Bo's gaze remained fixed on Dean, but his hand crept onto Sam's knee and gave a comforting squeeze.

Dean shrugged. "It's certainly possible. If you're coming down with a virus, that on top of the run in the heat this morning and being out in the sun most of the afternoon could have dehydrated you enough to cause a syncopal spell."

"A what now?" Sam asked, confused.

"Passing out." Bo rubbed his thumb over the curve of Sam's shoulder. "I'm sure that's exactly what happened. All I need is some fluids and a little rest, and I should be fine."

Sam laid his hand over Bo's. "Should he go back to the house, Dean? I know it would set y'all back some, but maybe someone could drive Bo and me back. I could stay with him."

"There's no need for that," Bo protested. "I could stay at the table and monitor the remote cameras via the laptop. I feel okay sitting down."

Sam still itched to get Bo out of the fort, but the need to leave didn't feel as urgent as it had a few minutes ago. Plus, he had a feeling trying to talk Bo into going back to the house would cause another argument, and instinct told him he needed to avoid anger between them right now. Whatever it was that had prodded at the margins of his psychic senses a little while ago, it had seemed somehow connected to the anger and frustration spiraling out of control inside him.

It reminded him too much of Oleander House for comfort. Just because he hadn't accidentally opened a portal since then didn't mean anything. It could still happen. Fort Medina's strong electromagnetic field and unstable energy made it a prime spot for a gateway to form. If Sam lost his temper here, the runaway emotions might trigger the psychokinesis he still couldn't entirely control, and open a doorway to the other side. And if that happened, they would all be in danger.

"Sam? What do you think?"

Turning, Sam met Dean's questioning gaze. "Sorry, what?"

Dean shook his head as he rose to his feet. "I was saying, I brought some bottled water. It's in the SUV. We'll take Bo to the front, and I'll stay with him and make sure he's okay while you go get the water. How's that sound?"

"Sounds fine to me," Sam answered. He aimed a stern look at Bo. "And don't tell me you feel fine and you don't need anybody to sit with you. I'm sure you'd be all right alone, but I'll feel better if Dean watches you for a few more minutes."

Bo let out a long-suffering sigh. "I'm not a child who needs babysitting, Sam."

"No, you're an adult who just passed out cold not five minutes ago and still isn't feeling quite back to normal. I'd ask any of our group to do the same in your situation." He laid a finger over Bo's lips before he could say a word. "Humor me, okay?"

Bo's expression softened. Taking Sam's hand, he kissed his fingers. "Okay. If it'll make you feel better."

"It will. Thank you." Sam stood, pulling Bo up with an arm around his waist. "Just lean on me. And let me know if you start feeling faint again. We can sit down."

"I'm fine right now. Just a little wobbly." Removing his arm from around Sam's shoulders, Bo slipped it around his waist instead. He hooked a thumb into the back pocket of Sam's shorts. "I'm sorry to put you both to this much trouble. Especially in the middle of an investigation."

"It's no trouble. I'm sure we'll all be happy to lose a few minutes of investigation time to make sure you're okay." Dean leaned down to pick up the thermal camera, then crossed to the corner to retrieve Sam's flashlight. "Let me know if you need to stop, Bo."

Bo looked like he was about to protest, but he just nodded. Sam was glad. He'd had more than enough of Bo pretending nothing was wrong.

The three of them left the living quarters and made their slow way across the tremendous open space in the midst of the fort. Bo leaned heavily against Sam's side, but his steps were steady. None of them spoke, though Dean kept a sharp, assessing eye on Bo. If the attention bothered Bo, he didn't let on. It was a little surprising, but Sam wasn't about to complain. This was the most normal Bo had been since his first visit to the fort.

It was only a day ago. The realization caught Sam by surprise. It seemed like much longer.

When they drew near the arched tunnel leading to the parking lot, Sam saw three shadowy figures huddled around the table. The low murmur of voices stopped as they approached.

"Oh God," Bo groaned. "What are they doing here?"

Sam shook his head. He knew Bo hated being the center of attention, especially for something he would perceive as a weakness.

"I asked Andre to meet us here," Dean explained. "He has the keys to the SUV. I didn't expect a party."

"Hey, it was almost time to touch base and switch out some of the equipment anyway." David sauntered forward to meet them. "Here, Dean, let me have the thermal. It's my turn for it."

Dean handed over the camera. "It's all yours."

"Thanks." Grinning, David clapped Bo on the shoulder. "Hey, boss-man. Heard you had an attack of the vapors. You okay?"

Bo laughed. "Yes, David, I'm fine."

Leading Bo under the arch, Sam pointed at the nearest chair. "Sit. I'll go get you some water. Andre, could you give me the keys?"

"Sure." Andre reached into the pocket of his pants, pulled out the SUV keys and tossed them to Sam, who caught them one-handed.

Keys in hand, Sam strode down the tunnel and out into the parking lot, which was empty except for their SUV. Joanne had left after she let them in, saying her brother had been hospitalized unexpectedly and she needed to drive over to Mobile to be with him. Another fort worker was supposed to meet them at three a.m. to lock up again.

A cool, salt-scented breeze sighed through the pines edging the parking lot as Sam jogged toward the SUV. Beyond the fence, the darkness was absolute. Something about the fact that the six of them were all alone in this place, which had seen so much pain and death, gave Sam the shivers. He opened the SUV, found the water bottles Dean had brought, grabbed one and started back as fast as he could.

When he returned, David and Cecile had already left to continue their work. Andre and Dean stood talking in low tones. Dean had positioned himself so he could keep an eye on Bo, who was sitting at the table with his gaze fixed on the laptop.

"Andre, heads up," Sam called. He tossed the keys to Andre, then plopped into the empty chair beside Bo and set the water bottle on the table. "Here's some water for you."

"Thanks, Sam." Smiling, Bo leaned sideways and planted a kiss on the corner of Sam's mouth. He twisted the cap off the bottle and took a long swallow. "Mm. I needed that."

Andre shoved the SUV keys into his pocket and started gathering equipment. "Okay, Dean, you ready to get started again?"

Dean nodded. "Yep. Bo, radio me if you start feeling bad again."

"We will," Sam promised, cutting off whatever Bo was about to say. "Thanks, Dean."

"Yes, thank you," Bo echoed. "Don't worry, I feel completely back to normal now."

"Good." Dean leaned both hands on the table and fixed Bo with a serious look. "I know you don't think this is anything to worry about, Bo, but I think you need to take what just happened seriously. Your passing out was most likely the result of you being dehydrated and feverish from whatever bug it is you've caught, but..." He glanced behind him to where Andre stood staring into the empty courtyard, evidently lost in thought. "But I'm not sure I'm ready to blame these blanking-out spells you've had on that. Not until I know more about it. I think you need to be watchful, and careful. And I think you should stay at the house tomorrow night."

Sam tensed. *Oh, fuck. Here we go.*

Bo's expression hardened. "Dean—"

"Look, if you're really sick, you should be resting, not staying up most of the night working." Straightening up, Dean took a video camera and audio recorder from the equipment scattered across the tabletop. "You and Sam can review evidence, if you really want to help. But my medical opinion is that you should do not a damn thing all day tomorrow except relax, then after a hard day lying around doing nothing, you should go to bed early."

To Sam's surprise, Bo laughed. "Whatever you say, Dr. Delapore."

"Good boy. I do love a cooperative patient." Dean winked at them and strolled off. He handed Andre the video camera. The two of them headed off into the darkness, and Sam and Bo were alone.

For a while, they didn't speak. All the things Sam wanted to say formed a hopeless jumble in his brain, preventing him from expressing any of it. It was probably just as well. Nothing he had to say was likely to make Bo happy.

They'd been sitting in silence, Bo watching the laptop screen and Sam pretending not to watch him, when Bo laid a hand on Sam's thigh. "Thank you."

Sam raised his eyebrows. "For what?"

"For putting up with me the last couple of days." Bo's lips curved into a wry smile. "I've been feeling a bit short-tempered lately. You may have noticed."

Sam laughed. "You could say that."

"At least I know *why* now. I've never handled sickness well."

"Don't I know it," Sam said with feeling. The days he'd spent taking care of Bo while he recovered from that near-fatal bite had been trying, to put it mildly.

"Forgive me?" There was a vague flinching quality to Bo's voice, as if he wasn't sure Sam *would* forgive him.

Sam didn't even hesitate. "Of course."

Relief flooded Bo's face. Scooting his chair closer, he leaned sideways to rest his head on Sam's shoulder.

Sam put an arm around him and nuzzled his hair. He drew a deep breath of the musky-sweet scent that was uniquely Bo.

I should talk to him, right now when he's relaxed and might actually listen. I should tell him about what I felt before he passed out. It might not have anything to do with what's been happening to him, but we can't ignore the possibility, even if it's a slight one.

The problem was, the last twenty-four hours had shaken Sam's faith in Bo's rationality. Maybe Bo would accept the possibility—however remote—that his most recent episode was related to whatever Sam had felt, and maybe he wouldn't. If he didn't, if he grew angry again, Sam wasn't sure he would be able to keep his own emotions in check. And none of them could afford for him to lose control here.

There was also the very real likelihood that he was wrong. He didn't believe he was, but what sort of hypocrite would he be if he berated Bo for denying some of the possible explanations, then did the same thing himself?

He had no answer to that. Still undecided about what to tell Bo and when, Sam cuddled closer to Bo and waited for the night's work to be over.

When they left two hours later, Sam still hadn't mentioned what he'd felt in the little stone room. Exhausted, with Bo falling asleep on his shoulder as the SUV bumped along the pocked road to the house, Sam decided it could wait until morning.

༃

Dark. Cold.

Bone-freezing blackness, terror like a fist in the throat.

Sam thrashed, struggling to breathe, to move, to get away from what was coming for him. He couldn't see it, but he felt its approach through the living dark, felt its malevolence thumping through his mind.

Out of the nothingness appeared a point of brilliant light. It writhed, stretched and elongated, and became a shining thread winding through the inky night. Sam followed its bright length with his eyes. One end disappeared into an aperture which led to a world of light, noise and life, so radiant Sam couldn't look directly at it. On the other end loomed the thing Sam had felt, a

presence which swallowed the thread's luminescence in shadow.
In an instant of blinding clarity, Sam realized the thing
wasn't coming for him at all. It was following the thread,
following its path to the door, and beyond...

Sam woke gasping and drenched in sweat. The moonlight
pouring through the curtains bathed the room he and Bo
shared in silver light. Sam sat up and looked around, peering
into the shadows pooled around the furniture. God, the dream
had been so vivid, he could almost believe he'd really been in
that other place, even though logically he knew he couldn't have
been.

Keeping his eyes open, Sam stretched out his psychic
senses. The house felt exactly like it always did. Nothing was
out of place, or different. No thread of light, no dark presence
filling Sam's mind with hate and bloodlust. Just the normal
energy of a peacefully slumbering house.

Reassured, Sam lay down and spooned himself around Bo,
who was curled into a ball and still fast asleep. A shudder went
through Bo's bare back. He let out a soft mewl. Something
about it sounded lost and terrified.

Sam frowned. He pushed up on one elbow and leaned over
to look into Bo's face. Bo's eyes were wide open, staring at
nothing. His hands clenched his pillow in a death grip. This
close, Sam could hear the faint clack-clack-clack of his teeth
chattering.

Adrenaline raced through Sam's veins. Slipping an arm
beneath Bo's shoulders, Sam hauled Bo's rigid body into his
arms. Bo's skin felt hot and damp. "Bo! Wake up. Come on." He
held Bo to his chest with one arm and gave his cheek a light
slap with his other hand.

Bo's body jerked violently a couple of times, then relaxed.
Awareness filled his empty eyes. He stared up at Sam, panting.

"Bo? Are you all right?" Silence. Sam stroked Bo's cheek. "Say something, huh? You're scaring me."

Without warning, Bo flung both arms around Sam's neck in a crushing embrace. He buried his face in Sam's shoulder. He was shaking hard.

"It's okay," Sam whispered, holding Bo tight against him. "It's okay. I think you had another nightmare."

Bo nodded. His fingers dug painfully into Sam's back. "It was bad."

"You want to talk about it?"

Another nod. Relaxing his grip a little, Bo pulled Sam down so that they lay face-to-face, arms and legs wound together. "It was similar to the one I had yesterday. I saw strange things, I think, but I can't remember what they were now. It was dark and cold and I couldn't breathe. But this time, something was after me. Something was following me, and I knew I couldn't get away. That it would catch me eventually." Bo stared at Sam with haunted eyes. "It seemed so real. For a second, when I woke up, I thought the thing had followed me here. I really expected to see it, and God, I didn't want to. I was so relieved to see you there instead."

Dread trickled down Sam's spine. "I just had a dream almost exactly like that. Except I wasn't being followed. I was in that same place, but I saw this thread of light leading to a doorway, and felt an entity following the thread to the door."

Bo's mouth opened, then closed again. He didn't say anything, but Sam saw the fear in his eyes, and knew he was thinking the same thing Sam was.

Somehow, the things from the other dimension had sensed the group's presence at the fort from across the barrier. And they were coming.

Chapter Nine

Unable to go back to sleep, Sam and Bo dressed and trudged downstairs. Bo made a pot of coffee, and the two of them sat on the back porch sipping the extra strong brew and watching dawn creep over the world. Neither spoke. Sam knew they'd have to talk soon, but he had no idea how to bring up the fears he suspected Bo shared. Bo evidently didn't either. So they sat in silence and watched the rising sun turn the water to molten gold.

When the first early riser appeared on the beach, a young woman jogging along the strip of damp sand stranded by the receding tide, Bo turned sideways in his chair and pinned Sam with a troubled look. "It bothers me that we had such similar nightmares. What do you think it means?"

Sam stomped hard on the part of himself that wanted to remind Bo of how he'd dismissed it when Sam had expressed that same concern only a day ago. Now wasn't the time.

"I'm not really sure," he said, watching Bo's face. "But I don't think we should ignore it, especially since both of our dreams have been so similar to what you said you felt during those weird spells you had."

Bo curled a leg underneath him. He turned and gazed out over the water, his coffee mug cupped in his hands. "You think Fort Medina is a potential portal site, don't you?"

"Yeah, I do. The EMF level is high enough, and the psychic energy is awfully unstable there."

Nodding, Bo lifted his mug to his lips and took a sip. The steam curled around his face. "Did you feel anything last night? Psychically speaking, that is." His gaze wouldn't meet Sam's.

He's afraid. Sam's stomach clenched. He wished he could tell Bo he'd felt nothing, that the episode last night and the dreams this morning were the result of Bo's illness and Sam's empathy for him, nothing more. But that would be a lie, and lying wouldn't help either of them.

Sam set his coffee on the porch railing, reached over and laid a hand on Bo's knee. "Right before you passed out, I sensed something. It was just for a second, right on the edges of my perception, but it was enough for me to know it wasn't anything that belonged there."

Bo's tongue darted out to probe at the corner of his mouth. "Was it a portal trying to open?"

"Possibly."

"That's why you said we needed to get out of there."

"Yeah. I didn't think you heard that."

"I did. Just barely." Bo set his mug beside Sam's and turned to look at him. "The portal didn't open, though. Why? And why do you think it was trying to open in the first place? Was it because we were fighting, do you think? That's what finally triggered the one at Oleander House."

Sam dropped his gaze to his lap. Nine months later, he still couldn't think about Oleander House without feeling nearly smothered by guilt and shame, even though he knew he wasn't to blame for what had happened. "I think my anger and frustration with you is probably what caused it to almost open, yes. I have no idea why it didn't." He raised his eyes to meet Bo's. "My control is better, but it's not *that* good."

"Well, it's not as if you've had very many portals to practice on, thankfully."

"True."

Bo stared into his coffee cup. When he looked up again, his expression was full of worry. "You don't think my...illness, or whatever it is, has anything to do with that portal, do you?"

"That's exactly what I've been wondering." Sam drew a deep breath and let it out. "Truthfully, I have no idea. I sort of feel like it does, but I don't have anything to base that on. Just a sort of gut feeling, and we all know how reliable those are. And to be honest, I don't know how the two could possibly be related. Unless you've suddenly become psychic." He nudged Bo with his elbow. "You haven't, have you?"

He was only half joking, and Bo's laughter at the idea was a relief. "No, Sam, I haven't become psychic. The only thing I felt last night was nausea and dizziness. I can't sense the fort's energy, and I certainly haven't felt anything that I would describe as portal-like, going by your accounts of them."

"Good." Sam glanced at the water glinting in the sun, then back at Bo. He was staring out over the Gulf, seemingly lost in thought. Stray strands of black hair pulled loose from his braid to blow across his face in the rising breeze. Sam's insides constricted with a sudden rush of desire. "Bo?"

"Hm?"

Sam waited until Bo turned toward him. Leaning over, he cupped Bo's face in his hands and kissed him. Bo's mouth opened with a soft sigh. He tasted of coffee and caramel creamer, mingled with a need equal to Sam's own.

Bo smiled as they drew apart, brown eyes bright with a familiar hunger. "Let's go back upstairs," he murmured, and flicked his tongue over Sam's lips. "The others won't be up for a while yet."

Sam answered him with another kiss. When it broke, he stood, took Bo's hands in his and pulled him to his feet. "You sure you feel up to sex right now?"

"I'm definitely *up...*" Bo thrust his erection against Sam's, "...to being inside you." He dipped his head and bit at the juncture of Sam's neck and shoulder. "But I'm still feeling kind of weak. You'll have to do all the work."

Sam knew what that meant—Bo on his back, Sam riding him. Sam grinned. He *loved* that position.

Arm snug around Bo's waist, Sam led him inside and up the stairs to their bedroom.

It was good, just like always, even though Bo seemed more passive than usual. Sam figured that, at least, could easily be blamed on sickness. When Sam's release hit, bowing his spine and blasting his senses wide open, he ignored the faint thread of *wrongness* he felt emanating from Bo. He'd never been able to sense anyone's personal energy field, and there was certainly no reason to think he could now. It was his imagination, the result of the loss of control which always went along with orgasm.

Watching Bo's face as Bo came deep inside him seconds later, Sam told himself the blank look in Bo's eyes was due to the surge of pleasure making his body jerk and his hips buck. The sudden, jarring sensation of something else looking out of Bo's eyes had to be Sam's imagination again. He was still riding out the aftershocks of his own release, and it was messing with his head. That was all.

He lay awake long after Bo had drifted off, still trying to convince himself.

℥

Eventually, Sam gave up on sleep. He pulled on his clothes and wandered downstairs. Bo didn't even move.

The rest of the group filtered in one by one. By noon, everyone but Bo was up and reviewing evidence. Sam started on one of the videos from the night before, thinking the work would distract him from his worry over Bo, but it was no good. He couldn't keep his mind on what he was doing. He excused himself with an apology to Andre and headed out to the beach.

Outside, Sam parked himself on the wooden bench tucked against the base of a huge sand dune. Over the past few hours the breeze had turned into a hard wind which whipped the sand against his legs and bent the sea oats almost double. The Gulf was still a clear green, though the waves were higher than they'd been the day before. The hazy sky spoke of rainy weather to come.

He'd only been out there a few minutes when he heard bare feet shuffle through the sand behind him. Dean plopped onto the bench a moment later. He slouched against the weathered wood, hands laced behind his head, and stared up at the sky.

"Looks like rain," Dean said, squinting against the glare.

Sam nodded. "Not today, though. I'm betting it hits tomorrow."

"Probably." Dean glanced at Sam. "What's wrong?"

Sam's shoulders tensed. "What makes you think anything's wrong?"

With a shrug, Dean unclasped his hands and leaned forward, forearms resting on his thighs. "You don't have to tell me if you don't want to. But you can. You know that, right?"

Sam did know, and was endlessly grateful for Dean's staunch friendship. Dean was always willing to lend a sympathetic ear. Venting over the phone to Dean after a fight with Bo had become so commonplace that Sam felt a little guilty about it, in spite of Dean's assurances that he was happy to help and would definitely let Sam know if he could ever return the favor.

"I think he's still having those spells," Sam confessed. "And we both had nightmares that were so much alike it was frightening." Sighing, he rubbed a hand over his forehead, where a dull ache had begun. "I'm worried about him. If it's this virus or whatever that's causing these episodes, that's bad enough, because you know he's liable to push himself too hard and make it worse. If it's something else..."

Dean cocked his head sideways, reminding Sam of a curious puppy. "Like what?"

"I don't know," Sam admitted after a moment's consideration. "I really don't know what's making me feel like it's anything more sinister. I just do. I can't help it."

"Okay, let's look at this logically." Dean shoved a hand through his hair, pushing his bangs out of his eyes. The wind blew them right back across his face as soon as he let go. "You say Bo's been acting strange for the last couple of days, right?"

"Oh yeah. Very right."

"And that's pretty much coincided with him having those spells, as you call them."

"Right."

"Hm." Dean scratched at a mosquito bite on his knee. "Describe the spells to me again."

"He basically just blanks out for a while. The first one was literally just a split second, but the others have lasted longer. He says when it happens, he feels like he's in a different place, where it's dark and cold and he has trouble breathing."

"What about last night, when he passed out? Was that an episode like those other times, or was it different?"

"It was different. At least I think it was. He's never passed out like that, for one thing. And he didn't say anything about having the sense of being someplace else with that one. At the time, I thought he was lying and that he really did have another spell, but now I'm not so sure. Maybe I'm seeing things in this situation that aren't really there." Sam turned sideways and leaned an elbow on the back of the bench. "It does seem likely that it's all related to him being sick, doesn't it?"

Dean was silent, staring thoughtfully into space. Sam frowned. "Dean?"

Blinking, Dean turned toward him. "Hm? What?"

"What were you thinking just now?"

"I was just wondering if..."

"If what?"

Dean shook his head. "Never mind, it's crazy. About what you were saying before, yeah, even a mild fever can make people feel pretty strange sometimes. Especially if they've been out in the heat all day and are dehydrated like Bo was last night."

Sam rubbed the stubble on his chin. It made sense. It could explain everything that had happened to Bo in the past two days, even the nightmares.

He should've been relieved. But he wasn't. Something was wrong. Something beyond a simple illness. Sam knew it. His bones ached with the dread of it.

"I felt something last night," he said, his voice nearly drowned out by the rising wind. "Right before Bo passed out."

Dean's gaze bored into him, needle sharp. "What was it?"

"I think it was a portal, Dean. I think I almost opened an interdimensional portal at the fort."

All the color drained from Dean's face. "Fuck."

"Yeah."

"Why? How?"

"Bo and I were fighting. I was angry. Furious, in fact." Sam laughed, the sound harsh and brittle. "Bo can get under my fucking skin like nobody else."

Dean arched an eyebrow. "I can believe that. But why would that—?" His eyes went wide. "Oh, shit. It's because of your psychokinesis. Uncontrolled negative emotions set it off, and if you're in a place with the potential for a portal to form..."

"Exactly." Sam dug a foot deep into the loose sand. "Ever since Bo and I went to the fort for the first time, I've felt like he was in danger there, and I didn't know why. I thought it must have something to do with those episodes he's had, but maybe it's not that at all. Maybe I'm the one putting him in danger, just by being there."

Dean leaned toward Sam, one hand on his knee. "Listen, Sam. We don't know that anyone's in danger at all. But even if you're right, y'all are both safe here at the house, right?" Sam nodded his assent, and Dean flashed a wide smile. "Well there you go. All you have to do is stay here. Bo's already said he wouldn't come to the fort tonight."

It was a seductive thought. Sam licked his lips. "What about the rest of you?"

"If you're right about your emotional reaction triggering a portal, then we should all be perfectly safe if you're here at the house."

"And if I'm wrong?"

Dean didn't answer right away. He held Sam's gaze, searching his face. "We'll talk to Andre and Cecile," he said finally. "Let's see what they think about it. If the consensus is that we're in danger, we can stay away. But if we're in danger even if you're not there to trigger the portal, then everyone who goes there is in danger. And I really don't think that's the case. There have been no reports of anything remotely like a portal in all the fort's history, and we sure didn't experience any such thing on the first night."

"Yeah. You're probably right. Everyone should be fine if I stay here with Bo." Sighing, Sam slumped against the back of the bench. As terrible as it was to be a potential danger to his friends once again, he wanted to believe Dean was right. After all, he and Bo weren't even supposed to be at the fort. "I hope you're right, Dean. I don't even know what to think anymore. It's all so damn confusing."

"I know." Leaning over, Dean wrapped his arms around Sam's neck and hugged him. "Don't worry, Sam. I'm sure Bo will be fine."

"Yeah." Sam smiled, patting Dean's shoulder as he drew away and stood. "I do think we should talk to Joanne about the possibility of a portal, though. If I can open it, anyone else with latent psychokinesis could too."

"That's true." Dean chewed his lower lip. "Actually, it seems kind of strange that there haven't been any reports of portal-type activity, if the place has the potential for it. There's no way other people with your abilities haven't been through there before."

"Another mystery," Sam said, sounding much calmer than he felt.

"Yeah." Dean's brow furrowed for a moment, then smoothed again. He smiled. "I better get back to work. See you later."

"Yeah, see you."

Dean strolled off, hands in the pockets of his shorts. Sam

sat there for a while longer, trying to arrange the puzzle pieces of the last two days in a way that made sense. When his growling stomach finally forced him back inside a couple of hours later, he still hadn't figured it out.

ℬ

Bo didn't stir from bed until nearly six o'clock that evening. Sam was just starting to wonder if he should check on Bo again—he'd looked in on him several times during the afternoon—when Bo shuffled into the living room, wearing Sam's pajama bottoms and nothing else.

Pausing the video he'd been reviewing, Sam jumped up and hurried over to his lover. "Hey, Bo. You okay?"

"Mm-hm." Bo yawned and pushed a hand through his hair, which hung unbound and tangled around his bare shoulders. "Sorry I slept so long."

"Don't be sorry, you needed to rest." Sam slipped an arm around Bo's waist and led him to the sofa, savoring the feel of Bo warm and sleepy against his side. "You're not as hot as you were earlier."

"Thanks a lot." Tilting his head up, Bo raised his eyebrows at Sam. "Maybe I should've fixed myself up."

Sam laughed, relieved that Bo felt like joking. "You know what I meant."

"I do." Bo sat beside Cecile and folded his legs beneath him. "My temperature does seem to be back to normal, or close to it."

Cecile gave him a surprised look. "Didn't you check it?"

"We don't have a thermometer," Bo explained, looking embarrassed.

Pausing his video, Dean pushed his chair back from the

134

kitchen table and turned his attention to Bo. "But you feel better, huh? You feel like your fever's gone?"

Bo nodded. "Pretty much."

"Sam's still gonna make you stay here," David said, glancing up from the thermal with a teasing grin.

The look Bo gave him in return was less than friendly. "I know. And yes, Sam, I'm going to stay out of it tonight, just like I said I would." Taking Sam's hand, he pulled him down to the sofa and curled up against him. "You're staying here with me, by the way."

"Nowhere else I'd rather be." Sam tucked his arm around Bo and planted a kiss on his forehead.

"Hey, Sam," Dean called. "Did you want to ask Andre and Cecile about the, uh...the thing?"

Sam couldn't decide whether to be amused or annoyed. Amusement won. He chuckled. "Subtle, Dean."

Dean let out an exaggerated sigh. "It's not enough that I'm smart, resourceful and devastatingly sexy, now I have to be subtle too. Will the pressure never end?"

Cecile threw a sofa cushion at him. "Ask us what?"

Sam glanced around the room. Andre had turned off the video he'd been watching and was staring at him with the same curious expression as Cecile and David. Bo's face revealed nothing, but the sudden apprehension in his eyes said he'd guessed what Sam was about to ask.

"I felt something last night," Sam began. "Right before Bo passed out. It was a change in the fort's energy field, and it felt a lot like a portal trying to open."

Cecile's face went dead white. "Oh, my God."

"What did it feel like?" Andre asked, breaking the silence he'd kept most of the afternoon. "I mean, was it localized and controlled like the one at South Bay High, or more random like the one at Oleander House?"

Andre's unflappable calm eased some of the tension which had knotted Sam's insides all day. "It felt like it did at Oleander House more so than South Bay, although it wasn't *precisely* like either one." Sam paused, going over the event in his mind with what he hoped was a dispassionate eye. "It was sort of in between the two, I guess. It felt more controlled than at Oleander House, but without the intense focus I felt at South Bay. It seemed to be triggered by my anger—"

"Sam and I were arguing again," Bo interjected, looking sheepish. "My fault, of course."

"It takes two to fight." Tilting Bo's chin up, Sam brushed their lips together. "Anyway, I sort of equated it with the Oleander House portal because it felt to me like I triggered it. If that makes any sense."

Cecile nodded. "It makes sense to me."

"Me too." Andre scratched his jaw, his expression thoughtful. "Anything else?"

"Not really. Of course whatever it was, it only lasted for a second. If it really was a portal, it never did open. So it's sort of difficult to be sure of anything."

"But you did feel as if whatever it was, was connected to your emotions in some way, right?" Bo curled a hand around Sam's knee, thumb caressing the old scar from a childhood bicycle accident. "So if you and I stay here, everyone else should be able to finish the investigation without unnecessary risk."

"Right." Sam scowled. Even though he was relieved that he and Bo would be staying at the house, it was galling to be reminded that he could be a source of danger to the people who mattered most to him in the world. "Andre, I think we should talk to Joanne about this. If there's even the slightest potential of a portal ever opening at the fort, they should know about the danger."

"Yeah, you're probably right." Andre let out a deep sigh. "She's not going to like it. She was hoping we could help her business, not hurt it."

"Well, there's no need to break the bad news just yet, is there?" Uncurling his legs from where he'd been sitting on the floor, David stretched out on his back with both hands behind his head. "I mean, we can see what comes up tonight, can't we? The fort's closed tomorrow anyhow. If we run into anything freaky tonight, we can call Joanne tomorrow and let her know."

"Andre, you and I should probably do a thorough psychic run-through tonight." Cecile brushed her bangs out of her eyes. "We both felt the energy of the potential portals at Oleander House and at South Bay. If there's anything like that at Fort Medina, we should be able to sense it."

"For that matter, we should've been able to sense it before, if the potential is there at all," Andre pointed out. "But we weren't really doing the full-out psychic sweep, so maybe we just missed it. We'll plan on spending some time concentrating our attention on that tonight. If it's there, you're absolutely right, we should be able to pick up on it."

"And if Sam's not there, there's no danger of the critters getting loose." David shot an apologetic look at Sam. "No offense, man."

"None taken." Feeling morose and out of sorts now, Sam stood and headed toward the kitchen. "I think I'll start dinner. What do y'all want?"

"Let's get pizza," Dean suggested. "There's a place up the road that delivers. Kyle says it's quick and really good."

"Who's Kyle?" Bo asked.

"Dean's new boy-toy." David grinned. "Speaking of which,

Dean, you never did give us the scoop on the kid yesterday. Was he good?"

Dean smirked. "Sorry, David, I don't suck and tell."

"Oh my God," David groaned. "I just had to ask."

A grin tugged at Sam's lips. Having Dean and David in the same room always felt like being in a buddy movie. Their teasing banter never failed to lift Sam's spirits.

Sam reached for the phone book sitting on the counter between the kitchen and breakfast area. "What's the name of the pizza place, Dean?"

"Mimzi's." Tucking a leg beneath him in the chair, Dean restarted his video. "Get a veggie one."

"And one sausage and onion," David said, sitting up to start the thermal video again. "No black olives."

"I like black olives," Cecile protested.

"Maybe they'll do half with and half without," Andre suggested, already watching his own video once more.

Bo leaned over to grab a notepad and pen off the coffee table and held it out toward Sam. "Here, you might need to write all this down, Sam." He smiled, brown eyes sparkling with amusement.

"No kidding." Shaking his head, Sam skirted the dining table, took the notepad and pen from Bo along with a brief kiss, and went back to the phone. "Okay. Let's see if we can work out what to get."

It took several minutes of argument, negotiation and frantic note-taking, but eventually they agreed on three medium pizzas with a bewildering variety of toppings. It took several repetitions on Sam's part for the girl on the other end of the phone to get their order right when he called it in. He was pleasantly surprised when the pizzas arrived twenty minutes later perfect to the last detail.

Cecile and Sam were cleaning up the plates, napkins and leftover slices when someone tapped on the back door. Sam glanced up from loading the dishwasher in time to see Dean fling open the door and melt into the arms of the tall, sunburned young man from next door.

"Kyle?" Sam asked, exchanging an amused look with Cecile.

She grinned. "Yes."

"Kyle, this is Sam and Bo," Dean said, pointing to Sam and Bo in turn. "You met David, Andre and Cecile yesterday."

Everyone greeted Kyle, who gave them a grin and a wave. "Hey. Um, Dean? Wanna go for a walk on the beach?"

Dean bit his lip. "I don't know if I have time or not. We still have videos and stuff to review, then we have to load up and be at Fort Medina by eight-thirty."

Kyle's face fell. "Oh. Okay." The boy looked so forlorn, Sam had to fight back the urge to offer him a hug and a cookie.

"Oh, babe, don't look like that." Dean stood on tiptoe to kiss Kyle's lips, then turned to Andre. "Andre? Please?"

Andre's glare fizzled when he saw Kyle's "poor me" expression and Dean's big, pleading eyes. "Okay," he assented. "But be back here by seven-thirty."

Dean beamed. "I will. Thanks." Turning back to Kyle, he grabbed the boy's wrist in one hand and the door handle in the other. "Let's go."

David snickered as the two hurried off into the gathering dusk. "Andre, man, you're a big softie."

"Shut up while you're ahead," Andre advised without looking away from his video.

At the kitchen window, Sam watched Dean and Kyle

descend the steps. Kyle's arm was around Dean's shoulders, and Dean's hand was firmly lodged in the back pocket of Kyle's shorts. The sight made Sam smile. Maybe he and Bo could take a walk later. There was no more romantic a setting than a moonlit beach.

Feeling the pull of Bo watching him, Sam turned away from the window. His gaze locked with Bo's across the room.

I love you, Bo mouthed, eyes shining.

Love you too, Sam silently replied.

They smiled at each other, and Sam thought maybe everything would be all right after all.

Chapter Ten

Dean came running into the house at seven twenty-five with two new bruises on his throat and sand caked on his knees. "I'm gonna shower," he called on his way down the hall. "I'll be done in two minutes."

Andre shook his head. "I swear to God, one of these days his sex drive is going to get us all in trouble."

Laughing, Bo got up from the sofa and headed for the broom closet. "For someone with Dean's experience and ability, we can put up with a little extra horniness." He opened the closet, took out a battered yellow plastic broom and started sweeping up the sand Dean had left in his wake. "Besides, he's never been late yet."

"True." Andre yawned and stretched, falling back against the couch cushions. "You know what, unless we find something tonight that warrants further investigation, I think I might call this the last night."

Surprised and hopeful, Sam closed the book he'd been halfway reading for the past half hour and looked at Andre. "Really? How come?"

"Well, Joanne's stuck in Mobile, for one thing, so we might not actually have anyone to let us in and lock up again after tonight. Plus I think we've really done everything we can do." Andre shrugged. "Hopefully we won't find anything tonight to suggest the potential for an interdimensional portal. To be honest, I don't know what the hell we'll do if we find anything like that."

With no answer for that, Sam fell silent along with the rest of the group. He opened his book and stared at the page, pretending he wasn't thinking about what might happen that night.

જી

Sam helped load equipment into the SUV while Bo lay curled up on the sofa watching a cooking show on TV. Bo had scowled when Sam insisted he stay inside instead of carrying around camera cases and long rolls of extension cord, but he hadn't argued. Whether that meant he'd seen reason at last or simply that he was feeling worse than he let on, Sam had no idea. Bo had acted normal enough through the evening so far, but he was paler than usual and seemed distracted.

Lifting the last camera case into the back of the SUV, Sam decided that as soon as the others left, he would ask Bo exactly how he felt, and whether or not he was still experiencing those strange, blank spells. If he was lucky, Bo might even answer him without getting angry.

After the SUV pulled onto the road to the fort, Sam stood on the front porch for a moment, mentally steeling himself for what was bound to be a difficult conversation. At least Bo's mood had mellowed since the previous day.

Inside, Sam found Bo flipping through the channels. He smiled and switched off the TV when Sam plopped onto the sofa beside him. "So. Here we are alone in the house." Bo nuzzled behind Sam's ear. "What should we do?"

The suggestion in Bo's voice went straight to Sam's groin. It took all his willpower to hold Bo away from him instead of crushing their mouths together.

"I think we should talk," Sam said, wishing he didn't sound so breathless.

Bo groaned, head falling forward onto Sam's shoulder. "Why does that sentence never precede a discussion about how well everything's going?"

Sam laughed in spite of himself. "I don't know."

Looking resigned, Bo sat back against the sofa cushions, drew his knees up and wrapped his arms around them. "What do you want to talk about?"

"You."

Bo let out a deep sigh. "Sam, come on."

"I just want to know how you really are. I know your fever's down, but you still don't seem entirely back to normal to me."

"I'm fine."

"Are you really?"

"Yes." Bo shoved his hair out of his eyes and pinned Sam with an irritated look. "Why are you so obsessed with the idea that I'm deathly ill, or possessed, or whatever the hell it is you're thinking is wrong with me?"

Biting back his frustration, Sam took one of Bo's hands between both of his. "I know I seem obsessed. I don't mean to. But I almost lost you once, and the thought of going through that sort of thing again scares me to death."

Being reminded of his near death and its effect on Sam always broke down Bo's defenses. It was a dirty trick, in a way, but Sam didn't care. He wasn't above playing the pity card if it got Bo to tell him the truth.

To his shock, Bo yanked his hand away and jumped to his

feet. "Don't you dare use that tactic with me. Not now."

Sam stared, stunned, as Bo started pacing a furious path back and forth across the living room. "Bo, I—"

"Shut up." Bo shot a glare full of simmering fury at Sam. "If you bring that up one more time, I swear to God I will punch that fucking lost-puppy look right off your face."

Sam eyed Bo's tense shoulders and twitching jaw warily. He had no idea what to say. For all their arguments, for all the ugly things they'd said to each other in anger, Bo had never threatened him before. Not since that night at Oleander House, before they'd become a couple, and Sam had to admit he'd goaded Bo into hitting him that time.

"Listen to yourself," Sam said, keeping his voice calm and his face expressionless. "Listen to what you just said. This isn't like you. You haven't really been yourself since that first night at Fort Medina."

"If I haven't been myself, it's because you have been driving me up the fucking wall." Bo stopped pacing and jabbed a shaking finger at Sam. "A couple of nightmares and a few bad reactions to a fever, and you have me..." He waved a hand around, as if trying to pull the right words out of the air. "I don't even fucking know what you think, but you obviously have the idea that something is horribly wrong with me. Yet when it comes down to it, we find out that *you* are the real danger here. You and that goddamn psychokinesis that you *fucking refuse* to control."

That hurt. Sam clasped his hands together, trying to tamp down his rising anger. "I'm trying to control it. It isn't easy, you know. There's not exactly a how-to book on it."

Bo barked a harsh laugh. He started pacing again, twisting a lock of hair hard around his fingers. "I can't believe you can't see what a fucking hypocrite you're being."

Exasperated, Sam pressed both palms to his forehead. "Are you being a prick on purpose now? I don't know what the hell you're talking about."

"No, you wouldn't, would you?"

That was it. Sam jumped up, grabbed Bo's shoulders and whirled him around so they were facing each other. "Then fucking explain it! Why don't you tell me what you're thinking? Or can't you handle being honest for a change?"

Bo's cheeks went red. He shrugged off Sam's grip. "You want honesty? Well, you fucking got it." He shoved a palm into Sam's chest, sending him stumbling backward. "First, you come up with this theory that anticonvulsants might dampen your psychokinesis to the point where your mind can't connect to those damned portals anymore. Then you flatly refuse to even explore that option. It didn't matter to you how much it scared me to think of the man I love—*you*"—this was punctuated by another jab to the chest—"facing that kind of danger all the time. It didn't matter to you how much I fucking *begged* you to at least get tested for seizure disorder so we could find out if your theory would hold water. It did not matter to you how I felt. Not once."

Sam swallowed. "I didn't mean—"

"Shut *up!*" Bo advanced on him, a dangerous glitter in his eyes. "My opinion didn't matter to you then. My fears didn't matter to you. You didn't want to hear it. Yet you have the *fucking gall* to whine about how scared you are of losing me? Well let me tell you something. I wouldn't be in any danger at the fucking fort if you'd fucking listened to me before, because you wouldn't be accidentally opening portals again." His lips curled into a rictus of a grin, making him look more than a little deranged. "Who's the prick now, huh?"

Sam's vision went red. Before he knew quite what he was

doing, he'd tackled Bo to the ground, pinning his wrists above his head. "Fuck you!"

Sam expected Bo to fight back. Maybe even wanted him to. Having an excuse to hit Bo right now would be welcome.

He didn't expect Bo to clamp a hand onto the back of his neck, rear up and kiss him.

Taken by surprise, Sam automatically reciprocated, opening wide for Bo's tongue. Bo growled deep in his chest. His hand clutched Sam's neck in a bruising grip, his mouth eating at Sam's. Sam groaned, excited in spite of his hurt and anger.

"Yes," Bo breathed.

"Huh?"

"What you said before." Bo hooked a leg around Sam's back. His erection dug into Sam's groin. "Fuck me."

Sam stared at him, wondering if he'd gone crazy. "You want to fuck? Right now?"

"Yes." Reaching between them, Bo twisted Sam's nipple through his T-shirt.

Sam yelped and shoved Bo's hand away. "No."

"Yes." Bo grabbed Sam's hair in both fists, yanked his head down and kissed him hard.

Sam felt his lip split under the assault. The taste of blood flooded his mouth. He dug a hand into Bo's hair and yanked his head back, feeling a rush of dark satisfaction when Bo winced. "Stop it! I'm not having sex with you when you're like this."

Eyelids dropping to half-mast, Bo licked Sam's blood off his lips. The movement was slow and sensual, and Sam's body reacted. He tried to extricate himself from Bo's determined grip before Bo could notice, but Bo's smirk told him it was too late.

"You're hard, you fucking liar. You want me, just like you always do." Bo ground his crotch against Sam's, heel digging into the small of Sam's back. "Do it, Sam. Fuck me."

Sam gulped. "No. Not like this."

Bo's laugh was harsh and ugly. "Bullshit. You want it." He shoved a hand between their bodies and pinched the head of Sam's cock hard. It hurt. Sam yelped and tried to jerk away. Bo's leg remained around him like an iron band, holding him down. "Come on, Sam. Fuck me hard. Or don't you have the balls to give it to me like I want?"

The sneer on Bo's face was what snapped Sam's wavering control. He pried Bo's fingers from his neck, grabbed Bo's hips and flipped him onto his stomach. A hand planted between Bo's shoulder blades kept him face down on the rug.

"Don't you fucking move." Keeping his right hand splayed on Bo's back, Sam wrestled Bo's pajama bottoms off one-handed and threw them aside. "Spread your legs."

"Fuck you," Bo spat. "Do it yourself."

Fury boiled up inside Sam. Somewhere in a calm corner of his brain, he knew Bo was manipulating him, deliberately goading him into being rough. He knew it, and he hated that it was working. Angry at Bo and even angrier at himself, yet so turned on he could barely see straight, Sam grabbed Bo's thighs and shoved them apart.

Shifting to kneel between Bo's open legs, he spread Bo's buttocks to stare at the dusky little whorl of his anus. God, but the sight excited him. He wished it wouldn't. Bending down, he sank his teeth into one firm ass cheek. He didn't let go until he heard Bo's hiss of pain.

Sam sat back on his heels, both palms still planted on Bo's ass, and pushed. Bo got the message. He tucked his knees under him and raised his butt into the air. Sam smacked the insides of his thighs, forcing his legs to open as wide as possible without making him fall flat on the floor again.

Sam took a moment to admire the sight of Bo in this vulnerable position—cheek pressed to the braided rug, ass in the air, cock and balls swinging beneath his spread thighs. A perfect set of tooth marks, still wet with Sam's saliva, blazed red on his right buttock.

Twisting his upper body, Bo glared over his shoulder at Sam. "What're you waiting for? Do it already."

Sam gritted his teeth. He lunged for the bottle of piña-colada-scented lotion Cecile kept beside the sofa, poured far more than he needed into his palm, and slicked his cock. He spread the rest over Bo's hole.

"You want me to fuck you? Fine." Not waiting for an answer, he spread Bo open with his thumbs and penetrated him with one swift, savage thrust.

"Fuck!" Bo's body tensed, fingers clawing at the floor. "Jesus. Move."

Sam clamped his hands onto Bo's hipbones and held still with a mighty effort, in spite of Bo's demand. Bo was so tight Sam knew even the slightest movement would hurt.

Bo was having none of it. He rocked backward, forcing Sam's cock deep inside him. He turned to look over his shoulder, his face contorted in silent agony, and Sam felt a flash of pure hatred toward Bo for making him do this to him.

"Don't stop." Bo's eyes screwed shut. His voice was tight with pain. "Fuck me, come on."

Angry and confused and hating himself for being this excited, Sam shut his eyes and let himself go. His hips pistoned, driving his prick into Bo with brutal force. With each thrust, he heard Bo grunt, felt the slap of his groin against Bo's ass, the hot clutch of Bo's insides around his shaft. The room smelled like sweat, sex and coconut.

Bo let out a soft little "oh", and Sam suddenly thought

about the night he'd spanked Bo and fucked him against the wall. That had been all about pleasure, not pain. Love and mutual desire, not anger or the need to punish. He wanted it to be like that again. He didn't like Bo this way. More than that, he didn't like *himself* this way.

The telltale pulsing of Bo's hole forced Sam's eyes open again. Bo's eyes remained shut, his mouth falling open and his back arching as his orgasm hit. His prick, untouched by either of them, spattered the floor with globs of white. Sam came almost in spite of himself, fingertips digging into Bo's hipbones as his cock emptied deep inside Bo.

He pulled out so fast it hurt. His own pained noise echoed Bo's. Letting go of Bo's hips, he stumbled to his feet, staggered backward and dropped onto the sofa. Bo fell forward onto the floor with a muffled thump. Sam thought he looked like a broken doll, lying face down with eyes closed and limbs splayed, semen leaking from his ass.

"I didn't want to do that," Sam said, sounding harsher than he'd intended. "I didn't want to hurt you."

The corner of Bo's mouth hitched up in a bitter half-smile. "Right."

"It's true." Sam drew his knees up and rested his chin on them. He felt tired and depressed. What he and Bo had just done wasn't their usual lovemaking. It was fucking, rough bordering on violent, and it left him hollow. "This isn't normal. You can't pretend it is."

Bo rolled onto his side. His eyes opened, and their icy regard made Sam wish he'd left them closed. "It's just sex, Sam. Just a little rough sex. Maybe I want that once in a while."

Sam blinked, surprised. "You do?"

Wincing, Bo pushed to a sitting position and climbed to his feet. He stood there swaying, his nude body glistening with

149

sweat and semen. "I'm not a china doll. I won't break. I'm sick of you treating me like some delicate little toy."

Sam's mouth fell open. "What the fuck? I've never done that."

"You're doing it right now! Sitting there telling me I'm not normal for wanting you to be rough with me sometimes—"

"I didn't say that, dammit!"

Bo plowed on as if Sam hadn't spoken. "And telling me I'm not fit to work just because of a few nightmares and...and things." His hands clenched into quick fists, then relaxed. "And, and now you're ignoring the fact that there was *no portal activity* at Fort Medina until *you* showed up, and trying to make out like I'm somehow causing it. You're the focus, Sam, *you're* the one with the fucking psychokinesis, not me. But oh no, Bo has a bad reaction to a virus so that must mean it's his fault. Well, fuck that, Sam, it's *you* causing it, not me! You're the one with an ability you won't even consider getting rid of, not me. Maybe it gives you a power rush to know you can manipulate those portals. Is that it? Huh? You like the power rush?" His voice, which had been rising, dropped to a husky whisper. He cupped his balls in one hand, his cold gaze turning soft and sultry. "You sure seemed to like fucking me till it hurt. I bet that's it. You get off on power, don't you?"

Sam gaped, speechless in the face of Bo's increasingly paranoid and nonsensical rant. If he hadn't been worried about Bo before, this would've done it. He had no idea what to say or do, if he should try to placate Bo or talk sense into him. He was out of his depth, afraid to say a word or make a move for fear of how Bo might react.

God, is he turning psychotic? What the fuck do I do?

He was saved from having to act by Bo turning on his heel and stalking out of the room, still naked. "Don't bother coming to bed," Bo sneered over his shoulder. "I don't want to look at you right now."

Bo's bare feet thudded up the stairs. The bedroom door squeaked open and slammed so hard the sound echoed through the house.

Sam sat there staring at the painting of a sailing ship cutting through stormy seas hanging on the opposite wall. He felt numb and shell-shocked. Bo was acting irrationally, without a doubt, but some of the things he'd said had a ring of truth Sam couldn't ignore.

Had he really dismissed Bo's fears to the extent Bo claimed? Had he truly been that insensitive to Bo's desire to see him safe from the portals? And what about Bo's unexpected confession that he liked near-brutal sex sometimes? Had Bo been giving him clues all along, and he just hadn't seen?

Did he really know so little about the man he claimed to love?

"God, I can't think about this right now." Pushing to his feet, Sam snatched the discarded pajama pants off the floor, un-wadded them and tugged them on. He shuffled into the kitchen and wet a hand towel under the faucet. Back in the living room, he scrubbed the congealing spunk off the rug. Leaving the towel wadded up on the floor, he curled up on the sofa and turned on the TV to drown out his racing thoughts.

Worn out with worry, hurt and fear, Sam slept. If the nightmares came, he didn't remember them.

∓

He woke to the sound of the front door opening and hushed voices coming closer. He sat up and squinted at the clock on the VCR. It read three-thirty a.m.

Cecile stopped, eyes widening when she saw Sam. "My God, Sam, what happened to you?"

"What to do you mean?" He yawned, grimacing when the twinge in his lip reminded him of what had happened earlier.

"Your lip's split," David pointed out, setting a camera case in the corner. He grinned. "What, did you and Bo get in a fist fight or something?"

"Not exactly." Sam turned his face away when Cecile sat beside him and tried to get a better look at his mouth. "It's okay. It's nothing."

"Not if Bo's the one who did that, it isn't." Grabbing his chin in a firm grip, Cecile forced him to look at her. A crease formed between her eyes. "Sam, what happened?"

Irritated, Sam pulled away. "He didn't hit me. It was just... I mean, we...um..."

He didn't know what to say that wouldn't sound crude. Evidently his blush gave him away, though.

David snorted. "They just had a little rough sex, Cecile. Stop fussing."

It was uncomfortably close to what Bo had said earlier. To his horror, Sam felt tears prick his eyes. He blinked until it went away and forced a smile. "I'd rather not discuss my sex life right now, if it's all right with you. Tell me about the investigation tonight. Did you find anything?"

Cecile gave him a sharp look, but let it drop. "I got some video of the woman some people have seen in the courtyard."

"And I caught something else on thermal," Dean added, wandering in at that moment with a bag of cables in his hand. Andre trailed behind him, a canvas bag in each hand. "Not sure what it was. It moved so fast I couldn't really tell. Maybe we can figure it out when we go over the evidence."

"Sounds like you had a productive night." Sam looked at Andre. "What about the portals? Did you and Cecile sense anything?"

Andre shook his head. "The EMF and the general energy of the place seem more unstable than they did the first night we went there, but they were unchanged from the past two nights. We didn't sense anything that felt like a portal, or even a potential one."

Sam let out a breath, the tension draining from his body. "God, that's a relief."

"It sure is." Yawning, Andre turned and shuffled toward the door. "C'mon, let's finish unloading. I'm beat."

"Coming." Cecile squeezed Sam's hand, then jumped up and followed Andre and David out the door.

Dean set his bag on the floor and walked over to sit beside Sam, his eyes full of concern. "You okay?"

"Bo and I had another fight. He was acting really irrational there at the end." Sam probed the cut on his lip with his tongue. "I'm going beyond worried into seriously alarmed here. I have no idea what to do."

Dean's brow furrowed. "What did he say?"

"He told me that if he was in any danger, it was because of me. Because my psychokinesis can open the portals. And he said..." Sam trailed off, not wanting to admit some of the things Bo had said and how ashamed they had made him feel. "He said a lot of things. Some of it didn't make much sense."

Dean pursed his lips. "Hm. Okay, I was gonna say something this morning, but I didn't because it just seemed so crazy to think Bo would do this. But after what you just told me..."

"What?" Sam prodded when Dean fell silent, frowning and chewing his lip. "Come on, you're scaring me."

Dean gave him an apprehensive look. "All right. Please don't get mad at me for saying this, but does Bo... Well, does he take any kind of medication?"

"Not for months now, no. They stopped the antibiotics only a couple of weeks after he was bitten, and he hasn't needed the pain pills since before Sunset Lodge. I don't see—" Suddenly Sam *did* see. His eyes went wide. "No, that can't be it. I'd know if he were still taking prescription drugs for pain."

"Maybe, maybe not. Lots of people pop 'em like candy without anyone ever suspecting, even the people closest to them. In any case, it's a possibility we can't afford to ignore. The blanking-out spells, the mood swings, the irrationality? Acting in ways that just aren't normal for him? Those are all signs of substance abuse. And prescription narcotics are some of the most commonly abused substances there are." Taking Sam's hand between both of his, Dean gave it a gentle squeeze. "I don't want to believe it either. Hopefully I'm wrong. But I think we should consider that that's what might be going on here. Addiction does funny things to a person, and it can happen to anyone."

Before Sam could think of anything else to say, the front door opened and Andre, David and Cecile came in carrying the last of the equipment. Dean glanced at them. "We'll talk later," he whispered. Patting Sam's hand, he stood and went over to talk to Andre.

Sam smiled and said good night to the group through a haze of shock and fear. Could Dean be right? Could Bo really be hooked on the narcotics Sam thought he'd taken the last of months ago? The possibility shook Sam to the core.

But he's never acted this way before now, Sam's inner voice murmured. *He's stubborn and irritating sometimes, but he's never been like this before. It all started with Fort Medina. He can't be hooked on pain pills. He just can't. There's no way he could hide it from me this long.*

Of course Sam's certainty proved nothing. He was no expert on drug addiction, but he knew Dean was right. A person could be hooked and no one ever suspect. He'd seen it from time to time in his previous job. Working in a hospital, even in computer support, you heard stories. Saw things. If a hospital vice president could successfully hide his narcotic habit from his wife, his children and co-workers, who was to say Bo couldn't do the same? Sam still didn't quite believe it, but Dean was right. They couldn't afford to ignore the possibility.

Yawning, Sam rubbed a hand across his face. In spite of everything that had happened that night—or maybe because of it—he could barely keep his eyes open.

I'll talk to Dean some more later, he promised himself, stretching out on the sofa. Maybe his friend would have some idea where to start looking for more clues, and how on earth to confront Bo if they needed to. The very idea made Sam shudder.

"God, I hope we don't have to do that," Sam mumbled, his eyes drifting shut. Sheer exhaustion sucked him in, and he slept.

Chapter Eleven

Toward morning, Sam dreamed again. Another nightmare of frigid, crushing blackness, alive with a sense of intelligent menace. He woke damp and shaking in the gray predawn light. Sitting up, he turned on the lamp beside the couch to banish the darkness. It was too easy to see things in the shadows.

He was in the kitchen making coffee when he heard the shuffle of bare feet behind him. Before he could turn, arms slid around his waist and soft lips brushed the back of his neck.

He laid his hand over Bo's where it pressed to his belly. This was Bo's "apology" posture. He'd seen it countless times, and it was usually followed by them making up from whatever their latest fight had been. But after what had happened the night before, Sam had no clue what to say. Especially in light of Dean's suspicions regarding Bo's behavior.

"I was way out of line last night," Bo said after a few moments of awkward silence. His voice was raspy and tremulous. "Can you ever forgive me?"

Sam swallowed, his throat constricting. "Have I really been that insensitive to you all this time?" He almost laughed at himself for being most interested in the answer to that question when there were other, more important things he *should* be asking.

Bo only hesitated a few seconds, but it was enough to give

Sam his answer. He groaned, dropping his head into his hands. "Shit. I'm sorry."

Bo's arms tightened around him. "You dismissed my fears for you, that's true. And you didn't listen to me about at least trying to get on anticonvulsants to see if they'd keep your mind from connecting to the portals and those things on the other side. But I understand why you don't want to do that. I really do. It makes sense for you to keep your connection to the portals, even if I don't like it. Everyone's safer that way, in the end. I never should've said those things to you last night."

It was true, so Sam didn't bother to argue. Turning in Bo's embrace, Sam stared into his eyes. They were swollen and bloodshot. "You didn't sleep."

"Not really, no." The ghost of a smile touched Bo's lips. "It took me a while to realize exactly how horrible I'd been to you. You were asleep when I came down to apologize, and I didn't want to wake you. Then the others came back, and I just...just couldn't face them."

It was on the tip of Sam's tongue to ask Bo if he had any pain pills stashed away upstairs. If he'd been taking them on the sly all this time. But he couldn't do it. Not right now, with Bo standing there red-eyed and clearly exhausted, apologizing to him. This was the Bo he'd fallen in love with, and he didn't want to do anything to drive him away and bring back the sneering, hurtful person from the night before.

He didn't even consider asking if Bo really enjoyed the sort of violent sex they'd had last night. He wasn't sure he wanted to know.

Cupping Bo's face in his hands, Sam pressed a gentle kiss to his lips. "I'll forgive you, if you'll forgive me."

Bo laughed. "Deal." He dropped his hands to Sam's ass and squeezed as Sam kissed him again, deeper this time.

After breakfast, they curled up together on the sofa and turned on the TV. Bo flipped around until he found a show about spectacular vacation homes and settled down to watch. Outside the rain, which had been threatening since the previous day, finally began pattering softly against the side of the house.

It was strange that everything could seem so normal after the events of the previous night. Sam knew this was simply the calm before the storm. Eventually, he would have to either ask Bo point-blank if he was still taking narcotics, or go through his things to find out. Neither option held much appeal. The thought of confronting Bo with Dean's suspicions knotted Sam's stomach. However, he didn't think he could go behind Bo's back. It would be wrong. Not to mention that Bo would never forgive him if he found out.

He didn't want to think about it. Not now. Not when everything between them was this peaceful, even if it was only temporary. He let his dread and worry slide to the back of his mind and concentrated on the perfection of lying in Bo's arms while the rain fell outside.

Predictably, Dean was the first of the others to rise. He came wandering in around midmorning, barefoot and shirtless, wearing a pair of oversize blue flannel boxers, which seemed in danger of falling off at any moment. "Hey," he greeted them through a yawn. "'S there any food?"

Bo's chuckle vibrated against Sam's back. "I didn't cook, if that's what you mean. Sam and I just had cereal. There's coffee, otherwise you'll have to fend for yourself."

"No problem." He yawned again and ran a hand through his mussed hair, making it stick up in several directions at once. He shot a swift, assessing look at Bo on his way to the kitchen. "How're you feeling this morning, Bo? Okay?"

"Mm-hm." Bo snuggled closer, nuzzling the back of Sam's neck. "I didn't sleep much, but otherwise I feel fine. No fever at all that I can tell."

"Good." From the kitchen came the sound of the refrigerator door opening and closing, followed by dishes rattling in a cabinet. "What about those weird spells? Are you still having those?"

Behind Sam, Bo's body tensed, but his voice when he answered was calm and relaxed. "Um. No. I haven't had any more of those."

"And no more passing out? I assume you would've told me if that had happened again."

"No, no more passing out."

"That's good to hear." Dean came back into the living room, a cup of coffee in one hand and a slice of cold pizza in the other, and plopped into the armchair on the other side of the room. "How's your leg?"

Sam felt his eyes go wide. *What're you doing?* he mouthed. Dean just smiled and bit off a huge mouthful of pizza.

"My leg's fine. Hasn't bothered me enough to mention since Sunset Lodge." Bo sounded honestly puzzled, which made Sam feel better. "Why do you ask?"

Dean shrugged. "Just wondering. I thought I saw you rubbing your thigh yesterday." He grinned over the rim of his mug. "Or was that Sam rubbing your thigh?"

Bo chuckled, and Sam breathed a sigh of relief. It wasn't easy to get information from Bo without him catching on, and Dean's question had been a little too bold for comfort.

"Well, anything more than mild physical stress makes it ache," Bo said, tracing one of Sam's ribs with his thumb. "So you probably did see me rubbing it. But that intermittent ache has been there ever since the surgery. Sunset Lodge is the only time it's actually been what I'd call painful in months. It certainly hasn't been more than mildly uncomfortable here."

"Good." Dean squirmed sideways and slung both legs over one arm of the chair. "So. Looks like it might rain all day, what do y'all want to do?"

"Doing it already," Sam mumbled, pulling Bo's arm tighter around him.

"Sounds like a good plan to me." Bo nipped Sam's shoulder.

Dean snickered around another mouthful of pizza. "You do realize the rest of us can't cuddle with you, right?"

"Your loss." Sam grinned, a little of his tension evaporating. "Are y'all going back to Mobile today?"

"Why, you trying to get rid of us? You want the house to yourselves so you can christen every room with your love juice?"

"We did that before y'all got here," Sam said while Bo groaned and hid his face in the curve of Sam's neck. "Now we just want the rest of you to go away so we can go back to walking around naked."

"Feel free." Dean waggled his eyebrows.

"Okay, stop it, both of you," Bo's muffled voice ordered. He raised his head, and Sam didn't even have to look to know his face was beet red. "Andre said something yesterday about making last night the final night of the investigation, unless you found a compelling reason to go back."

Nodding, Dean popped the last bite of pizza into his mouth and chewed. "Yeah, we're not going back tonight. No good reason to. Good thing, since we don't have anyone to let us in. Plus, it's probably going to be raining." Dean scrunched his nose up in clear distaste. "I hate investigating outdoors in the rain."

"Not all of the fort is outdoors," Bo pointed out.

"No, but even the parts that aren't might as well be, for all the protection you get from the weather. Which is to say, not much." Dean wiped his fingers on his boxers, stretched and got to his feet. He swiped his mug off the floor and started toward the kitchen. "In any case, Andre's already declared the field portion of this case to be officially over. They're heading back to Mobile this afternoon."

"They?" Sam craned his neck to give Dean a questioning look across the counter dividing the kitchen from the dining area. "Aren't you going?"

"Nope. I'm staying next door with Kyle for a couple of days." Dean emerged from the kitchen with a fresh cup of coffee and plopped into the chair again. "He invited me to stay. BCPI isn't taking on any other new cases at the moment, since we've been so covered up lately and we still have lots of paperwork to catch up on. I'm still owed some vacation time, so Andre said I could take a few days off."

Bo shifted his position a bit, resting his chin on Sam's shoulder. "I'm glad you're taking some time off. You've been putting in a lot of overtime in the past few months."

"Is it overtime if you don't get paid for it?" Dean wondered, scratching his chin. "Hm. Food for thought."

Sam laughed along with Bo. Even though he'd initially resented his friends' intrusion into his and Bo's vacation, the thought of being alone with Bo at this point scared him a little. He was relieved to know Dean would be right next door. Something told him he might need Dean's help before the end.

By three o'clock, Andre, David and Cecile had the SUV loaded up and were ready to leave. The rain had settled into a steady downpour. Water puddled on the driveway and drowned the thin grass of the front lawn in a shallow lake.

While Bo and Andre talked in the foyer, Sam and Dean stood on the front porch with David and Cecile. Cecile shivered, clutching David's jacket around her. "It *would* have to be raining today," she complained, tossing her dripping hair out of her eyes. "I can't believe we didn't even think to bring an umbrella."

David gathered her into his arms and kissed her head. "Don't worry, babe. I'll keep you warm."

Cecile laid her head on his shoulder, a smile curving her lips. "Mmm. Thank you."

"Oh my God, that's sweet." Dean sighed. "I want a girlfriend. Or a boyfriend. Or both."

Sam laughed. "So what's Kyle, then?"

"A summer fling, of course." Dean glanced next door, grinned and waved. "Speaking of which, here he comes."

Sam followed Dean's gaze. Sure enough, Kyle was crossing the open space between the two houses, a huge green and white striped umbrella curving over his head. He bounded up the porch steps just as the front door opened and Bo and Andre emerged.

"Hey, y'all." Kyle gave the group a sweet, shy smile before turning an adoring gaze to Dean. "You ready?"

"Yeah, all set." Dean bent to pick up his duffle bag. He leaned close to Sam and dropped his voice to a whisper. "Call me if you need me, okay?"

Sam nodded his thanks. Dean gave his arm a quick squeeze, then straightened up and went to Kyle's side. He hooked his free hand through Kyle's elbow. "Y'all have a safe trip back home. Be careful."

"David's not driving, so we should be safe enough." Andre ducked away from the smack David aimed at his head. "Sam, Bo, enjoy the rest of your vacation. Do *not* call us, we'll be fine." He arched an eyebrow at Dean. "That goes for you too. You're nearly as bad as Bo."

Dean clutched his chest. "Oh, ouch."

Shaking his head, Bo moved closer to Sam's side. "We'll see you in a few days. And I promise I won't call."

"Neither will I." Dean tugged on Kyle's arm. "Let's go. You promised me sex, alcohol and PlayStation. In that order."

Kyle turned red. "Um. Yeah." He darted a brief, embarrassed look at the group. "Nice to meet y'all. Bye."

Kyle and Dean descended the steps into the rain, followed by goodbyes and David's gleeful admonishment not to break the furniture while fucking on it. Dean leered back at them while Kyle hunched his shoulders and walked faster.

Cecile pinched David's arm, making him yelp. "Why do you have to embarrass the poor boy like that?"

"Hey, Dean started it," David protested, rubbing his arm.

"Well, you didn't have to make it worse." Pulling away from David, Cecile hugged first Bo, then Sam. "Have fun, guys. And don't worry about the business, we'll be okay. We're planning to spend this next week catching up on paperwork and reviewing evidence from Fort Medina."

"Sounds good." Bo slipped an arm around Sam's waist as David, Cecile and Andre hurried through the rain to the SUV. "Let us know if you find anything exciting, okay?"

Andre waved a noncommittal hand at them as he slid behind the wheel. The engine revved, the headlights came on and the SUV rolled down the driveway. Sam watched with a mix of relief and dread as it pulled onto the road and picked up speed. The taillights disappeared around a bend in the narrow street, and he was officially alone with Bo.

"Alone at last," Bo murmured, echoing Sam's thoughts. He pressed a kiss to Sam's neck. "Why don't I fix us a couple of Irish coffees, and we can go out on the back porch and watch the rain?"

"That sounds perfect." Turning, Sam cupped Bo's cheek in one palm and kissed his lips. Bo's mouth was warm and soft, his cheek rough with the stubble he hadn't yet shaved off that day. "I'm glad they're gone. They're my friends, and I love them, but I'm glad to have you to myself again." It was true, in spite of his fear of what might happen when he confronted Bo. "Is that selfish?"

Bo smiled, dark eyes shining. "If it is, then we're both selfish. Because I'm looking forward to being alone with you again."

Warmth swelled in Sam's chest. He brushed his lips across Bo's brow. "If the rain lets up, we can walk on the beach later."

"I'd like that." Bo squeezed Sam's butt, then stepped out of his embrace. "Come on. Irish coffee. Back porch."

Laughing, Sam linked his hand with Bo's and followed him inside.

ॐ

They spent the majority of the remaining daylight hours on the back porch, contemplating the roiling gray Gulf and talking.

By unspoken agreement, they didn't discuss Fort Medina, or interdimensional gateways, or any of the other topics that tended to cause friction between them. Instead, they talked about little things. Safe things. The weather, movies they wanted to see, the marathon they were still trying to decide if they should run together next spring. It was wonderfully peaceful, and Sam hated to disturb that rare atmosphere between them.

The rain eased over the afternoon hours. When the sinking sun filtered through the thinning clouds to tint water, sand and sky fiery red, Sam and Bo decided to brave the remaining misty drizzle and watch the sunset from the beach. They stood arm in arm on the damp sand at the water's edge while blue twilight crept over the world and the waves washed blood-warm over their feet.

As the last sliver of golden light slid below the horizon, Bo turned to Sam with a solemn expression. "Something's been bothering you all day. And I think it has something to do with me." He slipped both arms around Sam's waist. "Tell me what's wrong, Sam. Please. Whatever it is, I promise to listen and not lose my temper."

Sam wasn't at all sure Bo could keep that promise, but what choice did he have? All day long, he'd been looking for the right moment to ask Bo the hardest question he'd ever had to ask. And now, Bo had just given him the perfect opening. He had to take it.

"I have to ask you something," Sam began, choosing his words with care. He wound an arm around Bo's waist and rested his other hand on Bo's shoulder. "It's not... You're not going to like it."

Apprehension filled Bo's face, but he nodded. "Okay. Go on."

Sam cleared his throat. "The thing is, you've been acting...well, not quite like yourself lately. And I've been worried."

The corners of Bo's mouth lifted. "So you've said."

"Yeah, well." Sam tongued the healing cut on his bottom lip. He'd never been so nervous in his life. "Okay, there's no easy way to ask you this, so I'm just going to ask. Are you on drugs?"

Bo's eyebrows shot up. "Are you serious?"

Sam didn't say anything, but evidently the look on his face was answer enough.

Bo's mouth dropped open. He closed it again and shook his head. "I almost asked where in the world you'd gotten that idea, but I think I can see it. I *have* been acting irrationally lately. Especially last night."

Sam didn't bother to deny it. "So, you're not still taking those pain pills they gave you after your surgery?"

Smiling, Bo pulled Sam close and kissed his chin. "No, I'm not."

Sam stared into Bo's eyes, searching for any sign of deception. He found none. Bo met his gaze without flinching.

Relieved, Sam rested his forehead against Bo's. "I didn't really believe it, but I couldn't just let it go without knowing for sure. Dean—" He stopped, wincing.

Damn. The last thing he'd wanted was to bring up Dean's part in this. Bo hadn't been angry yet, but knowing Sam had talked to Dean about him just might do it.

Sam's fear melted away when Bo hooked one arm around his neck and pressed his cheek to Sam's. "So Dean's the one who told you I might be hooked on narcotics?" Bo laughed, the sound soft against Sam's ear. "I wondered if that might be the case. The man has a suspicious mind."

"And a medical background." Sam drew back enough to look into Bo's eyes. "You're not mad at me?"

"For thinking I was on drugs, or for talking to Dean about me?"

"Both."

"No. I know you and Dean are close friends. I know you confide in him. Of course you'd talk to him about this. And I know I gave him plenty of reasons to suspect what he did." A lock of hair came loose from Bo's braid, the wind whipping it around his face. He tucked it behind his ear. "I'm not angry. What I am is ashamed, and embarrassed. I've been absolutely awful the past few days. The way I treated you last night was unforgivable. It...It shook me to realize exactly how terrible I had been. The fact that you were willing to look for a reason instead of simply leaving me for good makes me love you even more."

Something hard and tight in Sam's chest loosened. He cupped Bo's cheek in his palm. "You weren't the only one out of line last night. I know I hurt you. I didn't mean to, and I didn't want to. I hope you know that."

"Of course I do." Bo gazed at Sam, eyes gleaming in the dimness. "I know you feel bad about what happened, Sam, but you shouldn't. It hurt, yes, but a part of me liked it very much. That scares me a little. But I can't deny that it excited me for you to take me that way."

Sam didn't know what to say to that. He'd been positive that whatever inner demon was riding Bo last night had made him do things he would never enjoy under normal circumstances. It disturbed Sam—and, to his mortification, intrigued him—to learn that Bo really did get off on an act that was more violence than sex.

"I don't want to do that again," Sam admitted. "Not like last night. If we play rough again at some point, I just…I don't want it to be that way. Angry. You know?"

"I know." Bo stroked Sam's cheek, thumb tracing his jawline. "No more anger. No more fighting. I don't know why I've been behaving the way I have lately. I've just been…I don't know. I've felt very strange, and I've been completely out of control. But it ends right here, right now. Our last days here are going to be all about the two of us."

It was far better than anything Sam had expected to hear. A wide grin spread across his face. "I like that plan."

"Me too." Bo's smile was seductive this time. "Kiss me."

Desire pooled in Sam's belly. Tilting his head, he leaned in and sealed his lips to Bo's. Bo's mouth opened beneath his. Their tongues slid together, sending a rush of heat through Sam's blood. He let out a low moan and dropped his hand down to caress Bo's ass.

"Let's go inside," Bo whispered, his voice low and rough. "I want you."

Unable to speak, Sam drew back, took Bo's hand and led him across the darkening beach to the house.

They climbed the stairs in a silence which was no longer heavy with tension. In the bedroom, Sam shut the curtains and switched on the bedside lamp. The heavy shade filtered the light to a warm gold which made Bo's dark skin glow.

Taking Sam's hands, Bo pulled him to the bed and grasped the hem of his T-shirt. "Arms up."

Sam obeyed, allowing Bo to strip the slightly damp shirt off and throw it on the floor. "You next."

"Whatever you say." Smiling, Bo took off his shirt, then skinned out of his shorts. He was naked underneath, his prick already hard and leaking.

Sam stared, licking his lips. "God, you have a beautiful cock."

"Thank you." Bo leaned close and drew his tongue up Sam's throat. "Take off your shorts, so I can see *your* beautiful cock."

Sam shivered. Maybe it was juvenile of him, but he loved hearing the word "cock" emerging from Bo's lips in that lust-rough voice.

He unbuttoned and unzipped his shorts, shoved them down and stepped out of them. Before he could do the same with his underwear, Bo hooked his thumbs in the waistband and sank to his knees, taking Sam's briefs down at the same time.

Kneeling at Sam's feet, Bo closed his eyes and rubbed his face against Sam's erection. His hands slipped around Sam's hips, caressing the swell of his ass. Sam moaned. His entire body erupted in gooseflesh. He buried his fingers in Bo's hair, massaging his scalp.

Bo rose to his feet again, trailing a feather-light caress up Sam's body. His thumbs found Sam's nipples and rubbed them in firm circles. He leaned forward, lips parting, and Sam met him in a deep, unhurried kiss.

His mouth still locked with Bo's, Sam put his arms around Bo's neck and set about unbraiding his rain-damp hair. Bo let out a muffled chuckle. His hands slid up to cradle Sam's face.

That tender touch was enough to make Sam's eyes burn and his throat constrict. Of all the different types of sex he and Bo had explored together, this slow, sweet lovemaking was still what Sam loved best. After the previous night, it was exactly what he needed. What they both needed.

Bo broke the kiss just as Sam worked loose the last twist in his braid. "Lie down," Bo ordered, giving Sam's chest a gentle push.

Sam shuffled backward, noticing for the first time that his underwear was still tangled around his ankles. Luckily, the bed was only a couple of steps behind him. Lowering himself to the edge of the mattress, he scooted up to the middle of the bed and lay back with his head on Bo's pillow. He bent his knees and let his legs fall open, his briefs holding his feet together. In this position, he felt wanton. Utterly shameless.

Grasping his prick in one hand, Sam slid his palm slowly up and down his shaft. "What do you want, Bo? You want to fuck me? Or would you rather have me suck you off?"

Shaking his head, Bo crawled onto the bed. "No. I want you to stay right there, and let me take care of you."

Sam tried to answer, but nothing came out. The raw hunger in Bo's eyes completely destroyed his power of speech. He nodded, watching with a racing pulse as Bo stalked him on all fours across the mattress.

Planting his hands on either side of Sam's hips, Bo leaned down and pressed open-mouthed kisses to Sam's lower belly. His hair cascaded around his shoulders, brushing silky cool along Sam's groin. Sam let out a ragged moan. "God. Bo."

"Mmmm." Bo drew Sam's balls into his mouth, rolling them with his tongue for a moment before letting go. He stared up at Sam with hooded eyes. "I love the way you taste, Sam."

"Oh, God," Sam breathed as Bo licked up his shaft and lapped at his slit. "Bo. Please. Please."

Another lick, then Bo's lips sealed around the tip of Sam's cock. His cheeks hollowed, and Sam gasped at the sudden sharp suction. He got a double handful of thick ebony hair and gave Bo's head a little push, just enough to remind him of what Sam wanted.

Bo allowed Sam's prick to slip from his mouth with a soft pop. "Let me get rid of your underwear. It's in my way."

The way Bo's breath teased the head of Sam's cock made Sam want to rut mindlessly into Bo's mouth, but he managed to concentrate enough to unclench his fingers and let go of Bo's hair. Bo sat back on his heels, freed Sam's ankles from the wadded briefs and tossed them aside. He ran his hands up the insides of Sam's thighs, urging them apart.

Sam obediently spread his legs. He gazed up at Bo with something like awe. Bo had never looked more gorgeous than he did now, hair tangled and lips swollen, desire bringing a rosy flush to his skin and a simmering heat to his eyes. His prick bobbed red and rigid in front of him, making Sam's mouth water.

Crawling forward, Bo straddled Sam on all fours, leaned down and kissed him. Sam opened with a soft sigh to let their tongues wind together. Bo tasted like cock, like sweat and precome, and God, it was exciting. Sam arched up as the kiss became deeper, more aggressive. Bo's hair fell around them in a dark curtain that smelled of rain and sea air.

A low groan emerged from Sam's mouth as Bo's cock dragged a damp trail across his stomach. Sam's hips canted upward, looking for friction. He let out a little whine when he found none.

Bo chuckled against Sam's mouth. "God, I love it when you're like this. So turned on you can't be still." Dipping his head, he sucked at the spot on Sam's neck that always made him tremble. His hand snaked downward, fingers curling around Sam's shaft. "I want to suck your cock, Sam. I want you to come in my mouth. Is that all right?"

If he'd been capable of any sounds other than breathless whimpers, Sam would've laughed. As if it had ever *not* been all right for Bo to suck him off. Sam laid his palms on Bo's shoulders and pushed.

Grinning, Bo shimmied down Sam's body. He stopped on the way to suck first one nipple then the other, until both were swollen and throbbing, and so sensitive the slightest brush of Bo's fingertips over them nearly sent Sam right out of his skin. When Bo reached Sam's navel, he halted a while to explore it with his tongue. The crease where Sam's right leg met his hip received the same treatment. Sam wanted to scream with frustration when Bo bypassed his cock, grabbed the backs of his thighs and pushed his hips into the air.

"Hand me a pillow," Bo said, thumbs caressing Sam's legs. "I'm going to make you feel so good, sweetheart."

The whispered endearment brought a lump to Sam's throat, even as Bo's touch twisted the pleasure tighter inside him. Reaching to his right, Sam snagged a pillow and tossed it to Bo, who tucked it beneath Sam's hips. Sam hooked his hands behind his knees, holding his legs up and apart. He drew a deep breath and let it out in a slow stream. Calm spread through him, tempering his arousal enough that he thought he might not come the second Bo touched his cock.

With a sweet smile, Bo lifted Sam's balls in one hand and kissed them. "Beautiful." He dropped his head, and Sam felt the slick warmth of Bo's tongue against his hole.

"Oh fuck," he panted, fighting to hold still. "Oh fuck. Bo. Yes."

Humming, Bo swirled his tongue in a slow circle around Sam's anus. It felt incredible. The portion of Sam's brain still capable of rational thought mused that Bo had become very, very good at this in the months since he'd first tried it. Sam expressed his approval with moans and gasps and encouraging noises.

As usual, Sam's hole opened right up under Bo's gentle licks and kisses. Bo plunged his tongue inside again and again, his fingers kneading Sam's ass cheeks like a cat. Sam rocked and moaned and wondered if it were possible to go insane from pure physical pleasure.

He was no more than a lick away from coming when Bo pulled back. "Oh, no, no no no," Sam keened. "Don't stop. Don't stop."

"Not stopping," Bo murmured. He popped a finger in his mouth, pulled it out and slid it into Sam's hole.

Sam let out a choked cry. His fingers shook where they gripped his knees. "Oh. Oh. God."

Bo licked his lips, as if trying to gather every last bit of Sam's taste. "Mmm. So good, Sam."

God, please, suck me now, please. Sam couldn't make the words come out. He whimpered, the sound faint and pitiful.

Bo's lips curled into a lustful smile. Then finally, finally, he bent and slid Sam's prick into that sexy, talented, wonderful mouth.

Sam let go of his legs and buried both hands in Bo's hair, moaning low and rough under an overwhelming rush of sensation. One hand across Sam's hips to hold him still, Bo bobbed his head up and down Sam's shaft. His tongue curled around the head each time he pulled up, his finger nailed Sam's prostate over and over, and Sam thought he would have to come soon or die.

Bo lifted his head, letting Sam's cock fall from his mouth to hit Sam's belly with a wet smack. The hand still working Sam's ass went still, the fingertip pressing his gland just hard enough to send rapid pulses of intense pleasure shooting through his blood. Sam groaned and squirmed in a painful, wordless ecstasy.

For a moment, Bo just stared, his eyes bright with love and desire and something else, something Sam couldn't quite identify. "I love you, Sam," he whispered in a voice hoarse with emotion. Then before Sam could react, he bent and swallowed Sam's cock to the root. His nose hit Sam's groin, his throat squeezing in rhythmic waves.

The feeling was so huge, so rapturous, it flung Sam beyond words, even beyond sounds. He came silently, mouth open and eyes rolled back, his body bowed and shaking.

Through an orgasmic haze, Sam watched Bo crawl to the bedside table and take out the bottle of liquid lube. He felt Bo slick his hole, felt his legs lifted and spread, felt Bo's cock slide into his unresisting body. Bo's hips slapped against his buttocks over and over, driving into him hard and deep. Almost too spent to move, Sam locked his ankles around Bo's back and cupped Bo's ass in his hands, feeling the muscles flex with each thrust.

Bo's breath hitched in that particular way it tended to do during sex, and Sam knew he was close. Reaching up, Sam pulled Bo's head down and kissed him. Bo opened with the sweetest little whimper Sam had ever heard, devouring his mouth as if it held the answers to all the mysteries of the universe. Bo tasted like Sam's semen, and the intimacy that fact implied made Sam's chest tight.

When Bo came, Sam stroked his back and drank down his soft, broken moans. He murmured a barely coherent litany of loving words into Bo's ear, hanging on as he rode out his orgasm. When Bo collapsed on top of Sam, his chest heaving and his heart thudding against Sam's ribs, Sam held him tight and kissed his forehead and thanked whoever was listening that Bo had come back to him.

They lay like that for a long time, not speaking, just

breathing together. Eventually, Bo pushed up onto one elbow and smiled down at Sam. "That was incredible."

"Yes, it was." Sam reached up to caress Bo's cheek. "I love you, Bo."

"Love you too." Bo bent and pressed a kiss to Sam's brow. "You're exhausted. Go to sleep."

The mere suggestion of sleep made Sam's eyelids feel like they weighed ten pounds each. "Mm-hm. I know it's early, but you're right. I'm wiped out." He yawned. "You must be pretty worn out yourself, are you going to go to sleep too?"

"Yes. In a minute." Bo raked the sweaty hair from Sam's forehead. His fingers mapped the contours of Sam's face. "Sleep, love. I'm right here."

Bo's voice was low and warm, his touch soothing. Cradled in Bo's arms, Sam let his body relax.

The last thing he remembered before sleep took him was the watchful gleam in Bo's eyes. When he woke some time later from a dream of dark and cold and gut-wrenching terror, Bo was gone.

Chapter Twelve

Sam pushed up onto his elbows, blinking his eyes open and looking around the room. The lamp beside the bed was still on, and the bedroom door was shut. A quick glance at the clock told Sam it was ten-thirty. He'd slept no more than a couple of hours.

Yawning, Sam scooted to the edge of the mattress, stood and wandered into the bathroom. After relieving himself, he retrieved his clothes from the pile on the floor and pulled them on.

The second he opened the bedroom door, he was struck by the absolute quiet. He should have been able to hear the TV with the volume turned low, or Bo singing to himself while he cooked. But there was nothing. Not even the quiet rustle of pages turning while Bo read.

Sam hurried down the stairs. A single lamp burned on the end table, but there was no sound from any part of the house. Bo wasn't in the living room or the kitchen. Sam turned on the back-porch light and opened the door. Bo wasn't on the porch. The rain had picked up again, thudding hard and steady against the roof and sand, so Sam didn't think Bo would've gone out onto the beach.

Growing more alarmed by the second, Sam ran back inside and started searching every available surface for a note or anything else to indicate where Bo might have gone. There was nothing.

It wasn't until Sam went back to search the table in the foyer for the third time that he noticed that the car keys were missing. A quick look out front confirmed that the car he and Bo had driven here was no longer there.

Sam leaned against the doorframe, cold dread churning in his stomach. Bo was gone. He'd taken the car and left. And Sam thought he knew where to find him.

Whirling around, Sam raced up the stairs, snatched his cell phone from the dresser and dialed Dean's cell. He swore when he got Dean's voice mail.

Spurred on by a sense of urgency bordering on panic, Sam yanked on the battered sneakers he'd left lying beside the dresser and leapt down the stairs two at a time. He knew they'd brought an umbrella with them, but couldn't remember where it was. Not wanting to waste time looking for it, Sam ran out into the rain and splashed across the space between the house and the one next door.

It wasn't far, but Sam was soaked to the skin by the time he got to the front porch of the house where Dean was staying with Kyle. He pounded on the door, belatedly noticing the distinct lack of apparent activity in the house. He hoped the group hadn't decided to retire early tonight.

He was just about to knock again, and maybe yell for good measure, when the door opened. Sam recognized one of the girls he'd seen on the beach before. She smiled at him. "Hey, aren't you from next door? What're you doing out in the rain?"

He managed to return her smile. "Sorry to bother y'all, but I need to talk to Dean. It's an emergency."

Her eyes widened. "Sure. C'mon in, I'll get him."

"Thanks."

He stepped inside and stood chewing his lip and dripping on the tiles while the girl hurried into the back of the house. He heard the drone of the TV stop, followed by low voices. A moment later, Dean came striding down the short hallway toward him. His brows drew together in concern when he saw Sam.

"What's wrong?" Dean asked, crossing to Sam and laying a hand on his arm. "Jill said it was an emergency."

"Yeah, it is. At least I think so." Sam drew a deep breath, trying to calm himself down. "Bo's gone."

Dean frowned. "What do you mean, gone?"

"I mean, he's gone. I fell asleep earlier, and when I woke up a little while ago he was nowhere to be found. I looked everywhere."

"Maybe he went for a walk or something. I mean, I know it's raining, but that wouldn't stop him if he really wanted to go."

Sam shook his head. "The car's gone."

Dean's face went white. "Oh shit. He went to Fort Medina."

"That's what I'm afraid of, yeah." Sam shoved his wet hair out of his eyes. "Will you help me find him? I don't know why he left, or if he's okay, and I just...I-I need you, Dean, will you help me?"

"You know I will." Taking Sam's hand in his, Dean pulled him close and kissed his cheek. "We need transport. Let me get Kyle, he can drive us."

Sam gaped as Dean dragged him toward the back of the house. "But he won't want to—"

"He won't mind, believe me. Plus we may need a third person if anything's actually wrong." They emerged into the living room. The whole group turned to look at them, bathed in the blue glow of the television. "Kyle, can I borrow you?"

"Sure." Kyle unfolded his long legs, stood and followed Sam and Dean into the hall. "What's up?"

Dean glanced at Sam, a question in his eyes. Sam nodded. He didn't really want Kyle to know about the situation with Bo, but he didn't see any way around it. Not if he expected Kyle to help them.

"Bo's gone missing," Dean said, linking his hand with Kyle's. "He took the car, and we think he might've gone to Fort Medina. He, um...he might not be entirely well. We need to find him. Can you help us out?"

Kyle nodded, his eyes huge and his face pale. "Sure. We can take my car."

Smiling, Dean stood on tiptoe and kissed him. "Thanks, babe. Bring your cell. I'm just gonna run get mine. Sam, have you got your phone?"

"Yeah." Sam patted the front pocket of his shorts. He watched Dean run down a short hallway which evidently led to the bedroom he and Kyle shared. "I tried calling you, but got your voice mail."

"Damn. Sorry, we were watching a movie and I didn't have it on." Dean came hopping out of the bedroom on one green-sneakered foot, pulling the second shoe on with one hand and clutching his cell phone in the other. "Kyle, we'll need your umbrella. Oh, and I stuck my raincoat there in the hall closet, Sam, will you grab it?"

While Kyle ran into the back, Sam obediently went to the closet and pulled out Dean's long, bright green raincoat. "Yeah, no point in both of y'all getting as soaked as I am."

"Oh, it's not for us. It's in case anything's happened to Bo. There's a blanket in Kyle's car, which we might need, but if something's wrong and we need to warm him up, we're gonna need to keep the rain off him too." Dean glanced up as Kyle joined them. "Did you tell everyone else you're leaving?"

Kyle nodded. He was still pale and looked nervous, but he seemed calm enough. "Yeah. Y'all ready?"

"Uh-huh." Shoving his phone in the pocket of his cargo shorts, Dean squeezed Sam's arm. "Let's get going. I'll make sure we all have each other's numbers in our phones on the ride over."

Sam followed Dean and Kyle out the front door in silence. Dean's words had brought home to him the fact that Bo might be in real danger, and not only from the creatures inhabiting the other side. By now, Sam was convinced something was wrong with Bo. Something which made him potentially a danger to himself. Sam had no idea what that might be, but after everything that had happened in the past few days he was sure he was right.

He climbed into the backseat of Kyle's ancient Nova, handed Dean his phone and tried to sit still as Kyle drove along the narrow road. Staring out the window into the night, Sam found himself silently pleading to whoever or whatever might be listening for Bo's safety.

The short drive to the fort seemed to last forever. Bo's car was parked in front of the closed and locked parking lot gate. Sam's insides twisted with a mix of relief and apprehension. "He's here."

"Yeah." Dean glanced back at Sam. "And the gate's locked. I'd forgotten about that."

"Me too," Sam confessed, feeling stupid.

"What do we do?" Kyle asked. He turned a nervous look to Dean. "If we go in it's breaking and entering. I don't want to get in trouble."

"We won't ask you to do that. You can wait out here while Sam and I go in." Dean turned to hand Sam his phone, encased in a plastic sandwich bag to keep it dry. "Sam, you and I can climb the fence. We'll separate and look for Bo. Whoever finds him calls the other."

"All right." Sam stuck his phone in his pocket. "You take the umbrella. I'm already soaked anyhow."

"Sure. You take the raincoat. That way we'll each have something to cover Bo with if we need to." Dean turned back to Kyle. "When we find him, I'll call you, okay?"

"Okay." With a self-conscious glance at Sam, Kyle hooked a hand around the back of Dean's head, pulled him forward and kissed him. "Be careful."

"Don't worry, we'll be fine." Smiling, Dean touched Kyle's cheek, then scooted away and opened his door. "Ready, Sam?"

"Yeah."

Sam got out of the car, with Dean a couple of steps behind. Pulling on the raincoat, he started scaling the fence. Within seconds, he and Dean were on the other side and jogging through the rain toward the floodlit entrance. Dean opened the umbrella as they went. An oval of brighter light swung across the parking lot as Kyle pulled the car off the road, into the shadows of the trees.

"We should've brought flashlights," Sam said, wiping the water from his eyes to peer at the blackness under the brick arch. "Shit. I was so anxious to get here I wasn't thinking straight. It'll be seriously dark in the inside rooms."

"I brought some lights. Hang on a sec." Dean stopped and dug through the side pocket of his shorts. He pulled out a small metal flashlight and handed it to Sam. "It's waterproof."

Sam took the light. It was heavier than it looked, and when he switched it on the beam proved to be quite powerful. "Thanks." He turned it off and stuck it in his pocket as he and Dean started moving forward again. "What are you going to use?"

"My penlight." Dean held up something that looked rather like a thick ballpoint pen made of fluorescent green plastic. He clicked it on, revealing a bright, narrow beam of light, then turned it off again and stuck it in his pocket. "It won't light up anything very far ahead, but I can see well enough with it. I have great night vision."

Sam nodded. "Why don't I start with the rooms inside the walls, since my light's stronger? You can search the courtyard and the walkway on top of the walls. The floodlights inside should be bright enough that you won't need a light at all."

"Sounds good."

They crossed the rest of the parking lot in silence. Beneath the sheer outer wall of the fort, Sam hunched his shoulders and scowled at the heavy steel gate guarding the interior. It was closed. The light on the lock's keypad winked on and off, waiting for them to input the security code. The code they didn't have.

Sam swore. "Shit. How do we get in?"

"Hm." Dean pursed his lips. "Maybe we don't need to."

"But he would've gone inside if..." Sam trailed off as he realized what Dean meant.

"If he could get in," Dean finished for him. "But obviously he didn't get in. Not through the gate, anyway."

It made sense. "So what do we do now?"

Hands on his hips, Dean turned in a circle, surveying their surroundings. "Let's each take a direction and scout the outside perimeter. He may have found another way in. We'll eventually meet up, but if either of us finds Bo or any sign of him before that, we'll call each other."

Sam nodded. "Sounds good to me. I'll take the beach side.

There's more floodlights on the inland side, and I have the strongest flashlight."

"Okay." Dean laid a hand on Sam's arm. "We'll find him, Sam. It'll be all right."

Sam managed a smile despite the fear curdling his stomach. "Yeah. Thanks."

Sliding his hand down to Sam's, Dean squeezed his fingers, turned and strode off to the right, following the line of the fort's outer wall.

Sam drew a deep breath and blew it out, willing himself to keep it together. Panicking wouldn't help anyone, least of all Bo. When he felt calm enough, he started making his way along the ancient brick wall.

The first leg of the search was easy. The security lights bathed the wall and most of the parking lot in a harsh yellowish glare in which nothing larger than a gnat could possibly hide. Raindrops glinted silver and gold in the glow. An occasional cockroach scuttled along the wall or flew into the night as Sam approached, and once he spotted a drenched brown rat darting through a crack in the bricks, but there was no sign of Bo.

The dark reasserted itself when Sam rounded the curved corner between one side of the pentagonal fort and the next. There were lights along the top of the wall, but their illumination seemed to dissipate as the scrubby grass gave way to sand and sea oats. The beach sloped away into the darkness beyond. Sam heard the thunder of the waves on the sand, though he couldn't see them. Overhead, the thick clouds obliterated the moon and stars.

Taking the flashlight out of his pocket, Sam switched it on and played it over the ground at his feet and the wall looming on his right. A candy bar wrapper half caught under a stone flapped in the rising wind, the only sign of recent human activity. Sam turned to shine his light toward the beach. Just beyond the edge of the beam, on the other side of the chainlink fence cutting across the dunes, something small and white darted between two clusters of sea oats. A ghost crab, Sam realized as the little creature stopped and raised its claws in clear threat.

Something about the presence of the normal nocturnal animals made Sam feel better. Hopefully it meant he wouldn't be dealing with a portal tonight.

Keeping the flashlight beam trained on the uneven ground, Sam made his way along the strip of grass and mud between the fort and the fence. He couldn't help thinking how easy it would be for someone to climb the fence as he and Dean had done to gain access, to the fort. Of course, the ramparts rose thirty perpendicular feet above the ground, with the sturdy stone parapet jutting outward at the top. A person would need some serious climbing gear to scale that wall. Since the fort contained very little in the way of removable objects with any value, Sam doubted most people would bother.

The obvious difficulty of getting in this way eased some of Sam's fear, since it seemed clear to him that Bo could not have climbed over the wall. Which meant he must be outside somewhere. Considering his near-pathological obsession with Fort Medina during the past few days, Sam figured Bo would keep close to the fort rather than wandering off to the beach, or into the woods on the inland side. With any luck, either he or Dean would find Bo within the hour.

With hope spurring him on, Sam hurried along the edge of the fort, swinging his flashlight this way and that as he went. The rain had slacked off a bit in the last few minutes, though the wind had picked up enough to lash the falling drops against Sam's face with stinging force. He brought his free hand up to shield his face as he went.

184

Sam turned the next corner of the pentagon without finding any sign of Bo. He stopped, playing his light around to survey the stretch of land ahead of him. The fence continued along the inside of the sea wall where the land curved and the Gulf met Mobile Bay. On this side, the fort stood with its feet practically in the water of the bay. The floodlights lining the top of the wall all pointed toward the interior of the fort, lending only a faint illumination to the outside. Enough to see by, barely. A rock jetty ran some way out into the water, sheltering the fort from the waves rolling in from the Gulf. The narrow space between the fence and the fort's outer wall was a jumble of rocks, all slick surfaces and sharp edges. The air was heavy with the smell of salt, fish and wet earth.

Turning to his left, Sam squinted through the rain and mist at the low hump of land just barely visible on the other side of the bay. A few scattered lights winked in the dark. Mobile was too far north for Sam to see, but he knew where it lay. He wished he and Bo were over there right now, safe and warm and dry in their cozy apartment.

When I find him, we're going straight home. No more Fort Medina, no more beach house. We'll finish our vacation at home.

Thus resolved, Sam switched his light to his left hand, put his right hand on the wall to steady himself and started picking his way across the jumble of rocks. It would have been tough going in any conditions, but the low light, the rain and the wind made it downright dangerous. Sam fought off the urge to hurry and forced himself to take his time. The last thing any of them needed was for him to fall and injure himself.

He was about halfway along that leg of the rampart when a movement behind the parapet at the top caught the corner of his eye. Heart pounding, he stopped and peered upward. A figure stood there, a smoky blackness in the yellow glow of the floodlights inside the fort.

"Bo?" Sam called, though something told him he was looking at one of the fort's many ghosts. "Bo, are you there?"

Moving faster than Sam would have believed possible, the apparition shot off toward the interior of the fort and disappeared. Sam didn't know whether to be relieved or disappointed. Turning his attention away from the parapet, he started making his way along the rocks once again.

He'd barely resumed his journey when a sudden wave of purposeful menace struck him like a hammer. Staggering under the psychic blow, he fell to his hands and knees. He lost his grip on the flashlight. It bounced on the rocks and went out.

Sam climbed to his feet. He hardly noticed the searing pain in his right knee, or the burn which told him his palms had been scraped raw. His entire being was focused on the alien thoughts pulsing through his brain.

He recognized the feeling of cold, malicious intelligence invading his mind. Somewhere nearby, a portal had just opened. And he hadn't done it.

Bo. Fuck.

Heedless of the danger of falling, Sam ran.

Chapter Thirteen

The portal was nearby. Sam could feel it. But he couldn't see it. He ran on, slipping along the rocks in the near-dark.

"Bo! Can you hear me?" His voice was almost lost in the howl of the wind and the pounding of rain on stone, but he kept yelling every few seconds anyway, hoping Bo would hear him.

He heard the sound he'd been dreading just as the end of the sea wall came into sight. A deep rasp almost below the level of hearing, accompanied by a flood of strange images and shades of meaning Sam couldn't quite grasp. Following the thread of alien energy in his head and the crackle of electricity in the air, he turned to peer into the dense shadows beneath the pines crowding near the next corner of the fort.

Bo stood on a rounded hump of rock a few feet from the spot where the sea wall gave way to grass. The floodlights atop this corner of the wall pointed outward, bathing Bo in a harsh glow. He had his back to Sam, and he was wearing only the shorts he'd had on earlier in the day. Not fifteen feet from him, beneath the spreading boughs of a gnarled old pine tree, crouched a shadowy, nebulous shape—one of the things which still haunted Sam's nightmares. The air around it swirled and sparked. That, plus the dense, pulsing darkness around it, told Sam he was looking at a newly activated portal.

For a heartbeat, Sam stood frozen. Then the monster

darted straight toward Bo, mud flying from its claws as they dug into the rain-soaked ground.

Sam was halfway to Bo before he even knew he'd moved. His stomach lurched when he realized the creature would reach Bo long before he would.

"Bo!" he shouted. "Bo, *run!*"

Bo turned toward Sam. The glare of the lights high above revealed blank eyes in an expressionless face. His bare feet remained rooted to the rock.

The thing flowed toward him, one serrated claw held high, and time slowed to a painful crawl. Sam kept running, trying to focus his mind enough to send the thing back where it came from. The creature wavered and slowed, but didn't stop. It felt to Sam like beating his mind against a stone wall. He had a torturous eternity to watch the gleaming black claw slice downward, down through the rain, inevitably down toward Bo's naked back. Sam let out a wordless cry as the razor-sharp claw hit Bo's body and he stumbled forward.

Time jerked into motion again. Sam lunged the last few feet and caught Bo before he hit the ground. Laying Bo as gently as he could on the rocks, Sam flung himself between his lover and the horror in front of him.

"Go away!" he screamed. "Just go the fuck away!"

The monster seemed to hesitate, as if uncertain of whether or not it could harm Sam. It was only a split second, but it was enough. Gathering his psychokinetic powers, Sam followed the umbilical cord of energy linking the thing to its world and focused every ounce of his mind on that spot.

His vision dimmed and he felt as if someone was sitting on his chest, but he didn't dare relax his concentration. This portal was strong, resisting his efforts to send the entity back through and close it. If he lost control of it, he and Bo were both dead, and a terrible threat would be loose.

Just as Sam felt unconsciousness closing in, the balance of power shifted. He felt the pull of energy from the other side as the portal began to close. The air swirled, the fabric of reality twisting in a way that hurt Sam's eyes.

Calling on reserves of strength he didn't know he possessed until that moment, Sam redoubled his efforts. With a shriek more felt than heard, the creature collapsed in on itself and vanished. Sam felt the gateway seal behind it.

Sam's knees buckled and he dropped to the ground, gasping for breath. He no longer sensed the portal in his head. In fact, the inert residual energy felt almost exactly like what he'd experienced at Sunset Lodge. That, more than anything, told him this particular gateway must now be permanently closed.

Relieved, Sam turned to Bo, who lay huddled on his side on the rocks, facing the fort. Sam tried to get a look at Bo's back, to see how badly he was injured, but Bo's position kept his back in shadow and Sam couldn't see anything useful. He cursed, wishing he hadn't dropped his flashlight.

Leaning down, he brushed the streaming hair from Bo's face. "Bo? Are you all right?"

No answer. Sam laid a hand on Bo's cheek. His skin was cold, the jaw muscles tense and quivering beneath Sam's palm.

Heart in his throat, Sam pressed two shaking fingers against the proper spot in Bo's neck. Bo's pulse beat fast and thready beneath Sam's fingertips. He bent closer, until his ear nearly touched Bo's lips. Bo's breathing sounded shallow and harsh, but at least he *was* breathing.

Sitting up on his knees, Sam slipped the raincoat off and laid it over Bo, then reached for his phone. He had to call Dean, and they had to get Bo out of here.

"Sam! Where are you?"

Dean. Sam looked up, and saw the flash of Dean's penlight coming around the corner of the fort. "Over here!" He raised a hand and waved.

Dean was beside him in a matter of seconds. "I heard you yelling. What happened?" He knelt on the rocks beside Sam and handed him the open umbrella. "Hold this over us. I need to examine him."

"A portal opened. I don't know how, or why, other than it was nothing I did this time." Sam watched, shivering, as Dean shone his light into both of Bo's eyes, then pulled the raincoat down to sweep the narrow beam over his body. Bo didn't respond, and the cold knot of fear in Sam's belly grew. "I called him, and he turned around, but he wouldn't answer me. He seemed completely out of it. Then that…that thing attacked him right before I sent it away. I think it cut him."

"I'll say." Dean was gazing at Bo's back, where he had his light trained. "His back's sliced up pretty badly. If whatever cut him had hit him in the front, it would've torn him open." Dean glanced at Sam, his face solemn. "Looks like you saved his life by getting him to turn around like that."

Against his better judgment, Sam leaned over to look, and instantly wished he hadn't. A deep gash ran from Bo's right shoulder diagonally to his left hip. Blood poured from the wound to form a red river that trickled over the rocks and washed away in the rain.

Sam sat back, fighting nausea. "We need to get him to the hospital."

"I know." Jumping to his feet, Dean hurried around to kneel at Bo's other side. He pulled his T-shirt off and used both forearms to press it hard against Bo's back.

"How are we gonna get him out of here? The gate's locked."

Sam's eyes widened as he realized what would have to happen. "Shit, Dean, we'll have to get the police or somebody to open it. They'll find out Bo broke in."

"And us," Dean added, his face grim.

"They'll arrest us all. Fuck." Sam grimaced. "But we don't have any choice. We have to get him out of here, fast." He reached for his cell phone.

"Wait."

Sam looked up at Dean, eyebrows raised, one hand curled around the phone in his pocket. "Yes?"

"There's a spot about twenty feet up the inland side where the fence has been cut." Dean nodded to a spot behind Sam and a bit to his right. "I noticed it the other night when we were investigating out here. Call Kyle first, tell him to meet us there with the car. There's a road to the right of the gate that goes straight down this side of the fence. We'll call the ambulance, then take Bo out through the break in the fence."

Sam took his phone out of his pocket and was already dialing while Dean talked. Kyle picked up on the second ring. "Sam?"

"Yeah. Listen, Bo's hurt. Dean says drive down the side road to the right of the gate. We're on the other side of the fence, near the end. Dean says there's a place where the fence is cut. I'm not sure where exact—"

"I know the place," Kyle interrupted. "I'm on my way."

Sam clicked the phone closed. "He knows where the cut in the fence is. He's on his way."

Dean looked surprised, but pleased. "Okay, good. You go ahead and call 911, then we can carry him out to Kyle's car."

Nodding, Sam opened his phone again and dialed 911. He wished his hands wouldn't shake so much. He told the operator

Bo had been attacked by an unknown assailant, with what Sam believed to be a knife, just outside the fence on the north side of Fort Medina. It surprised him how easily the lie rolled off his tongue. Maybe because Bo's injury and his unconscious state—and Sam's resulting worry and fear—were all too true.

Once the operator hung up, Sam clicked his phone closed and pocketed it. "They'll be here in five minutes. I hope this place isn't far." He glanced toward the road, which lay about twenty yards away on the other side of the chainlink fence.

At that moment, Bo stirred and opened his eyes. He blinked, looking confused. "Wh...? Where...? S-Sam?"

"Right here." Giddy with relief, Sam leaned down to kiss Bo's brow. "Bo, we need to move you, okay?"

Bo's throat worked. "Sick."

For a second, Sam had no idea what he meant. He got it just as Bo turned his head to the side. Sam held Bo's head off the rocks while he threw up.

When he finished heaving up the contents of his stomach, Bo curled into a ball. Violent shudders shook his body. His lips looked almost purple, and Sam couldn't tell if it was just the faint, sickly yellow light or something more sinister.

"Hurts," Bo whispered, his voice raspy.

"I know it hurts." Sam stroked Bo's shoulder. "An ambulance is on the way. We just need to move you a little ways before they get here, all right?"

Bo nodded, his eyes fluttering closed. Dean, who still had his T-shirt pressed to Bo's back, glanced toward the road. "Kyle's coming. I can see his headlights. Let's go ahead and start moving. We need to get Bo in the car and out of the elements. We'll do what we can for that wound while we wait for the ambulance to get here."

The thought of tending the bleeding slash in Bo's back made Sam's stomach roll, but he nodded. Moving as carefully as he could, he slipped an arm beneath Bo's shoulders and hauled him into a sitting position. Bo let out a soft whimper.

"Sorry, baby." Sam pulled Bo flush against his chest. Bo's chilled cheek lolled on his shoulder. "Put your arms around me, okay? Hold on to me."

With slow, obviously painful movements, Bo wrapped his arms around Sam's neck. His ribs heaved in rapid, shallow breaths. Digging his shivering fingers into Sam's shoulders, he buried his face in Sam's neck. Icy lips brushed Sam's skin.

Worried, Sam glanced up at Dean. "He's really cold."

"I know. It's kind of strange." Dean frowned, shifting along with Sam to keep the T-shirt pressed to Bo's back as Sam hooked his other arm under Bo's knees. "Or maybe not. Depends on how long he's been out here. It's not cold, even with the rain, but being out in it for a while could've dropped his temperature enough to be dangerous."

Sam didn't answer. A renewed fear for Bo's life gave him the surge of strength he needed to stagger to his feet with Bo in his arms. Dean kept both arms pressed to the wound in Bo's back.

Together, they made their way off the rocks and diagonally across the wide strip of grass to their destination. As they approached, Sam could see the place where a corner of the fence hung loose at the bottom next to one of the metal support poles. It wasn't as far as he'd feared it would be, for which he was grateful. Bo was shorter and slimmer than Sam, but not by much, and Sam's body was feeling the strain.

By the time they reached the spot, Kyle was there and had pulled a section of fence nearly as tall as himself loose from the pole. Long fingers hooked into the links, he lifted the loose part up and out as far as possible. "It was already loose when the guys and I found it last week," he explained, looking guilty. "There were just a few pieces of wire twisted around to hold it down and make it look like it hadn't been cut."

Dean shot him a grateful smile. "Thanks, babe."

Puffing with exertion, Sam shuffled through the opening. Dean moved with him, hunched over to keep from scratching his bare back on the broken ends of fence wire.

"Kyle, can you open the car door?" Dean lifted one arm a bit to check Bo's wound. "Shit. This thing's bleeding really bad. Kyle, babe, take this raincoat and lay it on the seat. Then get the blanket out. We'll need to cover him."

Kyle scrambled to do as Dean said. Pulling the raincoat off Bo's legs, he flung the back door of his car open and spread the coat on the seat. He snatched a dark blue blanket off the floorboard and jumped out of the way.

"Dean, you're going to have to move," Sam said. "There's not room enough for both of us in there."

"You're right. Hang on, I'll get in on the other side and help you."

Dean ran around to the other side of the car, his bloody T-shirt clutched in one hand. Grunting under the strain of Bo's weight, Sam bent down and laid Bo's upper body gently on top of the raincoat. Bo let out a little pained noise when his torn back came in contact with the wet plastic. By that time Dean was kneeling on the opposite seat. He grabbed the raincoat and pulled, sliding Bo fully onto the seat. If Bo's sudden agonized cry affected him, he didn't show it. Sam watched, wishing he could stop Bo's suffering and hating that he couldn't.

With one hand on Bo's hip and the other beneath his shoulders, Dean rolled him onto his side, facing the back of the seat. "Kyle, hand Sam the blanket, would you please?"

Sam took the blanket from Kyle and tossed it over Bo's legs. Dean arranged it so that Bo was completely covered except for his back. "Kyle, keep an eye out for the ambulance. Make sure they see us when they drive up. Sam, you try to keep Bo awake and talking. I need you to brace his chest too, so I can keep holding pressure on this cut."

While Dean knelt on the floorboard, both forearms pressed to Bo's back, Sam sat next to Bo's head, leaned over and planted both hands on the vinyl between Bo and the back of the car seat. He stiffened his arms so that Bo's chest was sandwiched between Dean's arms and Sam's. Bo gasped, his body going tense.

"I'm sorry," Sam whispered. "I know it hurts. I'm so sorry."

Bo's head tilted back, his eyes opening to fix on Sam's face. "S...Sam. There was...a portal. I-I couldn't...couldn't stop it."

Dean glanced at Bo, then Sam. He raised his eyebrows in question, but said nothing. "The portal's closed," Sam told them both. "I sent the thing back and closed the portal. I think it might be closed permanently. It feels the same now as the one at Sunset Lodge."

A tiny smile curved Bo's lips. He didn't answer, but his shaking eased. He closed his eyes again.

Sam studied his face in continued concern. His lips didn't look purple like they had outside, but the car's bright overhead light showed a worrisome bluish tinge, and his face was gray beneath his normal dusky complexion. The parts of his skin not covered by the blanket were cool and mottled.

"Bo? You having any numbness in your hands or feet?" Dean's voice sounded tight, and Sam figured the effort of keeping pressure on Bo's wound must be tiring him.

Bo shook his head. "No. Cold. I'm cold. Not numb though."

"Good." Sam planted a kiss on Bo's shoulder. "You're gonna

be all right, Bo."

"You'll probably need a blood transfusion." Dean tossed his dripping hair out of his eyes. "You've lost a lot of blood. But I'm not seeing any sign of infection like we did with that bite, so that's good."

Bo licked his lips. "I f-feel. Weird. Wrong. Felt it...all night."

Sam stared at Bo's ashen face, heart racing. Instinct told him Bo's feeling of wrongness had as much—or more—to do with his recent behavior as with the injury he'd sustained. And he had a sinking feeling it was all related somehow to the portal which had unexpectedly opened where there had been none before. The juxtaposition couldn't possibly be a coincidence.

He felt as though his subconscious mind knew what the link was, but he couldn't quite grasp it. *If I could just think of it, maybe it would help Bo. Think, Sam, come on...*

The sound of approaching sirens startled Sam out of his thoughts. He glanced up. Lights flashed red and white through the back window. Relief washed through him. "Thank God."

Outside, Kyle ran toward the approaching ambulance. Sam could see him out the back window, waving his arms. The siren cut off. Sam heard the hiss of tires on the wet road, followed by the sound of the vehicle's doors slamming.

"Bo?" Sam stroked Bo's wet hair. "Bo, the ambulance is here. We're gonna get you to the hospital now."

There was no answer. As Sam watched, Bo's body began to shake. Frowning, Sam looked more closely at Bo's face. His jaw muscle was twitching, and this time there was no mistaking the alarming purple hue to his lips.

Sam shot a panicked look at Dean. "He doesn't look very good."

Dean craned his neck to look at Bo's face. His eyes widened

when Bo's tremors spread into his arms. "Shit. Sam, you need to get out of the car now."

Before Sam had a chance to ask why, a large hand grabbed his arm and yanked him none too gently out the door. "Sorry, sir, but I need to get in there."

Sam stumbled out of the way and stood there trying to make out what was going on. The tall, broad-shouldered paramedic who'd pulled him out of the car was hunched over Bo's upper body. On the other side of the seat, a young woman—the big man's partner, evidently—straddled Bo's legs. She took a syringe out of what looked like a toolbox and dipped out of view. Sam could see Bo's arms and legs jerking, but he couldn't see Bo's face, and he was unable to tell what the paramedics were doing to him.

After what felt like years but couldn't have been more than a few seconds, Dean squirmed out through the front seat and came around to stand beside Sam. "He's having a seizure," Dean explained before Sam could ask. "I was able to tell them he's not allergic to the medicine they needed to give him to stop it, but I didn't know if he has anything else in his system or not."

The look in Dean's eyes was enough to tell Sam what he meant. Sam shook his head. "No, he didn't. At least that's what he said when I asked, and I believe him."

"Good. We can let the paramedics know once they have him stabilized." Dean lowered his voice until Sam could barely hear it above the wind. "I told them the same thing you told the 911 operator. That Bo was attacked and that you were here and witnessed part of it, but couldn't see exactly what happened because he was under the trees where it was dark. Other than that, I told the truth."

Nodding, Sam squeezed Dean's arm. "Thank you."

Kyle edged up to join them, shoulders hunched against the windblown rain. "Dean? Do y'all need me to drive you to the hospital?"

"Probably so, yeah. I don't know if Bo has his car keys with him or left 'em in the car, but either way we don't really have time to find out. They're gonna be loading him into the ambulance any minute now." Dean took Kyle's hand, threading their fingers together. "Do you mind? If you can't drive us that's okay, we'll get a cab or something."

"No, I don't mind at all." Kyle glanced at his car, chewing on his bottom lip. "I hope he'll be okay."

Dean didn't answer, and Sam's heart clenched. If Dean couldn't muster enough optimism to reassure the boy, Bo must be worse off than Sam had thought.

Don't think about it. You'll drive yourself and everyone else crazy if you do.

As Sam watched, the two paramedics eased Bo out of the backseat, lying strapped in on his side on a narrow gurney. The folding legs of the gurney snapped open, the wheels hit the wet pavement, and the medics rolled it toward the ambulance. The man held an IV bag in one hand, feeding fluids into a vein in Bo's arm. Clear tubing ran from an oxygen mask over Bo's nose and mouth to a green tank sitting on the stretcher beside him. A large bandage was secured to Bo's back with what looked like elastic tape.

Sam trotted over, Dean and Kyle at his heels. "Is he okay?"

The female paramedic—Julia, according to the nametag pinned to her shirt—glanced at Sam while she and her partner loaded Bo into the ambulance. "He's breathing and his vital signs are stable, but he's unconscious. That's probably partly the seizure and partly the lorazepam we gave him to stop it."

"Your friend there said Bo was unconscious for a little

while before the seizure," the man said from inside the vehicle. "Did he hit his head when he fell?"

"No. Well, not that I know of," Sam amended. "The...um, the attack happened right after I got here. I'd just spotted him. But I caught him before he hit the ground so if he *did* hit his head it wasn't then."

"What about the attacker? Did they hit him in the head?"

"I don't think so. I just saw...a shadow behind Bo. It looked like whoever it was stabbed him with a big knife or something. Oh, and he hasn't taken any medications or anything. Dean said you asked."

"We did, thank you." With Bo safely in the ambulance, Julia turned and touched Sam's arm. "We're taking him to the hospital in Foley. It's about thirty miles away, but it's the closest one we can get to from here. Y'all know how to get there?"

"I do." Dean grabbed Sam's elbow, stopping his protest. "We'll follow you as far as we can, but if we lose you I can get us there."

The young woman nodded. "Good. Oh, are you relatives of his?"

Sam and Dean glanced at each other. Dean grimaced. "We're just friends. He's divorced, his sons are minors, and I have no idea how to get in touch with his parents. Hell, I don't even know if he has brothers and sisters."

"Three sisters," Sam added, wrapping his arms around himself. "I don't know how to reach them, though."

"Hm. Well, it's okay for right now, but you may need to find his next of kin if he doesn't come around." Julia slammed the ambulance doors shut. "We're going. We'll tell them you're on your way. What're your names?"

"I'm Dean Delapore," Dean said. "This is Sam Raintree and Kyle DuPree."

"Got it." She gave them a smile. "Try not to worry. We'll take good care of him." She turned and jogged to the driver's side door.

Sam followed Dean and Kyle to Kyle's car and climbed into the backseat. A few drops of blood dotted the gray vinyl seat. It amazed Sam that there wasn't more. Most of it seemed to be puddled on Dean's raincoat.

Picking up Dean's ruined T-shirt from the floorboard where it had fallen, Sam wadded it into the middle of the raincoat. The blanket seemed to be largely blood-free, so he left it on the floor. He told himself he was trying to keep Kyle's car as clean as possible, but the truth was he didn't think he could stand to look at Bo's blood any longer. It made him focus on the fact that Bo was gravely injured, and there was no guarantee he'd be all right.

This is exactly what I was afraid of. Exactly. I knew he shouldn't be here. I knew we should've left. Why didn't he listen to me?

Sam's eyes stung. He blinked away the gathering moisture and stared out the window as the Nova zoomed along the dark, empty road in the wake of the ambulance. Now that the immediate need for action was over, reaction had set in, leaving him weak and shaken. Everything had happened so fast. A few hours ago, he and Bo had been safe in bed. Now, Bo was lying unconscious in the back of an ambulance after having been attacked for the second time by one of those fucking *things* from the other side. And this time, Sam had no idea how or why the portal had come into existence.

Another mystery to solve. Another twist in the sketchy tale of the interdimensional gateways and the beings who called the other side home. Why had the portal opened this time? What did Bo have to do with it? And why, *why*, did those creatures keep coming here in the first place? What did they want?

Sam didn't know, and wasn't sure he wanted to. But something told him he'd eventually learn those answers whether he was ready for them or not.

Chapter Fourteen

It was fifteen minutes after midnight when Sam, Dean and Kyle finally reached the Baldwin County Medical Center. They'd lost the ambulance in the string of lights and surprisingly heavy traffic along Highway 59 between Gulf Shores and Foley. By the time they entered the emergency room doors, nearly forty-five minutes after leaving Fort Medina, Sam was frantic with worry and ready to explode at the least provocation.

He marched up to the desk at the far side of the crowded room, Dean and Kyle at his heels. "We're looking for Dr. Bo Broussard," he said to the young man on the other side. "Where is he?"

The man raised his eyebrows. "I don't know a Dr. Broussard. You sure you're at the right hospital?"

Dean's hand on his arm stopped Sam's angry outburst. "He's a patient," Dean explained. "The ambulance should've brought him in not long ago. I'm Dean Delapore, and this is Sam Raintree and Kyle DuPree, we're Bo's friends."

"Oh, yeah. Julia said y'all would be coming in." The nurse gave them a critical look. "You can't all go back there. Two at the most. Sorry, but there's not much room back there."

"I'll stay out here," Kyle offered. "Y'all go on back."

Sam gave the boy a nod and a smile. "Thanks, Kyle."

"No problem." Kyle brushed his fingers against Dean's hand. "Let me know if you need me to do anything, okay?"

"Sure thing. Thanks, babe." Dean pressed close to kiss Kyle's chin. Kyle blushed to the roots of his hair, but his eyes shone.

After clipping on the white plastic "Visitor" badges the triage nurse handed them, Sam and Dean hurried through the double doors leading to the ER treatment rooms. Any other time, Sam would've teased Dean about Kyle's transparent adoration. Right now, however, he was too worried about Bo to concentrate on anything else.

Julia the paramedic was standing at the nurse's station, filling out paperwork. She nodded when they approached her. "Bo's in room twelve," she said. "He wanted to see you both as soon as you got here."

Relief made Sam's knees weak. He put a hand on the desk to steady himself. "So he's awake?"

"Not exactly. He's been fading in and out, but he woke up and was fairly lucid for a minute right before we got here. That's when he told Pete—that's my partner—to make sure y'all came to see him the second you got here. He was sort of fixated on that." She scrawled her name on the bottom of the form, clicked her pen off and stuck it in her shirt pocket. "I know it's kind of frightening, but try not to worry too much. It's normal to be drowsy and confused, or even completely out of it, for quite a while after a generalized seizure like the one he had. He'll come around."

Dean nodded. "Thanks, Julia. Where's room twelve?"

She pointed to her left. "On the corner there. I think they're getting ready to take him to the OR to clean and stitch that wound, so you better hurry."

Sam pushed away from the desk and strode off in the

indicated direction. He managed to mumble a thank you to Julia on the way. He heard Dean saying something to her, but couldn't make out the words. His attention was completely fixed on getting to Bo's side.

He walked along the row of cubicles to number twelve. The curtain hung open, revealing a tiny room packed full of people and equipment. Bo lay on his side on a narrow stretcher, his lower body covered by a white blanket. A clean bandage was taped across his back. IV lines snaked into both arms, feeding clear fluids from two different bags into one vein and blood into the other. The oxygen mask had been exchanged for nasal prongs. Three wires led from electrodes on Bo's chest to a heart monitor sitting on a shelf beside the bed. A fourth wire ran from the monitor to what looked like a bandage around the end of Bo's finger. Sam stared, wondering if it was even possible to attach more equipment to one person.

One of the nurses clustered around Bo's bed caught sight of Sam and Dean at the door and made her way over. "Is one of you Sam, by any chance?"

Sam gulped. "I am."

"Good. He wants to talk to you before surgery." She nodded toward Bo. "Go on, but be quick."

Sam edged his way through the crowd to the side of the stretcher, dimly aware that Dean had stayed behind to talk to the nurse. He gently brushed a lock of wet hair from Bo's face. "Bo? It's Sam. I'm here."

Bo's eyes fluttered open. The panicked look in them sent a jolt of fear through Sam's blood. "Sam," Bo whispered, his voice rough and raspy. "I think I know. We have to stop it. Have to...to figure out how to stop it." His hand clamped onto Sam's wrist, fingers digging in with surprising strength. "It could happen anywhere, Sam. Anywhere with the right conditions. It's in me, and we have to stop it."

Sam wasn't sure what exactly "it" was, but he'd already decided that whatever had caused the portal to form that night, it had something to do with Bo. Bo must've come to the same conclusion, then taken it a step further to theorize that whatever it was in him that had caused the gateway to open, it could happen anywhere with the correct conditions.

They didn't have any clue how or why Bo had brought the portal into being. And if they didn't know what it was, how could they possibly control it?

Dread flowed like ice water through Sam's veins. He opened his psychic senses, and swiftly shut them down again under the barrage of living human energy. Overwhelming, but entirely normal.

"It won't happen here," Sam said, hoping he was right. "Just let them get your back fixed, and we'll figure it out after you wake up, okay?"

Bo shook his head. Before he could say anything else, another nurse leaned over to pat his hand. "Let me have your arm, sweetie. I need to give you some medicine to make you sleepy for surgery, okay?"

A quick flash of irritation crossed Bo's face, and Sam smiled. Bo despised being talked to like a child.

As the nurse slid a needle into one of the rubber ports in Bo's IV tubing, Bo tugged Sam closer. Sam leaned down until his ear nearly touched Bo's lips.

"All these electronics produce an electromagnetic field," Bo murmured. "Probably all well-shielded, but still, it's there. Don't know if that's all they need. Probably not. But what if it is?"

Sam's heart stilled for a second. He knew that, of course, but had never really thought about how the electronic gadgets they all took for granted might interact with the

205

interdimensional gateways. Could the EMF produced by the electric appliances all around them form the right conditions for a portal to open? The possibility was terrifying.

"If that were going to happen, it probably would've happened already," Sam speculated, keeping his voice low so no one else would hear. "EMF can't be the only factor needed for a portal, otherwise one would've opened at the house. Right?"

Bo smiled, clearly relieved. "You're right." He blinked, his gaze going unfocused. "Oh. Sleepy."

His hand relaxed around Sam's wrist, and his eyelids fell shut as the drugs hit him. Sam kissed Bo's brow, then straightened up. Too late, he realized what that relatively innocent kiss might tell the people around them.

He glanced at the people gathered around Bo's stretcher. No one seemed to have noticed, as they were all busy with equipment or paperwork. Sam backed away from the stretcher and reluctantly left the room.

Outside the little cubicle, Dean still stood talking to the nurse. She glanced at Sam. "All done?"

He nodded. "Yes. Do you need us to sign anything for him?"

"No. He woke up and was clearheaded enough to sign his own consents for surgery and blood transfusion, luckily. You couldn't have signed for him anyway, you're not next of kin." She stepped aside, motioning Sam and Dean to come with her as three nurses wheeled the stretcher out into the hallway. "You two can wait out in the waiting room. I'll send the doctor out there to talk to you as soon as he's out of surgery."

Leaving Dean to handle the talking, Sam leaned against the wall and watched the stretcher turn the corner into a corridor and roll out of sight. All he could see was the top of Bo's head.

A cold knot of foreboding coalesced in Sam's stomach. What if Bo's fears were right? What if *any* electromagnetic field was enough to allow a portal to form? What if Bo didn't even have to be conscious for it to happen? He hadn't felt anything remotely portal-like here, but then again he hadn't felt it at Fort Medina either.

What if those things get free while he's in surgery? He'll die. They'll all die.

Bo hadn't mentioned any such thing, but Sam couldn't entirely discount the possibility, in spite of his reassurances to Bo that a portal wouldn't open here. Suddenly sick with fear, Sam leaned forward, bracing his hands on his knees. He thought he might throw up, or pass out. Or both.

He heard the nurse's voice as if from a great distance, asking if he was all right. He shook his head. Dean's arm slid around his waist, holding him up. Someone shoved a chair beneath him and pushed him down into it. He bent over, his shaking hands covering his face.

He heard Dean telling the nurse how Sam had witnessed the attack, how traumatized he must've been by the whole thing, and how reaction must now be setting in. She told Dean they could stay there until Sam felt able to get up, then hurried off to attend to another patient. Sam sat hunched in the chair and let it all wash over him while Dean's hand rubbed soothing circles between his shoulder blades. Dean didn't speak, and Sam was glad. He didn't feel up to explaining himself just yet.

After a few minutes, Sam felt calm enough to sit up straight and meet Dean's gaze. Dean gave him a worried smile. "You okay?"

"Better." Sam glanced around and motioned Dean closer. "We have to talk. Bo said something that scared the shit out of me."

"I figured so." Dean pursed his lips. "I tell you what. I'll go tell Kyle he can go on back, since it looks like Bo's gonna be here at least until tomorrow sometime. We're gonna need to call Andre and the rest of the crew anyway, so one of them can come get us whenever we're ready to leave. After Kyle leaves and I call Andre, you and I can find a private spot to talk and you can tell me what Bo said. Sound good?"

"Yeah." Sam pinned Dean with a solemn stare. "Not everything he said made sense. But some of it did, and *that's* what's so scary."

Dean didn't answer, but Sam saw the sudden apprehension in his eyes.

Taking Sam's elbow, Dean tugged him to his feet, and they headed back into the waiting room.

Half an hour later, Sam and Dean sat huddled in a corner of the hospital cafeteria, sipping strong, bitter coffee made barely palatable by liberal amounts of creamer and flavored syrup. Dean had sweet-talked a young nurse's aide into giving them some hospital scrubs to wear, and it felt good to be dry for a change. Kyle had taken their soaked and bloodstained clothes with him, saying he might as well wash them since he needed to wash his blanket anyway.

"That was nice of Kyle to take our things," Sam said, cupping his hands around his coffee mug.

"It was, yeah." Dean took a sip of his coffee and wrinkled his nose. "I guess you gave him Bo's car keys?"

Sam nodded. A nurse had found Bo's keys in the pocket of his shorts, so Kyle had offered to take one of his friends with him and retrieve Bo's car from the fort. "Kyle's a sweet kid."

A grin tugged up the corners of Dean's mouth. "He sure is."

"And he's crazy about you." Sam peered at Dean over the rim of his cup. "Any chance of this being more than a summer fling?"

Dean looked away. "I didn't think we came here to talk about my love life."

Sam studied Dean's face. Dean wore the closed-off expression he only ever got when someone suggested the possibility of him having a serious relationship. It bothered Sam—and worried him a bit—that Dean never let any one lover close enough to become something more, but Dean was right. They had more pressing matters to discuss at the moment.

Putting his concern for his friend to the back of his mind, Sam leaned his elbows on the table and dropped his voice low, even though there was no one nearby to hear. "When I went to talk to him, Bo said something was in him that caused the portal to open. Well, not in so many words, exactly, but that was the gist."

"What do you think he meant was in him? Just the ability to open a portal?"

"I'm not sure. I don't think he's sure either, honestly, but it seemed to me like he literally meant something was inside him that didn't belong there. It doesn't make much sense, but that's what he said. Maybe he was still confused from the seizure."

"Maybe." Dean rubbed his chin. "We're going to have to talk with Bo some more later, after he recovers from the anesthesia. He's not one to jump to unsupported conclusions, so there must be something specific that's making him think he's..." Dean snapped his fingers, as if he could summon the right word out of thin air. "Possessed. Infected. Whatever. The point is, even if he was confused, I bet there's something in particular that's making him believe something abnormal is inside him."

"It's all connected somehow," Sam muttered, half to himself. "The portal, Bo's seizure, the weird way he's been acting lately. Maybe whatever Bo thinks is in him is the common denominator." He rubbed a hand across his face. "I wish I'd had more time to talk to him."

Dean gave him a searching look. "You said some of what he told you *did* make sense. What else did he say?"

Hunching his shoulders, Sam traced the rim of his coffee mug with one finger. "He's afraid of another portal opening here."

"What do you mean, 'here'? You mean at the fort?"

"No. *Here,* as in here at the hospital."

Dean's eyebrows shot up. "What makes him think that?"

"All the electronics. No matter how well shielded they are, they produce an electromagnetic field. Bo's afraid that field could create favorable conditions for a portal to form." Sam took a sip of his cooling coffee. "We don't know what it is about Bo that caused the portal to open at the fort, if that really is what happened. What if that unknown factor plus the electromagnetism here is enough to make another one open?"

A visible shudder ran through Dean's body. "God, what a fucking nightmare." He raked his damp, tangled hair out of his eyes. "What do you think, Sam? Is it possible?"

Having had time to calm down and think about it, Sam had his answer ready. "I think it's *possible,* theoretically speaking, but I also think it's pretty unlikely. If there's really something inside Bo that made the portal open, he must've acquired it before tonight. If that's the case, and if all you need to open a portal is that unknown factor plus an electromagnetic field, what happened tonight would've happened before. In fact, the damn things would've been popping up all around us for days. I think there must be other conditions that have to be present for a portal to form."

"Like a certain level of EMF? Or a certain type? Because natural and artificial fields do have different characteristics."

"Either or both of those, yeah. I mean, the background EMF from a houseful of electronic gadgets is usually higher than most natural fields, so I'm thinking probably a strong *natural* rather than artificial field would be necessary."

"Yeah, that makes sense." Dean lifted his cup and took a long swallow of coffee. His expression was thoughtful. "Of course, there might also be a particular catalyst we're unaware of. Something that activates the X factor and sets off a chain reaction leading to a portal."

Sighing, Sam shook his head. "God, there're so many unknowns here it's impossible to form any sort of real hypothesis."

"You said it." Dean yawned. "I think we should stop speculating about this whole thing until we can talk to Bo. Knowing him, he already has a testable theory."

Sam had to laugh, because it was true. Bo's mind was so quick and agile it was scary. He could think through any problem and arrive at a logic-based conclusion in a fraction of the time it took most people. When his ideas started flowing, Sam had trouble keeping up.

They finished their coffee in silence, then went back to the ER waiting room. While Dean napped with his legs curled in the chair and his head resting on the wall, Sam sat awake and watchful, his psychic senses wide open. Most likely he was right, and there was little to no danger of a portal opening, but there was no point in taking chances.

He ignored the inner voice telling him that if the unthinkable happened, he'd never be able to get to Bo in time to save him.

Chapter Fifteen

Sam's concentration had begun to waver by the time the doctor came out to the waiting room with a report on Bo's surgery. Keeping his senses on full alert always tired Sam, but trying to hold his psychic focus while he was already tense with worry was exhausting. When the surgeon—"Dr. Curran, call me Jack"—sat in the chair next to him and started talking, Sam let his mind relax, keeping only a slight connection with the psychic energy of the hospital.

"Bo came through the surgery just fine," Jack told them. "He's lost a lot of blood, of course, and we're replacing that, but he should make an excellent recovery."

While Sam sagged in relief, Dean leaned forward with a serious expression. "Jack, this is going to sound like a strange question, but you didn't find any signs of infection, did you?"

The surgeon's pale eyebrows lifted. "No, we didn't. But then again we wouldn't expect to find anything like that so soon."

"No, of course not." Dean flashed his most winning smile. "Thanks, Doc. We were really worried about Bo."

The man's gray eyes flicked between Dean and Sam with a calculating look. "You're good friends of Bo's, right?"

"Right," Sam answered, doing his best to ignore the heat in his cheeks. "We have some other friends looking for contact information for his parents, just in case. Do we need to call them or anything?"

Jack let out a soft laugh. "No. But I need to ask you gentlemen something about your friend. It's... Well, pretty personal. But it's important."

Sam glanced at Dean, who gave a tiny shrug as if to say he didn't know what the doctor was talking about either. "We'll tell you anything we can to help Bo."

"Okay, good." Glancing around, Jack leaned forward, elbows on his knees. "The ambulance report said Bo had no substances in his system, as far as you're aware. But I have reason to suspect otherwise, and I need you both to tell me the truth. I won't get him in trouble, but I need to know what he's on, otherwise I can't treat him."

Alarm jolted along Sam's nerves. "You found drugs in his system? What kind?"

"Well, that's the thing." Frowning, Jack rubbed the back of his neck. "We did a toxicology screen—drug screen, that is— when he came in. It's standard procedure for any trauma patient. It showed up negative for all the standard substances except benzodiazepines, but we expected that one to be positive since he had lorazepam after his seizure. However, some of the medications we gave him before and during surgery had either paradoxical or exaggerated effects. Of course, there are other reasons why that might happen with one drug. But we saw several medications all having unexpected effects, and that tells me Bo must have some sort of drug on board that we aren't aware of. Whatever it was may have caused his seizure as well." He turned his sharp gaze from Sam to Dean and back again. "If you two know of anything he might have taken in the last couple of days—anything at all—you need to tell me."

Stunned, Sam shook his head. "Dean thought he might be still taking the pain pills he had after his surgery back in

November. We wondered if he might be hooked on them, because he'd been acting really strange lately. But I talked to him last night. He swore to me he hasn't been taking anything." Sam glanced at Dean, who seemed to be deep in thought, then turned back to the doctor. "I believed him. I still believe him."

"Hm." Jack scratched his chin. "You said he'd been acting strange. How so?"

Sam didn't want to bare Bo's recent behavior for inspection by this stranger, but there wasn't much choice. Bo's health, maybe even his life, was on the line.

"He's been very angry," Sam said, staring at his hands so he wouldn't have to see the doctor's expression. "He flies off the handle for no reason. He's been having nightmares lately, and he never used to. Overall, I guess he just hasn't been acting like himself."

He wasn't about to mention the angry, brutal sex, or the portal. Some things, he figured, it was best to keep quiet about.

"So the tox screen was negative," Dean spoke up. "What sort of drug do you think might've been in his system? What should we be looking for?"

"Honestly? I have no idea. Most drugs would've shown up on the screen, even if it's something we haven't run across before, because the tests look for the *type* of substance rather than the particular drug." Jack stood, joints cracking. "If you think of anything, please let one of the nurses know, and they'll pass it on to me. In the meantime, we'll have to be very cautious in what medications we give Bo, until we find out what, if anything, he's been taking. I'll talk with him about that later today, once he's awake."

"Okay." Rising to his feet, Dean held out his hand. "Thank you, Jack."

"Sure." The surgeon shook Dean's hand, then Sam's. "Bo's

in recovery right now. They'll be taking him to a room shortly. Someone will be out in a few minutes to let you know where he's going."

With that, Jack turned and strode off. Dean plopped back into his chair, shaking his head. "Okay, that was weird."

"Bo was telling the truth." Sam turned a pleading look to Dean. "I know he wasn't lying. I can tell. So what the hell could possibly be in his system?"

"I have no fucking clue." Sighing, Dean leaned back in the chair and rubbed both hands over his face. "None of it makes any damn sense. I mean, even Bo taking the prescription this long seemed pretty far-fetched to me, it was just the only reason I could come up with for him acting so weird. I can't believe Bo would even *know* about any drug so new and different it wouldn't show up on a tox screen, never mind actually be taking it. Hell, I can't see him taking any drugs at all, ever."

Sam was inclined to agree. Getting Bo to take his pain pills in the days after his surgery in November had been a never-ending struggle, in spite of all the sleep Bo lost because he was hurting. It was impossible for Sam to wrap his head around the thought of Bo being addicted to *any* drug.

It was only a few minutes until the nurse they'd talked to before came bustling up to them. "They're taking Bo to his room now. He's going to the general surgery floor, room 412. Just go down that hallway to the right of the triage desk"—she pointed in the right direction—"and take the visitor's elevators to the fourth floor. When you get off the elevators, the nurse's station will be right in front of you. Turn to the right, Bo's room is at the end of the hall."

Pushing to his feet, Sam smiled at her. "Thank you very much."

"You're welcome." She smiled back and patted Sam's

shoulder. "I hope Bo recovers well."

She hurried away again, and Sam and Dean set off to find Bo's room. They arrived just as two nurses were helping Bo off the stretcher and into bed. After a few minutes' wait while the staff got Bo settled, Sam and Dean were ushered into the cramped little room.

Sam heard the nurse telling them Bo would be groggy for a while and that someone would be coming to check his vital signs every half hour, but he barely listened. All his attention was focused on Bo, curled on his side beneath a white sheet and a thin blue blanket. His hair was in knots, his lips were uncharacteristically pale and he still had the green plastic prongs feeding oxygen into his nose, but overall he looked better than he had before. Sam felt some of the tightness ease from his shoulders and neck.

Moving closer, Sam perched on the edge of the recliner beside the bed, reached through the rails and touched Bo's hand. "Hi, Bo. How are you feeling?"

Bo's eyelids opened. He looked confused for a second, then his eyes focused on Sam. A faint smile curved his lips. "Like shit. But better now you're here." His cold fingers curled around Sam's, squeezing.

A warm glow pulsed in Sam's chest. He bent and pressed a kiss to Bo's hand, not caring if anyone saw.

Bo's smile faded into a solemn look. "We have to talk. About what happened tonight. I think I know..."

Sam glanced toward the door. The nurse was tapping on the keyboard of the computer in the corner. Dean was leaning against the doorframe, talking on his cell phone. "Later, okay? You've been through a lot, I know you're exhausted, and you need to rest." He bent closer, lowering his voice to a whisper. "I don't think a portal's going to open here. I kept my senses wide open while you were in surgery. I didn't feel anything. It's okay for you to sleep now. We'll figure all this out later."

A soft sigh escaped Bo's lips. "Good." He blinked, the movement so slow and languid it made Sam sleepy just to watch it. "Stay with me?"

"Of course." Sam laid his free hand against Bo's cheek. "I love you."

Bo's eyes shone. "Love you too." He turned his head to kiss Sam's palm before settling against the pillow once more. His eyes drifted closed.

"Sleeping, huh?" Dean leaned against the wall to Sam's left and smiled affectionately at Bo. "Good. Been a rough night for him."

"Yeah." Sam yawned. "Do you think they'll let us stay with him?" He looked up. The nurse was gone.

"They'll let *you* stay with him. There's not room for both of us."

"Oh." Sam glanced around the small room. "Damn."

Dean grinned. "Don't worry about it. Kyle's coming back to get me."

"He is?"

"Yeah. That was him on the phone just now." Dean's shoulder hitched up, and Sam could've sworn he saw a faint rosy flush coloring Dean's cheeks. "He said he missed me."

Sam laughed. "That is so cute."

Crossing his arms, Dean studied a spot on the far wall with great interest. "So, will y'all be okay if I go?"

"Yeah, we'll be fine. Go on back and get some sleep. And tell Kyle how much we both appreciate all he did for us tonight." Reaching up, Sam touched Dean's arm. "Thanks, Dean. For everything. Especially for always being such a good friend."

The shuttered look vanished from Dean's face, replaced by a beaming smile. He bent and hugged Sam hard. "Call me later and let me know how Bo's doing, okay? Oh, and let me know what he has to say about... You know."

"Sure." Sam smiled as Dean pulled away. "Talk to you later."

Dean left the room with a grin and a wave. Letting his hand slip from Bo's, Sam scooted the chair as close as possible to Bo's bed and studied Bo's sleeping face. He looked wan and tired, but peaceful. Sam hoped it would last. He didn't think he could go back to the kind of turmoil he and Bo had lived in for the past few days.

Kicking off his shoes, Sam curled his legs beneath him and slipped his arm through the bedrail to lace his fingers through Bo's. He let himself drift into a half-doze.

ॐ

In his dream, Sam felt eyes watching him. Unlike the malicious intelligence which populated his most recent nightmares, the mind whose attention was currently focused on him felt benign. Loving. The gaze was warm and comforting as sunshine on his face. He smiled and hummed, basking in the regard of the person he couldn't see.

A soft laugh slid beneath the dream and nudged him up into the waking world. He opened his eyes. Bo's smiling face was inches away, on the other side of the bedrail. "Good morning," Bo said.

"Hey." Sam sat up and gave Bo a once-over. The oxygen tubing was gone. He was still too pale, throwing the dark smudges under his eyes into sharp relief, but other than that

Sam thought he looked remarkably good for all he'd been through. "How long have you been awake?"

"Not long. A few minutes." Bo extended a hand through the railing, took Sam's hand and wound their fingers together. "I didn't mean to wake you up."

"You didn't." Sam lifted Bo's hand, rubbing his cheek against the cool, dry fingers. "How do you feel?"

A rueful smile crossed Bo's face. "Honestly? I feel like I've been filleted with a butter knife. But if what I remember is right, I'm lucky to be alive, so I'm not complaining."

"What *do* you remember about last night?" It was the last thing Sam wanted to talk about, but they had to discuss it at some point. Now was as good a time as any.

Bo's eyes clouded. "The last thing I remember with any clarity is being in bed with you. I think I went to sleep for a little while. When I woke up, everything seemed...strange. Fuzzy. I only remember parts of what happened after that, but I know I wasn't in control of myself."

"How do you mean?"

Bo was silent for a moment, stroking his thumb across the back of Sam's hand. "This is going to sound ludicrous, Sam, but I felt as if I were being literally *compelled* to go to the fort. I couldn't act for myself. I couldn't even think for myself. It was like my mind and body had been completely taken over. I...I heard things. Saw things. And the feel of those things was very similar to what I felt in my nightmares. Then the second you closed that portal, the compulsion was just...gone. Just like that. I still didn't feel normal, but the feeling of something else taking me over was gone."

Sam stared into Bo's eyes, his stomach churning. "What exactly are you saying?"

Bo frowned, looking as if he were trying to think of how to

explain himself. "After that juvenile bit me back in November, my blood grew out an unidentified organism, remember?"

"Yeah. The same bug showed up in the thing's teeth."

"Along with an unknown inorganic chemical." Bo's hand tightened around Sam's. "I think that chemical's been lying dormant in my body all this time, and something about the fort activated it."

Something cold squirmed in Sam's belly. "What makes you think that? And what does it mean?"

The corners of Bo's mouth lifted, as if he knew Sam had begun to figure it out. "First of all, the way my leg acted around the closed portal at Sunset Lodge tells me something in the wound must've been reacting to the residual energy of the portal. The chemical from the juvenile's teeth is the most logical possibility, especially since the organism was no longer there when they rechecked for it. The chemical is from the same world the portals link to. That means it's based on the same chemistry and physical properties as that world. So it seems reasonable to think it might react in some way to the energy left over from a sealed portal."

"Makes sense."

"Yes. The rest is pure speculation, but..." Bo glanced toward the closed door of his room. "Ever since the first time I went to Fort Medina, I haven't been myself. I didn't see it then, but I do now. I understand why Dean believed I might've been addicted to drugs, because that's exactly how I was acting. And he was right, in a way."

"Do you mean you think that chemical is addictive?"

"Not exactly." Bo shifted in bed, grimacing with the movement. "Ever since that first night at Fort Medina, I felt this irresistible pull toward the place. I couldn't stop thinking about it. I felt like I'd do anything to be there, even though I couldn't have given you a reason for it if you'd asked me. Addiction is a good analogy for how I felt."

Sam's mouth fell open as the memory of his recent nightmares hit him like a hammer. In his mind's eye, he saw the thread of glowing energy leading from the sentient blackness, through the empty cold of another dimension to his own world. At the same time, he remembered the strange sensation of something *other* looking out of Bo's eyes, and realized with a sickening jolt what it meant.

"Oh, my God. Those things used that chemical to draw you to the fort and track you. Then once they had you pinpointed, then they opened a portal and..." Sam trailed off, not wanting to consider *why* the fucking monsters had targeted Bo. "Shit."

"Yeah." Bo's solemn gaze held Sam's. "I think the chemical may have bonded with the primitive parts of my brain—the same parts that activate to allow you to manipulate portals— and allowed those things to enter my mind in a limited way. Once the chemical was activated and they were able to get into my head, all they had to do was nudge me toward the fort by 'addicting' me to it, for lack of a better phrase."

It made a horrible sort of sense. A hard chill raced up Sam's spine. "But they're gone now, right? They're gone from your head?"

"Yes. At least I assume so. I feel back to normal now."

Sam licked his lips. His fingers gripped Bo's tighter. "If that chemical's still in your body, then this could happen again."

Bo didn't say anything, but the fear in his eyes said it all. Dread knotted Sam's stomach.

"Dr. Curran was here earlier," Bo said after a silent moment.

"When? I thought you said you just woke up."

"I did. I went back to sleep for a while after he left."

"What did he say?" Sam asked, thinking of the doctor's conversation with him and Dean the night before.

"He asked me if I was taking any drugs. Said my tox screen was negative, but something was interfering with the meds they gave me during surgery. I told him I took some valerian root to help me sleep." Bo's lips curved into a faint smile. "I have no idea if valerian would actually interact with any of the drugs they gave me, but he didn't seem to know either, so I suppose it doesn't matter. In any case, he said that definitely wouldn't have caused a seizure, or the fever I had, which means I'm in for more tests before they'll let me go."

"What sort of tests?"

"MRI of my brain. EEG. Blood and body fluid cultures, chest X-ray to rule out pneumonia although his index of suspicion for that is pretty low. Of course, I believe the chemical caused both the seizure and the fever, but I can hardly tell the doctor that." Bo shifted again. The over-large hospital gown slid off his shoulder, revealing a corner of surgical tape from the bandage covering the better part of his back. "They're giving me anticonvulsants, Sam. You know what that might mean."

Sam did, and the realization gave him a surge of hope. "If your brain connected with those fucking things and the portals the same way mine does, the anticonvulsants could keep it from happening again."

"If your theory is correct, yes."

"I really hope it is."

"So do I." Letting go of Sam's hand, Bo pushed the button to raise the head of the bed. He stopped, wincing, after it lifted a few inches. "Damn. I think I'm going to ask for that pain medicine now."

"It's about time."

Sam reached inside the bedrail, feeling for the nurse call button. Bo's hand on his stopped him. He looked at Bo, eyebrows raised.

"Thank you, Sam," Bo whispered.

Sam smiled. "I haven't pushed the button yet."

"Not that." Bo's fingers caressed Sam's. "Thank you for sticking with me through these past few days. For saving me last night. And most of all, for still believing in me in spite of everything." His dark gaze bored into Sam's, serious and intent. "That means more to me than I can possibly tell you."

Sam's throat constricted. Rising to his feet, he leaned over, cupped Bo's face in his hands and kissed him. Bo's lips parted, his tongue stroking warm and soft against Sam's. It felt wonderful, even more so than usual because of all that had happened. Morning breath and chapped lips didn't matter. Bo was alive and safe, and he was himself again. To Sam, everything else paled beside that simple fact.

When they broke apart, Sam curled back into the recliner while Bo pushed the call button. The day shift nurse came in a few minutes later and injected morphine into Bo's IV line. By the time she left the room, Bo was already blinking drowsily at the wall. He drifted off a few minutes later, one hand still tucked beneath his head and the other hanging off the edge of the mattress.

For a long time, Sam sat and watched Bo sleep. His mind whirled with thoughts of the theories he and Bo had just discussed, and what they might mean for Bo's future and his own. If Sam was right, the anticonvulsants would keep the otherdimensional beings from finding their way into Bo's brain again. And if he was wrong...

If he was wrong, the possibilities didn't bear thinking of.

He reached out and stroked Bo's fingers, from the short,

blunt nails to the rough skin over his knuckles. "I'd better be right."

Epilogue

"It looks different."

"Must be the sunshine."

"And the crowd."

Sam smiled, his shoulder just brushing Bo's. "I think I like it better this way."

Bo nodded. "So do I."

They stood at the center of Fort Medina's courtyard, which did indeed look different than it had during the investigation, or during their brief visit after hours the previous month. The bright July sun and the swarms of tourists made the place seem smaller and friendlier.

"Do you feel anything?" Bo asked, his voice barely audible.

Sam shook his head. "No. But I didn't expect to. The portal's closed, for good." He glanced at Bo. "What about you?"

Looking around, Bo smiled. "Nothing. Of course, that's what I expected as well."

They'd both gone with Andre and the rest of the BCPI crew in June, when the group returned to present the findings of their investigation to Joanne. Sam and Bo had gone with the sole purpose of making sure the portal was closed, and things on the other side could no longer get into Bo's brain.

Neither of them had any idea whether having been

activated once would make the unclassified chemical easier to reactivate. Because of that, Sam hadn't wanted Bo to go, even though Bo had been on Dilantin for three weeks by then. Bo had pointed out that if the chemical in his body could still be activated in spite of the Dilantin, he'd rather find out then, when they were both ready for it and there were relatively few people around.

Even Sam hadn't been able to find any logical flaw with that argument. So they'd both gone back, wandering through the closed and darkened fort while their friends were gathered in the office with Joanne. Nothing had happened. Relieved, they'd held a private celebration in bed that night.

"Where are the boys?" Bo asked, frowning. "I don't see them."

Sam shaded his eyes with his hands and turned in a slow circle. "They're over there," he said, spotting Sean's tousled golden brown head and Adrian's sleeker, darker one in front of a plaque on the north wall. "They're reading one of the plaques."

Bo blew out a breath. "Come on, let's go get them. I don't like them wandering off like that."

Sam swallowed a frustrated sigh as he followed Bo across the grass. He hadn't been terribly enthused about taking Bo's sons here during their weekend visit, mostly because he'd known Bo would be nervous every time they were out of sight for more than a few seconds. Why, he thought irritably, were they even here if Bo was that worried about their safety?

Of course, he knew the answer to *that* question. The kids had overheard them discussing the fort, and the idea of bloodstained steps and a haunted weapons bunker had captured their fertile young imaginations. They'd begged to go. And Bo, as usual when his children were persistent enough, had caved.

Not that it wasn't safe here. It was. Bo wouldn't have agreed if he hadn't known in his heart that there was no danger here anymore. Neither would Sam, for that matter. But seeing Bo so tense and jumpy over the boys was getting on Sam's nerves.

"Boys, what did I tell you about wandering off?" Bo admonished as he and Sam approached the children. "You need to stay with Sam and me."

"Yessir." Sean, the youngest at eight years old, turned and flashed a gap-toothed grin. His hazel eyes shone with excitement. "Dad, can we go see the bloodstains now?"

"I don't care about the stupid bloodstains." Adrian gave Bo an unreadable look over his shoulder. "You said we could go see the weapons bunker first. You *promised*."

"You don't get to be boss just 'cause you're the oldest," Sean shot back. He grabbed Bo's T-shirt in both small hands and started bouncing up and down. "I wanna see the bloodstains, c'mon. Pleasepleaseplease?"

With a strained smile, Bo raked a hand through the boy's hair. "In a little while. I did promise Adrian we'd go see the weapons bunker first."

Adrian turned back to the plaque, looking smug. Sean scowled. "How come we always have to do what *he* wants?"

Bo pretended not to hear. Sam knew better. He knew Bo tended to favor Adrian these days, and he knew *why*.

Adrian was far more sensitive and perceptive than most eleven year olds. Learning his father was gay and in a relationship with a man had been a huge blow to him. While Sean had shrugged the whole thing off and cautiously accepted Sam as a friend and occasional video game opponent, Adrian had become even more quiet and withdrawn than usual. He'd never overtly rejected Sam—in fact, he barely acknowledged

Sam's presence most of the time—but the big, dark eyes so like his father's simmered with wounded rage every time he glanced Sam's way, and Sam knew Bo saw it.

Hurt and angry, Adrian was systematically distancing himself from his father. Bo, in a desperate attempt to keep from losing his son's love, bent over backward to try and make Adrian happy. The despair behind Bo's smile every time it didn't work broke Sam's heart.

An idea came to Sam, and he acted on it before he could change his mind. "Hey, Bo, why don't I take Sean over to see the bloodstains while you and Adrian go to the weapons bunker?"

Sean whooped, let go of Bo and scampered to Sam's side. "Cool! Dad, can I? Sam can tell me the story about the headless soldier again. I like how he tells it."

Sam caught Bo's eye. They grinned at each other, the worried crease vanishing from between Bo's brows for the first time since Janine had brought the boys over the previous night. The way Sean hung on Sam's every word during his tales of the fort's apparitions was adorable.

"All right." Bo laughed when Sean whooped again, drawing amused looks from the people around them. "You be good and mind Sam, okay?"

"Sure." He launched himself at Bo, flinging his arms around Bo's middle. "Love you, Dad."

Bo's throat worked. He wrapped his arms around Sean and hugged him close. "I love you too, son."

Sean let go of Bo and ran back to Sam. "Let's go!" He grabbed Sam's hand and started dragging him in the direction of the bloodstained steps.

"See you in a few minutes," Sam called as he was pulled away.

Bo nodded and waved. Before being swallowed by the crowd, Sam saw Adrian shrug off the arm Bo rested across his shoulders. He caught a glimpse of the sorrow in Bo's eyes and the fury in Adrian's before they were lost in the sea of people.

Forcing back the sympathetic ache for Bo, Sam turned his attention to the child hauling him with single-minded determination toward the flight of stone steps leading to the ramparts.

When they reached the steps, Sam showed Sean the bloodstains splattered across the gray stone. Sean's eyes widened with transparent awe as Sam related the story of the headless soldier who haunted this stairway. The boy had heard it all before, of course, but he never seemed to tire of it. He spent several minutes speculating on what the soldier's head must've looked like bouncing down the stairs before snagging Sam's wrist and pulling him toward the ramparts.

Up on the narrow walkway, Sam and Sean surveyed the glittering ocean beyond the fort's walls and the teeming courtyard far below. Sean kept up his usual nonstop stream-of-consciousness chatter. Sam listened with a smile, Sean's small hand clutched tightly in his. The boy could be exhausting, but he was sweet-tempered and outgoing, and made friends everywhere he went. He was an easy child to like.

Unlike his brother.

Sam nipped that thought in the bud. He knew he had to work harder to win over Adrian, but it was a daunting prospect, and he didn't want to think about it right now. He was enjoying himself, and he wanted to hang on to that fragile feeling.

With a start, Sam realized Sean had fallen silent. He glanced down. The child seemed lost in thought.

"Hey." He gave Sean's hand a gentle shake. "Earth to Sean."

Sean looked up at Sam with an uncharacteristically thoughtful expression. "You know what?"

"What?"

"I like it that Dad lives with you now. I like you. You're cool."

Sam returned the child's smile and gave his fingers a light squeeze. "I like you too. You're pretty cool yourself."

Sean beamed, his round little face aglow, and a feeling Sam couldn't put a name to twisted sharp and sweet in his chest. He'd never been close to his parents and sister. He didn't hate them, but he hadn't really loved them since he was small. The only honest conversation he'd ever had with them had ended with his mother calling him an abomination, his father threatening violence if he ever mentioned his homosexuality again, and his sister refusing to speak to him for a month. His father died the month after Sam came out, without ever speaking to him again. To this day, Sam wasn't allowed to spend time alone with his niece and nephew. Bo was the first person he'd ever loved completely, and who had loved him back without condition or reservation. Their relationship was his only experience with true intimacy. He had no benchmark for the fierce, protective tenderness suddenly bubbling up inside him.

Sean's delighted squeal broke into Sam's thoughts. "Hey, there's Dad and Adrian!" He jumped up and down, waving his free hand frantically in the air. "Dad! Hey, Dad! Up here!"

Sam laughed as nearly every head in the courtyard swiveled toward Sean. He was a bit small for his age, but he had a powerful set of lungs and wasn't shy about using them.

After a moment, Sam spotted Bo and Adrian making their way toward the steps. They started up the narrow stone flight side by side. Watching them, Sam marveled for the thousandth time at how alike they were. Adrian had inherited Bo's intelligence, his reserve, his stubbornness and his temper, along with his straight black hair, deep brown eyes and mocha skin. Sam often wondered if they clashed as often as they did because they were so similar.

Sean let go of Sam's hand and bounced up to his brother as Bo and Adrian approached. "Hey, Adrian, did you see the bloodstains?"

Adrian gave the younger boy a disdainful look. "I told you, I don't care about the stupid bloodstains. I bet it's just paint anyhow."

Sean's shock was almost comical. "It's not paint, it's *blood!*" He grabbed Adrian's wrist. "C'mon, I'll show you."

"Be careful," Bo warned as Sean dragged his protesting sibling toward the stairs.

Sam moved to stand beside Bo. They watched the boys crouch beside the red splotches on the last few steps and put their heads together, apparently holding quite a serious discussion about the stains.

"I appreciate you taking Sean," Bo murmured. His hand crept into Sam's, holding on tight. "It was nice to have a few minutes with just Adrian."

"I figured you could both use it. Besides, Sean and I get along great." Sam glanced at Bo. His expression was pensive. "Did it go all right?"

"I think so. He really loved hearing about the apparitions the BCPI team saw in the bunker. For a few minutes there, he seemed almost normal again." Bo turned his head and pinned Sam with a serious look. "Thank you for being so patient with me. With all of us. I know how hard it is for you when I have the boys with me, but you've been absolutely wonderful lately, and I just want you to know that I've noticed, and I appreciate it."

Sam glanced toward the bottom of the steps, where Sean

and Adrian were now involved in what looked like an impromptu reenactment of a long-ago battle. Both were laughing, and it warmed Sam's heart to see Adrian looking just as happy and carefree as Sean.

"I want us to be a family," Sam said, and instantly knew he meant it. "I know it won't be easy. But I love you, and Sean and Adrian are your sons. I care about them, and I...I want to be a part of their lives."

The startled expression on Bo's face melted into a glowing smile. "I knew there was a reason I love you."

Standing there in the summer sun, hand in hand with the man he loved while that man's children played below, Sam felt more content than he'd ever believed he could. Was this what it felt like to have a real family? One that fought and laughed, and loved each other through good times and bad?

Sam didn't know. But for the first time in his life, he wanted to find out.

ꝏ

Two hours later, after the boys had thoroughly explored every nook and cranny of the fort, Sam and Bo finally managed to drag them away. Sean clung to Bo's hand as they walked to the car, relating his own version of the day's adventures with infectious enthusiasm. Sam strolled a few paces behind. Adrian paced silently beside him, just far enough away to convey his distaste for Sam's presence.

Sam glanced at Adrian. His expression was as closed off as ever. Struck by an urge to draw him out, Sam moved closer. "What did you think of the fort? It's an interesting place, isn't it?"

Adrian shrugged. "I guess."

Encouraged by the lack of outright hostility, Sam decided to keep going. "What was your favorite part?"

Another shrug. Sam tried again. "I know you were looking forward to the weapons bunker, how was that?"

"It felt wrong."

A chill crawled up Sam's spine. "What?"

Adrian shot him a swift glance full of the undiluted hatred Sam had come to know quite well over the past few months. But behind that was a faint spark of fear which sent an unpleasant jolt through Sam's blood. "Adrian? What do you mean, it felt wrong?"

"Nothing," Adrian mumbled, looking away.

Sam plowed on, in spite of Adrian's obvious desire for him to drop it. "Adrian, look, I know you don't like me, but I...I feel strange things too, sometimes. You can tell me if—"

"I told you, I didn't mean anything. Just leave me alone."

Sam studied the boy's profile. His jaw was tight, his gaze fixed on the ground and his hands stuffed in the pockets of his shorts. Tension rolled off him in waves. The resemblance to his father was eerie, and Sam knew from experience that the similarities didn't end on the outside.

Part of Sam wanted very much to push the issue. To find out what exactly Adrian had felt in the fort. But a larger part of him didn't want to destroy what little progress he'd made with the child over something that was most likely his imagination.

If you push it, it'll only make him angry, and if that happens he'll make everyone else miserable. There's no point in that, when all you have to go on is your own fear.

It was a justification, and Sam knew it. But he couldn't bring himself to ruin what was left of Bo's weekend with his children. Not without a damn good reason, and this didn't qualify.

When they reached the car, Bo laid a hand on Sam's arm while the boys clambered into the backseat. "You were talking to Adrian."

Sam nodded. "A little bit, yeah."

"About what?"

"I asked him how he liked the fort."

"And what did he say?"

Sam was torn. He didn't want to lie to Bo, but he didn't have the heart to snuff out the hope in Bo's eyes.

"He said it was okay," Sam told him. "That was about it, but he said actual words to me, and he wasn't even insulting about it. It's an improvement, I think."

Bo's smile made the small deception worthwhile. "That's wonderful, Sam. Wonderful." He slipped his hand into Sam's. "The boys want to stop at Pizza Palace for dinner. Is that all right with you?"

"Absolutely. I love Pizza Palace."

Smiling, Bo gave Sam's fingers a squeeze, then let go and moved around to the passenger's side. Sam opened the driver's side door and slid behind the wheel.

As he drove down the shaded road toward town, Sam glanced at Adrian in the rearview mirror. The boy's dark eyes met his for a second before cutting away. What Sam saw there wasn't exactly acceptance, but it wasn't the usual resentment and brooding anger either. Adrian looked thoughtful, as if considering whether Sam was really the demon he'd always believed him to be.

Sam smiled. It wasn't much, but it was a start, and that was good enough.

About the Author

Ally Blue used to be a good girl. Really. Married for twenty years, two lovely children, house, dogs, picket fence, the whole deal. Then one day she discovered slash fan fiction. She wrote her first fan fiction story a couple of months later and has since slid merrily into the abyss. She has had several short stories published in the erotic e-zine Ruthie's Club, and is a regular contributor to the original slash e-zine Forbidden Fruit.

To learn more about Ally Blue, please visit www.allyblue.com. Send an email to Ally at ally@allyblue.com or join her Yahoo! group to join in the fun with other readers as well as Ally! http://groups.yahoo.com/group/loveisblue/.

In this world, trust is hard to find...
and the one thing they need to survive.

Poison
© *2008 Joely Skye*

Tobias Smator lives down his late father's execution by avoiding the spotlight—and responsibility. He doesn't mind what people think of him as long as they leave him alone. Still, in this unremarkable half-life he's fashioned for himself on deceptively low-tech Rimania, he's not safe from political intrigue. Someone wants him dead.

Alliance operative Geln Marac's orders for his first assignment were simple: Stay uninvolved. Those orders go out the window, however, when he delivers an antidote to save Tobias from death by poisoning. His reward? Possible betrayal that lands him in the hands of police interrogators. To protect the Alliance, Geln resorts to a temporary mindwipe.

Tobias is fascinated by the amnesiac man who saved his life. But Geln has attracted the attention of the high-powered Lord Eberly, who would use him as a pawn. Rather than sacrifice Geln to the political wolves, Tobias chooses to embrace his heritage.

Geln's memory reawakens to a precarious situation with no source of protection—except Tobias. There's only one way forward for both of them.

Trust—or die.

Warning: this book contains hot nekkid otherplanetary manlove.

Available now in ebook and print from Samhain Publishing.

Enjoy the following excerpt from Poison...

After Tobias returned from the outside world, Geln told him, "Take off your clothes."

That brought Tobias up short. But then he walked to Geln and stopped, a gleam in his eye that made Geln a little breathless.

"You first," said Tobias.

Geln slowly shook his head.

"I was naked last time," Tobias pointed out.

"Half-naked," Geln amended.

Tobias shrugged one shoulder to indicate he didn't think it made a difference.

"All right." Geln decided this wasn't an impasse he was interested in keeping. "Strip yourself," he added as he pulled off his shirt. A naked, responsive Tobias would be easier to work on. Dressed, Tobias wasn't quite vulnerable enough.

They stood nose to nose. "Lie down," said Geln.

A small half-smile played on Tobias's face. He gripped both of Geln's arms, gentle but firm, and pulled him to the bed so they sat together, Geln's legs draped over Tobias.

"I don't want to lie down," Tobias said softly, an edge there that surprised Geln. He could feel his heart kick up and couldn't tell if it was exactly lust or fear or both. His cock hardened though.

Tobias still had hands wrapped around each of Geln's arms, an odd kind of embrace, as if Tobias didn't fully trust him. Perhaps, Geln's earlier ministrations had made him uneasy. Geln skimmed a hand down Tobias's side, the movement restricted by Tobias's clasp.

His lover sucked in a breath and Geln did it again, enjoying the response.

"If you let go of me, I'll touch you all over," Geln promised. "In case you haven't noticed, you like it."

"I like it," Tobias admitted, "but I'd rather you come this time."

"Don't worry about that," Geln murmured and clasped Tobias's wrists, lifting his hands off. Before he could do more Tobias was kissing him, palms back on him, one on his neck, the other just under his arm. A thumb stroked the sensitive underside.

Geln shuddered and Tobias angled his mouth to kiss more deeply, tongue playing with Geln's, insisting, asking for more.

He wanted to give way, he did, but it was hard.

"Trust me, even if I don't know what I'm doing." This said against Geln's ear and then he was pushed onto his back. Well, whatever "stuff" Tobias and the stable boy had gotten up to... That thought got lost as Tobias's teeth came down on Geln, grazing the sensitive skin around his nipple, and Geln sucked in a long breath. A palm lay flat on his stomach now, warm, reassuring and he turned to see question in Tobias's eyes.

"Whatever," said Geln.

"Whatever?" repeated Tobias, somewhat taken aback, and his lust-darkened eyes seemed to lighten.

"I mean"—Geln swallowed—"whatever you want, I want."

Very slowly, Tobias wrapped a hand around Geln's dick, all the while watching.

"I guess I don't make a great top," Geln said dryly, "though I was trying."

Tobias cocked his head as he ran a thumb across Geln's slit. "I don't know what you're talking about."

Geln gave a small hoot of laughter, which just made Tobias more baffled. "Don't worry, neither do I. Besides, I don't make a great bottom, either." Geln pushed up, deciding that he'd better stop talking before he caused Tobias to lose all confidence.

He ran fingers through Tobias's hair. "I don't think I've ever been with someone so lovely." He kissed lightly, with some tongue. "I'm sorry I'm such a mess."

Tobias, he noted, hadn't released his dick. "Don't be sorry about this, about us," Tobias said in low tones.

"No. No." To his dismay, Geln's voice was shaky. He wrapped himself around Tobias's neck and buried his face in Tobias's throat. Strong arms held him and Tobias started up again, kissing, touching, exploring; and Geln gave it back. He didn't care if he came first, he just wanted to be with someone who noticed what was going on in bed.

When he was close, just from Tobias's hand, Tobias shot him a glance, bashfulness there. "I don't have much practice, well, any practice..."

"Yes."

Tobias scooted back and bent over, hot breath touching Geln's dick before his mouth took him in, a little unsteady, a little unsure while finding a rhythm.

GREAT
CHEAP
FUN

Discover eBooks!

THE FASTEST WAY TO GET THE HOTTEST NAMES

Get your favorite authors on your favorite reader, long before they're
out in print! Ebooks from Samhain go wherever you go, and work with
whatever you carry—Palm, PDF, Mobi, and more.

SAMHAIN
PUBLISHING, LTD

WWW.SAMHAINPUBLISHING.COM

Printed in the United States
217263BV00001B/52/P

9 781605 041445